## Praise for MARTA PERRY

"Marta Perry illuminates the differences between the Amish community and the larger society with an obvious care and respect for ways and beliefs.... She weaves these differences into the story with a deft hand, drawing the reader into a suspenseful, continually moving plot."
—*Fresh Fiction* on *Murder in Plain Sight*

"*Leah's Choice,* by Marta Perry, is a knowing and careful look into Amish culture and faith. A truly enjoyable reading experience."
—Angela Hunt, *New York Times* bestselling author of *Let Darkness Come*

"*Leah's Choice* takes us into the heart of Amish country and the Pennsylvania Dutch and shows us the struggles of the Amish community as the outside world continues to clash with the Plain ways. This is a story of grace and servitude as well as a story of difficult choices and heartbreaking realities. It touched my heart. I think the world of Amish fiction has found a new champion."
—Lenora Worth, author of *Code of Honor*

"Marta Perry delivers a strong story of tension, fear and trepidation. *Season of Secrets* (4.5 stars) is an excellent mystery that's certain to keep you in constant suspense. While love is a powerful entity in this story, danger is never too far behind."
—*RT Book Reviews,* Top Pick

"In this beautifully told tale, Marta Perry writes with the gentle cadence and rich detail of someone who understands the Amish well. *Leah's Choice* kept me reading long into the night."
—Linda Goodnight, author of *Finding Her Way Home*

# Available from Marta Perry and HQN Books
## MURDER IN PLAIN SIGHT

# MARTA PERRY

# VANISH
*in*
# PLAIN
# SIGHT

DOUBLEDAY LARGE PRINT HOME LIBRARY EDITION

HQN™

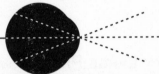

This Large Print Book carries the
Seal of Approval of N.A.V.H.

Dear Reader,

Thank you for deciding to read this second book in my Amish suspense series. As a lifelong resident of rural Pennsylvania, I have always lived near the Plain People. My own family heritage is Pennsylvania Dutch, so it has been a pleasure and a challenge to draw on those experiences in my books.

It can be difficult for outsiders to understand the tight bonds of the Amish community, so that it is sometimes seen as secretive or unkind in its efforts to avoid conforming to the world. For many people, the extent of their knowledge about the Amish is derived from the movie Witness, but there is far more to be understood about a unique people trying to live as they believe God wishes.

In this story, Marisa Angelo is the outsider whose personal needs require that she penetrate Amish society to learn about her mother's disappearance. She comes in with a great many preconceptions, most of which are put to the test as she tries to uncover the truth about her mother's background and the events that led up to her disappearance. I've tried to present Amish belief and practices as honestly and respectfully as I can, and any errors are my own.

I hope you'll let me know how you like my book, and I'd love to send you a signed bookmark and my free brochure of Pennsylvania Dutch recipes. You can email me at marta@martaperry.com, visit me on the web at www.martaperry.com or on Facebook at Marta Perry Books, or write to me at HQN Books, 233 Broadway, Suite 1001, New York, NY 10279.

Blessings,

Marta Perry

This story is dedicated to my husband, Brian, who always believes I can find another story to tell.

## Acknowledgments

I'd like to express my thanks to all those whose expertise helped me in writing this book: to Erik Wesner, whose Amish America blog is enormously helpful; to Donald Kraybill and John Hostetler, whose books are the definitive resources on Amish life and beliefs; to the Plain People I have known and respected; and to my family, for giving me such a rich heritage on which to draw.

The righteousness of the blameless
makes a straight way for them, but the wicked
are brought down by their own wickedness.
—*Proverbs* 11:5

# CHAPTER ONE

Link Morgan narrowed his focus to the heavy sledgehammer and the satisfying thwack it made when it broke into the old paneling.

The paneling shattered beneath Link's sledgehammer, its shoddiness a contrast to the solid double-plank construction of the rest of the old farmhouse. Setting the sledgehammer down, he pulled fragments loose with gloved hands, tossing them into a pile in front of the fireplace. The last bit of the section came free, revealing what lay behind it.

He stared, methodically wiping the sweat from his forehead. Shaking off the foreboding that gripped him, he reached into the wall and pulled out the object that lay there. A suitcase. Not empty, by the feel of it.

Carrying it to the makeshift worktable, he set down his find. An inexpensive suitcase, its fabric sides coated in dust and marred by stains. How long had it lain there, inside the wall of Uncle Allen's house? More important, why was it there?

He snapped open the latch and swung back the lid. Women's clothes, by the look of it—slacks, a skirt, several blouses. Beneath them something black. He picked it up, shook it out and recognized it. An Amish woman's black apron. His stomach twisted, rebelling the way it had in Afghanistan when they were coming upon a perfect place for an ambush.

Taking out the apron revealed what lay under it: a white Amish prayer kapp. At the very bottom was a framed photograph. He picked up the picture, bad feelings growing. A woman and a young girl, looking at each other, faces lit with laughter and love. Mother and daughter, he'd guess from the similarities in the faces. The child looked to be about four or five.

He set the picture down gently and took a step away from the table. Something was wrong here. The pair in the photo wore typical, though a little outdated, clothing. So how did that square with the Amish clothing in the suitcase? The pressure that had driven him for months urged him to ignore this, to get on with his plans. Whatever had led to this suitcase being placed inside the wall of the old house his uncle had left him, it was no concern of his.

If he hadn't opened the suitcase, maybe he could have bought that. But the contents raised too many questions. Too late now to take the easy way out. He pulled the cell phone from his pocket and dialed the Spring Township police.

Ten minutes later a police car pulled into the driveway. The occupants got out and headed for the back door, as country people always did, and he walked out to the back porch to meet them. Before he had a chance to speak, his brother Trey's pickup drew to a stop behind the cruiser.

He'd called Trey right after he'd called the police, figuring he would want to know. After all, he was the one who'd been here for the past six years while Link was off at college and then in the army. Maybe he'd be able to shed some light on this, but even if he couldn't, Trey was the kind of person you turned to when there was trouble.

Besides, Trey knew everyone. Adam Byler, now the township police chief, had been friends with Link's big brother since they were kids, running around together, usually trying to brush off Link, the bratty little brother tagging after them and getting into trouble.

"Hey, Link." Adam pulled off sunglasses and started toward him, followed by another cop...Dick McCall, fiftyish, balding, with a paunch that strained his uniform shirt a bit more each year. Mac had been a township cop when Link had been soaping windows at ten.

"Sorry to call you out." Link leaned against the porch post, hoping it didn't look as if he needed its support. "It's probably nothing, but I figured you'd want a look at this."

"No problem. That's what you pay taxes for, right?" Adam punched his shoulder lightly, the tap a hint of the power that lay behind it. Adam was as solid now as he'd been in high school, with not an ounce of fat on his muscular frame. "Let's have a look."

Trey joined them, giving Link the worried look he'd been using since Link got out of the military hospital and came home to recuperate.

"What's up?" Trey's voice was so much like Dad's that it still shocked Link sometimes. "Adam said you found something inside the wall of the addition."

He jerked a nod and headed inside. "See for yourself."

The family room, stretching across the rear of the centuries-old farmhouse, seemed smaller with four men in it. They stood in an awkward circle around the opened suitcase.

Adam took the photo, setting it so they all could see. He glanced at Link. "You know who the woman is?"

Link shook his head, frowning at a

vague memory that teased at the back of his mind. "The face seems a little familiar, but that's all."

"Yeah, me, too," Trey said, sounding annoyed with himself that he didn't have the answer.

Mac picked up the photo. "You three boys are too young to remember, that's all. It's Barbara Angelo, that's who it is."

"Angelo." The frown on Adam's stolid face deepened. "Wasn't there a scandal or something about her?"

"Ran off from her husband and kid, that's the way I heard it." Mac looked gratified at their attention. "Russ Angelo, the husband, said she'd gone back to Indiana to her family, leaving the little girl with him and his mother. Barbara was Amish, see, left the church to marry him, but the marriage didn't work out." He shrugged. "It happens. Nobody questioned her leaving all that much, as I recall."

"But if her suitcase is here..." Trey let that trail off.

No point in going on. Trey was thinking what they were all thinking. If Barbara Angelo had deserted her husband

and small daughter, what was her suitcase doing in the wall of Allen Morgan's house?

Adam closed the suitcase, scanning the sides with his eyes, not touching. "No ID tags. The kind of cheap bag you could pick up at any discount store."

To Link's eyes, the bag looked worn and battered, but maybe that was just the effect of being inside the paneling all these years. It was thick with dust, splattered with darker stains and a few nicks here and there.

Adam seemed to scan the stains more closely, then looked around the room. "Where was it?"

"Right here, next to the fireplace." Link showed them, concentrating on not limping as he crossed the room. Maybe that sledgehammer had been a bit much. The army said he was as well as they could make him, after what had happened in Afghanistan.

Adam squatted down, studying the area as deliberately as he did everything. "Well, it's not a crime to put a suitcase inside a wall. You two know when this work was done?"

"We were kids when Uncle Allen built the addition, that's as close as I can come," Trey said. "Mom would know exactly, though."

Adam let his gaze move around the room. "I hate to say it, but I think we'd best make sure there's nothing else inside that paneling." He shot a glance at Link. "You mind?"

"Hey, I'm tearing it off anyway. I'll take any help I can get. One thing's sure—if there is anything, it has to be in this room. The rest of the house has solid double-plank walls. Not room even for a mouse."

Let alone a human body, if that's what they were talking about.

"Well, let's have at it." Trey picked up the sledgehammer before Link could reach it. He managed a grin at Link. "You sure this isn't just a ploy to get us to do the work for you?"

"How else would I get you to do it? You're still dead set against my selling the old place, aren't you?" Link softened the question with an attempted smile, but he'd be glad if everyone would stop hovering over him.

"I just wish you'd stick around for a while, that's all," Trey said. He punctuated the words with a swing of the sledgehammer. "Seems like Morgans belong here in Lancaster County."

Trey didn't understand this drive of Link's to leave—that was clear. Link wasn't sure he understood it himself, but life had to be easier someplace where people weren't worrying about him all the time. A buddy of his was keeping a job for him in California. He had a simple plan: renovate the house, sell it, move to California and forget what had happened to his team in Afghanistan and the career he'd once thought to have in the military.

With four of them working, the job didn't take long. Soon all the old paneling lay in dusty stacks on the floor.

"Nothing." Adam summed it up, brushing off his hands. "Maybe that's what the whole thing amounts to. I guess there could be some innocent explanation for the woman's suitcase being inside the wall of your uncle's house."

"Can you think of one?" Trey challenged. Link could hear the worry in his voice. He'd be thinking about how Mom would take this.

"Not off the top of my head," Adam admitted. "But that doesn't mean there isn't one. Still, crime or no crime, I guess I'd better look into it." He shrugged. "Sorry."

That was aimed at both him and Trey, Link supposed. After all, it had been their uncle's house. There would be talk, speculation about the possible relationship between Allen Morgan and the Angelo woman. Adam might want to keep it quiet, but they all knew how impossible that was in a place like Spring Township.

Link picked up the photograph, looking into the big brown eyes of the little girl, feeling again that sense of something wrong he'd had the first time he looked at her face, reminding him of those other children who saw death and destruction everyday. Stronger than that—it was a sense of empathy, as if the child meant something to him.

"One thing I do know," he said. "This kid, or rather, the woman she is now—

she deserves to know what happened to her mother."

Marisa Angelo felt as if she hadn't taken a breath since she left Baltimore. Cutting the car engine, she stared at the house in front of her. It stood on the fringe of the village of Springville, but still gave the illusion of privacy, hidden as it was behind a hedge of lilac bushes so high that nothing could be seen from the road.

Marisa got out slowly, pushing the strap of her bag onto her shoulder, unable to take her gaze from the house. It was probably like a hundred other farmhouses in this rural area of Pennsylvania; a two-story white frame with black wooden shutters on the windows. But instead of being surrounded by neat flowerbeds, it hid behind overgrown trees, its windows shielded by blinds so that it seemed to sleep.

A shiver slid through her. She was being morbid. She shouldn't let this experience get to her. From the moment the police chief called her, after being unable to reach her father, she'd been focused on one thing only: get here. Find out what this place had to do with the disappearance of her mother that had left a hole in her heart nothing seemed to fill. She'd packed a bag, collected the materials she needed for her current set of illustrations, and set off.

She'd been five when her mother left, six when she and her father and grandmother moved to Baltimore. This area ought to be familiar to her, but she seemed to have only fragments of memories that didn't amount to anything—an image of herself jumping rope on a sidewalk, the scary feeling of standing onstage in what must have been an elementary-school program.

They'd left, they'd never come back, she'd forgotten this place, even though her dreams were haunted by the need to know. To understand what happened.

Gradually, over the past few years, when every line of inquiry came up empty, she'd thought she was accepting the fact that she'd never know. But when the call came, it was as if she'd been waiting for it all her life.

She closed the car door and walked

toward the house. Blank and shuttered, it looked deserted, but someone must be here. The police chief had said the owner was renovating the place. Seeming to understand her need to see for herself, Chief Byler had agreed to meet her here.

She had one foot on the porch step when she heard the noise—a steady series of thuds coming from the rear of the building. Maybe the renovator was still at work.

The yard behind the house proved just as secluded as the front. A stand of pines pressed close, reaching over a fieldstone wall to threaten a garage and a couple of outbuildings that tilted into each other in a dispirited manner. The source of the noise was instantly obvious.

The man, in jeans and a T-shirt, worked steadily, oblivious to her presence. Pick up a short log, set it on a stump, split it with an axe, toss it aside. His movements were smooth, efficient and almost angry in their intensity.

From the top of the stone wall, a large black cat watched with the casual indifference of its kind. He put up a lazy paw to swipe his face, his eyes never leaving the figure.

The contrast between the lean ferocity of the man and the lazy feline grace of the cat had her fingers itching. She pulled the ever-present pad and pencil from her bag, intent on capturing the scene in quick strokes. With a few changes, this might fit into the children's book she was illustrating. Even if it didn't, she couldn't resist.

The image was nearly complete when the man clutched his side with a grunt, dropping the axe. The cat vanished over the wall. She must have made some move, because the man spun and strode toward her, transferring that angry intensity from the logs to her.

"What are you doing?" He reached her, grabbing the pad from her hand and giving the drawing an angry glance. "What right do you have invading my privacy? Well?"

Panic clutched her throat at the angry voice. She forced it back, a millimeter at a time. She would not give in to it.

"I'm sorry." She found her voice. "I

didn't mean to intrude. I'm afraid I couldn't resist the contrast between your work and your cat's laziness." She tried for a smile that felt stiff on her lips.

"Not my cat." He handed the pad back to her and made a visible effort to contain himself, strong mouth firming, lashes shielding piercing green eyes for an instant. He yanked a handkerchief from his jeans pocket and wiped away the perspiration that beaded his forehead in spite of the coolness of the October day. He ran the cloth back over short dark brown hair and along his neck. "Are you looking for directions, Ms...?"

"Angelo. Marisa Angelo," she said, and saw his face change when he heard the name. This must be the man who'd found the suitcase, then, the man who'd inherited the house from an uncle, according to the police chief.

"Sorry." His voice went softer, rougher. "I didn't realize you were coming here. The person you want is Adam Byler, the township police chief. If you head back down the road—"

"I've already talked to him. He's meeting me here. Didn't he let you know?" She couldn't let him send her away, not when the only clue she'd ever had to her mother's disappearance had been found here.

"No." The word was so blunt that for a moment she thought he'd still send her packing. Then he managed a smile that gentled the harsh lines of his face. "I've been outside most of the day. Not paying any attention to the phone. I'm Link Morgan, by the way. Sorry to meet you under such circumstances."

The words were conventional. Could Link Morgan begin to understand what this meant to her? Or was her arrival just an unwelcome interruption to his work?

"Chief Byler said that you found my mother's suitcase while you were renovating the house?" She made it a question, since he didn't seem very forthcoming.

"Right." His jaw tightened. "I guess you want to see where?"

"If it's not too much trouble."

He sent a harassed glance toward the lane, as if willing the police car to appear. "Fine." He brushed his hands on his jeans. "I guess I'd better get washed up."

She followed him to the back door. His gait was ever-so-slightly uneven, reminding her of how he'd ended his woodcutting. "Are you all right?"

"What do you mean?" He turned on her, his lean, strong-featured face forbidding.

"I just... You looked as if you'd hurt yourself when you were cutting wood."

"I'm fine. Just got a stitch in my side." He held the door for her. "This leads into the addition to the house, where I've been working."

She went up the two steps into the house, steeling herself. No matter how much this affected her, she didn't want to show her pain in front of this stranger.

But it was just a room—long, running across the width of the farmhouse, with a fieldstone fireplace in the middle of the back wall. The walls were bare to the studs, with broken paneling stacked on the floor.

"I'll get washed up. Adam will probably be here by then." He disappeared into a room that must be a kitchen, and she heard the sound of running water.

She set her bag on a rough worktable and looked around. There was nothing to see. Just a virtually empty room, a shell waiting for renovation. If Link Morgan hadn't decided to tear off the old paneling, he wouldn't have found the suitcase. She'd have gone on for maybe the rest of her life knowing nothing more than that her mother had abandoned her.

Morgan came back in, pulling a flannel shirt on over his T-shirt. He was thin, she realized, not just lean. Strongly muscled but underweight, as if he'd been sick. Maybe her question about being hurt hadn't been too tactful.

"It was there, next to the fireplace." He indicated the spot with a nod. "When I saw what was inside—well, I had to call the police."

Delaying his renovation, obviously. "I guess you're eager to get the work done so you can enjoy your house."

He shook his head sharply. "I'm renovating it to sell. I want to get it finished and put it on the market before winter."

His priorities were clear, it seemed.

But so were hers. She'd governed her life by the knowledge that her mother hadn't loved her enough to stay with her. Now she had a hint, the tiniest thread, which seemed to say that might not be true. No matter who it inconvenienced, she wouldn't stop pulling at that thread until she knew the truth.

Link couldn't help but compare the woman in front of him with the child in the photograph who'd taken such a hold on his emotions. The adult Marisa had a slender, delicate build, like the little girl. Her brown hair, a bit darker than the shade in the picture, reached her shoulders, curling slightly.

The eyes in her oval face were those of the child in the picture—golden brown, with a touch of vulnerability that seared him. He couldn't let anyone lean on him, especially not this vulnerable stranger with the familiar eyes.

"Is something wrong?" She brushed her hair back, flushing slightly. "A smudge on my face?"

"No." It was his turn to feel embarrassed. "You just... I guess I was comparing you with the photo in the suitcase."

"Photo?" She was clearly at sea.

"Adam didn't tell you? There was a picture of your mother and you in the suitcase. That's how we were able to identify the owner so quickly. I'm surprised Adam didn't mention it."

"Maybe he did. I guess I found the news all a bit hard to take in."

"You must have dropped everything to get here so quickly." Was it odd, her showing up so fast? He wasn't sure.

"Once I heard, I couldn't think of anything else." She rubbed her arms, as if she felt a chill. "My work is freelance, so I just packed it up and brought it. I couldn't not come, once I heard."

He considered how that must have felt. "That almost sounds as if you were expecting something of the kind."

"Of course I wasn't."

There was a hint of something held back in her tone that bothered him.

No getting involved. Stay out of it. But he had to ask. "Did your mother know my uncle?"

"I have no idea." The brown eyes flashed. She clearly resented the implication.

Had he been implying anything? He just wanted to understand this, so he could put it behind him.

Marisa turned away, seeming to glance around the room almost at random, as if searching for something to take them away from an awkward place. "It looks as if you're making good progress in here."

"I wasn't, but once the police got into the act, the paneling came down pretty fast." Almost instantly he regretted the careless words, because she paled, obviously understanding why the police had gotten involved.

"We didn't find anything."

He rushed the words. It didn't help. His hands curled into fists. The whole situation angered him. Talking to this woman was like walking through a minefield, where any step could end up maiming someone.

Relief flooded through him at the sound of a car. "That'll be Adam." He went quickly to the door.

Adam got out of the police car, alone this time, and pulled out the suitcase. So, he was going to show it to her. Well, Marisa had probably as much right to it as anyone.

"Adam." He could only hope the relief didn't show in his voice. "Ms. Angelo, this is Adam Byler." He made introductions as Adam walked in. "Adam, Marisa Angelo. But I guess you've spoken on the phone."

Adam nodded, shaking hands gravely before swinging the suitcase onto the worktable where it had lain the previous day. Link was glad to retreat into the background while Adam went over the circumstances of finding the case and identifying her mother from the photograph.

"Yes, Mr. Morgan told me about it." Marisa reached toward the case, her hands hesitant. "May I see?"

"Of course. We've already run a few tests on it, just to be on the safe side." Adam took a step back, as if giving her space.

Marisa opened the case. The photograph now lay on top, faceup, so that it was the first thing she saw. Link could hear the way her breath choked at the sight. His throat tightened in response.

She picked up the photograph, holding it for a long moment, her fingers caressing the pictured faces. Then she cradled it against her chest.

"This is mine." She looked at Adam, as if expecting an argument.

"I suppose it is." His voice was gentle. "Or maybe more accurately your father's, but we haven't been able to reach him."

He knew Adam well. Maybe that was how he detected the hint of suspicion underlying the words.

Marisa didn't seem to. "Dad won't mind if I have the picture. I'm sorry you weren't able to reach him, but since he retired, he takes off in that RV of his at a moment's notice."

"Doesn't he have a cell phone?" Adam asked the question lightly, as if intent on not alarming her.

"He does, but half the time he doesn't check it from one week to the next." She didn't seem to find that odd, which argued that father and daughter weren't very close. "I've left a message for him to call me, and I'll let you know as soon as I hear from him."

"That'll be fine." Adam glanced at his watch. "It's getting late, and I know this is a lot to take in. If you don't mind staying over in the area tonight, maybe we can meet in my office tomorrow to talk things over."

She looked at him, blinking a little. "Tonight? I'll be here longer than that."

Adam seemed taken aback. "That's really not necessary, you know. We'll continue to look into the situation, and we'll let you know if and when we learn anything. I'm sure you want to get back to your own life."

In other words, Adam didn't want her here, dogging his every step. Link couldn't agree more.

Marisa's shoulders stiffened. She looked very deliberately from him to Adam. "I can see why you feel that way, but I have no intention of going anywhere. I intend to stay in Springville until I know why my mother's suitcase was inside the wall of this house."

# CHAPTER TWO

Marisa could see how unwelcome that announcement was to both men. With her unfortunate knack for empathy, she could easily put herself in their places.

The police chief was simplest to figure. He clearly wanted a free hand with his investigation, and he didn't want to tell her anything he didn't have to. Not that he suspected her—he could hardly believe that a five-year-old child would be involved in her mother's disappearance.

But her father was another matter.

Didn't the police automatically suspect the spouse when a woman disappeared?

Or died. She forced herself to finish that thought.

"Ms. Angelo, I hate to see you do that." The police chief sounded as harassed at the thought of her staying as she expected him to. "You'll just be kicking your heels around here to no purpose. It's hardly likely that we can find anything else out about what happened after all these years."

"You found the suitcase," she pointed out.

"Link did." Chief Byler shot a look at the other man. "If he hadn't been renovating the house, we wouldn't have known anything about it."

"But you have to investigate." A thought struck her with the force of a blow. "You must have investigated then. Well, I mean not you personally." He was far too young for that, probably not much more than in his early thirties. "But the police must have."

She'd never known. She could only wonder at herself. A child accepted what she was told by the authority figures in her life, of course. But later, when she'd wanted to understand, it hadn't occurred to her to ask her father what the police had thought.

"True, they did." Adam Byler leaned against the rough table, seeming to resign himself to the questions. "I've looked into the reports, talked to officers who were working then."

"And what did they say?" Was she going to have to drag information from the man? Ordinarily she probably wouldn't have had the nerve to confront him, but these weren't ordinary circumstances.

She couldn't read anything in his square, impassive face. She suspected he was trying to decide what and how much to tell her.

As for Link Morgan—well, he'd backed away, as if trying to disassociate himself from the whole business. He probably regretted that he hadn't thrown the suitcase on the trash heap without opening it.

"People noticed that your mother wasn't around any longer," Byler said. "Your father said she'd left him. That she hadn't been able to go on living English and she'd gone back to her people in Indiana. For the most part, the police accepted that."

Byler's lips clamped shut on the words. Was the implication that he wouldn't have?

"You know that your mother was Amish?" Link Morgan asked the question with a kind of reluctant concern in his voice.

She nodded. That she did know, but only because she'd pried it out of her grandmother, who was easier to talk to than her father. "I know. And my father said she'd gone back to her family because that was what he thought she'd done."

A shiver skittered along her nerves. She believed that. She had to.

"My grandmother said my mother had talked about going back to her family," she went on. "Grandma said my mother found it hard to give up her people and her faith the way she had."

*But how could she leave me behind?* The child who lived inside her asked the question she couldn't.

"You might want to see what else is in the suitcase," Link suggested.

She shot a look at him. That fine-drawn face, with the skin taut against the bones—she still had the urge to draw it every time she looked at him. What made him look that way? Illness? Grief? Guilt?

Slowly she lifted out folded clothing. Her fingers hesitated when they touched the black garment. Then she lifted it, shook it out.

"It's the kind of apron an Amish woman wears. And there's the prayer covering they always have on their heads." He nodded toward the object in the bottom of the case, not moving.

She picked it up, her fingers tingling a little. White organdy, a kind of small hat with long strings. She'd seen pictures of Amish women, looking almost like nuns in their dark dresses and identical hair styles, with the white covering on their heads. She'd taken a book out of the school library, she remembered, and hidden it under the mattress so Daddy wouldn't see.

"That would seem to confirm that she

was planning to leave," Chief Byler said. "As to how that suitcase ended up here, and where she went—we're as much in the dark as we were twenty-three years ago."

For her father's sake, she had to ask the question. "Is this a criminal investigation?"

Byler's expression didn't change, but Link Morgan's mouth tightened, as if in pain.

"Not at this time," Byler said. "For all we know, your mother did disappear back into an Amish community somewhere. That's possible, even in this age of instant communication. If so, and if she doesn't want to be found, the Amish would never give her up."

"I know." Her thoughts flickered to her own futile effort to find out something from her mother's relatives in Indiana. "So, if it's not a criminal investigation, will you do anything?" She didn't mean that to sound critical, but she had to understand.

"We'll pursue the leads we have." That sounded final, and the police chief closed the suitcase and lifted it from the table. "If you're intent on staying, please let my office know how to reach you. We'll contact you if we find anything."

She nodded, watching him walk to the door. He hadn't sounded particularly hopeful.

He turned at the door, hand on the screen. "Don't forget, Ms. Angelo. Let us know as soon as you hear from your father. We'd like to speak with him." He didn't wait for a response.

Her stomach tightened in apprehension as she watched him walk toward the patrol car. The fact that the police would suspect her father hadn't occurred to her when she'd rushed off in response to the phone call.

"He thinks my father had something to do with this, doesn't he?" The moment she asked the question, she regretted it. Link obviously didn't want to be involved in her troubles, and she certainly had no reason to confide in him.

"Adam is a fair-minded person. He wouldn't jump to any conclusions."

"But the husband is always a suspect. That's what you're thinking, isn't it?"

"I'm not thinking anything." His tone

was cool and dismissive. "I'm sorry for your—" he hesitated, and she suspected he'd been about to say *her loss* "—your situation, but it's nothing to do with me."

"You found the suitcase. It's your uncle's house. You have a responsibility—"

"I don't have any responsibility at all." The words came quick and angry. "There's nothing I can do."

He'd walk away, she thought, except that it was his house, which meant she was the one who had to walk away. Marisa took a deep breath and realized she was trembling. Confrontation definitely wasn't her strong suit.

"I see." She managed to keep her voice calm. "Thank you for your trouble."

She turned and walked to the door. She'd come here looking for answers, but it seemed all she'd found were more questions.

Link scowled at the high-school photos that still adorned the wall of the room that had been his as a kid and yanked open a drawer to find a clean shirt. Mom wouldn't hear of his being on his own when they'd finally released him from the military hospital, of course, and he'd been too weak to argue the point. But looking at the remnants of the life he used to live wasn't doing a thing for his morale.

Well, it would soon be over, and he'd move on. This business with the suitcase could have been worse. Now it was in Adam's capable hands, and Marisa Angelo's troubles were Adam's concern.

He'd been telling himself that all afternoon. So why did he still feel like such a loser? He wasn't responsible for the woman.

Trouble was, he'd always been a sucker for vulnerable brown eyes.

He pushed away the image of that heart-shaped face. Marisa wouldn't stick this out, anyway. She'd get tired of waiting around for news that didn't come and go back to wherever she'd come from—Baltimore, Adam had said.

Adam didn't want the woman here. But he did want to see her father. Marisa had been right about one thing. The police did always suspect the husband when a woman disappeared.

Funny that the cops hadn't looked

into it more thoroughly at the time. He'd have thought—

No, he wasn't going to obsess about Marisa Angelo.

He started down the stairs, running his hand along the railing that four or five generations of Morgans had touched. He never used to spare a thought for things like that. Trey was the oldest son—he'd always figured Trey was responsible for carrying on the family traditions.

But somehow the tour of duty in Afghanistan had made Link look at things differently, like this old house and the countryside that surrounded it. Morgan land, just like probably half of Spring Township was Morgan land.

*We have a duty to the land,* Grandpa used to say. *And to the people who live here.*

A stickler for duty, the old man had been, accepting no excuses for not doing what you should. Like dealing with Marisa Angelo's problem. And Uncle Allen's possible involvement.

But he wasn't going to see Marisa Angelo again.

Voices came from the living room.

Mom had said that Jessica Langdon, Trey's fiancée, was coming for dinner tonight, so apparently they were gathering there. He paused for a moment and then headed toward the archway.

Not that he didn't like Jessica—she was a smart city attorney who'd recently gone into partnership with an old friend of his father's. But tonight he wasn't in the mood to be sociable. Maybe he could—

He reached the living room and stopped. Jessica and Trey were there all right, talking to Mom, who was poised like a butterfly in flight, waving a tray of appetizers while she talked to the woman who sat in the Queen Anne armchair. Marisa Angelo.

"Link, there you are." His mother spun with one of her quick moves, the sleeves of her filmy top fluttering and the tray waving.

"Here I am," he agreed, taking the tray from her. "And these cheese puffs are about to be on the floor."

"Nonsense. I had a firm grip on them." She patted his cheek as if he were about four. "Now, you've already met Marisa, haven't you? I stopped by Adam's office while I was in town to see what he'd found out about that suitcase, and Marisa was there. So I just brought her along home for supper so we could all talk it over." Mom beamed, obviously pleased with her solution.

He had to suppress a groan. Geneva Morgan was known far and wide for her warm hospitality and her habit of adopting any stray that crossed her path, but he wished for once she'd restrained herself.

He nodded to Marisa, trying to look as if he wasn't aghast to find her in his mother's living room. "Marisa. I didn't realize you were headed back to the police station after you left my place."

Her eyes said it wasn't any of his business where she went. "I thought of a few more things I wanted to say to Chief Byler."

Trey must have thought that sounded ominous, because he frowned. "Adam Byler's a good man. If there's anything to find, I'm sure he'll find it."

That was not exactly what worried Marisa about him, Link suspected.

"Yes, he...he seems very capable." Marisa's expression suggested that she didn't want to discuss it, and probably also that she was wondering what had induced her to accept Mom's invitation.

Plenty of people had occasion to wonder how Geneva Morgan became entangled in their affairs. Trey had had his hands full since Dad's death. Their mother never saw a problem that she didn't consider it her duty to resolve.

"You must have been so shocked at Adam's call." His mother leaned over to pat Marisa's hand. "Poor child. And with your father out of touch, it all falls on you."

Marisa stiffened. Mom wouldn't understand that the subject of her father's absence was a touchy one, of course. His mind scrambled for something to say that would divert the conversation, but he couldn't come up with a thing.

"I understand you'll be staying around for a few days." Jessica broke what was becoming an uncomfortable silence. "It's fortunate you were able to take time off work."

Marisa turned to her gratefully, maybe

glad to see someone who wasn't a Morgan. "That wasn't an issue. I'm a freelance illustrator, and as long as I turn projects in on time, it doesn't matter where I do them."

"Really? That's fascinating. I don't think I ever met an illustrator before. What are you working on?" Jessica leaned forward, her interest sounding genuine.

"Right now I'm doing illustrations for a children's book. The story is set in a rural area, as a matter of fact, so these surroundings are perfect."

The first smile Link had seen from her curved Marisa's lips and lit her eyes. With the stress momentarily wiped from her face, she seemed to glow with enthusiasm for her work, drawing him closer. Too bad she couldn't look like that all the time. He hadn't given much of a thought to women since his injury, but now he felt that flicker of interest that was the first step toward attraction.

"But about this suitcase." Mom perched on the edge of a chair, clearly not distracted. "Have you any idea how it got there? Did your father ever mention that it was missing?"

"I don't think so." Marisa's lips tightened again. "Not to me, anyway. I was just five when my mother left." She hesitated. "If she did leave."

Trey's hand clenched. He was probably thinking, as Link was, about the implications of Uncle Allen being involved in the woman's disappearance. Mom had had enough grief in her life with Dad's death. She shouldn't have to face any more.

"Surely the fact that the suitcase was packed indicates that she at least planned to leave," Trey said.

"That's true, but why—?"

Mom's question was interrupted by a movement in the archway. Katie Zeller, one of several Amish teens who helped Mom around the house, stood there, probably waiting patiently for a break in the conversation.

Mom turned. "Oh, Katie, I'm sorry. Is everything ready?"

Katie nodded. "Ja. Did you want me to dish up already?"

"Please. I'll come and help you." Mom rose, waving toward the dining room. "The rest of you find seats. We'll get the food on right away. I'm sure Marisa is starved, and here we've been keeping her talking instead of feeding her."

"I'm not..." Marisa began, and let the word trail off when Mom vanished toward the kitchen.

"Pretend you're hungry," Trey advised, taking Jessica's hand as they moved into the dining room. "Our mother is only happy when she's feeding people."

"Well, now, I might resent that if it weren't true." Mom and her helper carried steaming bowls and platters to the table. "Katie and I made chicken pot pie for supper. I thought Marisa ought to sample some traditional Pennsylvania Dutch food while she's here."

Link held Marisa's chair while she sat down. Manners might be a vanishing art some places, but not in his mother's house. Marisa, he noticed, was staring at Katie, something almost tragic in her eyes.

Thinking about that Amish apron and kapp in her mother's suitcase? Both looked identical to the ones Katie wore at the moment. He sat down next to Marisa, turning that over in his mind.

By the time the food platters had circled the table, Marisa had regained her poise, as far as he could tell.

His mother glanced around the table, blue eyes sparkling. "This is nice, having a full table again. And you know, I think I can answer at least one of the questions that's perplexing Marisa."

Marisa's fingers tightened on her fork. "What question is that?"

"How the suitcase came to be in Allen's house, of course."

Link exchanged glances with Trey. What was their mother up to now?

"How would you be able to explain that?" He had a feeling he wasn't going to like the answer.

"It's simple, really. I thought of it last night, but then I never had a chance to tell you because you left so early this morning, Link."

"Tell me what?" Dealing with his mother required more patience than he possessed at the moment, and Marisa's tension seemed to vibrate through the space between them.

"Why, that Barbara Angelo was your uncle Allen's housekeeper, of course."

. . .

Marisa found that Link's hand was in her line of vision, lying on the white tablecloth next to hers. Hers was clenched around a fork. His had tightened into so hard a fist that the tendons stood out on the back of it.

Did that mean he was as shocked at Geneva's revelation as she was? Or did it mean that he hated the fact that it had come out?

"What are you talking about, Mom?" Across the table from her, Trey had found his voice.

Marisa studied him. A year or two older than Link, maybe, but his face, while serious, didn't carry those lines of tension which marked Link. At the moment Trey was staring at his mother in what seemed honest surprise.

"About Marisa's mother, Barbara Angelo. She worked for your uncle for a while, taking care of the house for him. Although why he needed a housekeeper, I never understood. There he was all by himself, practically a hermit. You'd think he could easily have done for himself..."

"Give it a rest, Mom." Trey seemed to

relax during his mother's wanderings. Maybe he was used to the track her thoughts took. "We all know you didn't like Dad's brother."

Geneva straightened, her shoulders back. "Trey, that is absolutely not true. I didn't dislike your uncle. I just said he didn't need a housekeeper. He could easily have taken care of things himself. Why, your father—"

"Dad was a paragon," Trey said, smiling a little. "But you know perfectly well he never washed a dish in his life. You wouldn't let him."

"You always thought Uncle Allen was lazy," Link said. "Typical younger son, taking life easy while his older brother did all the work."

That sounded like a teasing comment. Certainly the others took it that way, joining in kidding the older woman. But Marisa had heard an undercurrent in Link's voice that made her wonder. Was that how they'd seen Allen Morgan? Or was Link feeling guilty over something he had or hadn't done?

She expected Geneva to come back to the subject of her mother working as

Allen Morgan's housekeeper, but that didn't happen. At first she thought Geneva didn't care to talk about it, but as Marisa watched them, she realized that Trey and Link were steering the conversation away from that revelation.

They were protective of Geneva. Even Jessica joined in, keeping the talk light as they ate their way through the delectable chicken pot pie and a sweet and nutty squash casserole. At least, Marisa tried to eat. She ought to be hungry, but her stomach seemed tied in a permanent knot since she'd come to this place.

How normal was their protectiveness? She couldn't really compare them with her family. With Daddy away so much working, family had usually consisted of just her and her grandmother.

Finally everyone was finished, and Geneva suggested a move back into the living room for dessert and coffee. Jessica sat down next to Marisa, while Geneva disappeared into the kitchen and the two men halted in front of the fireplace, heads down in a low-voiced conversation.

"Don't mind them," Jessica said, nodding toward the two men. "I try to tell Trey he shouldn't be so protective of his mother, but everyone does it." She smiled. "I even find myself doing it sometimes, and the truth is that she's probably wiser than all of us put together, despite that scatterbrained façade."

"Is it an act?" She couldn't help voicing her doubts.

Jessica seemed to consider. "Not entirely. I think she has the sort of mind which jumps ahead of logic, very often arriving at the right answer without apparent effort. Of course, sometimes she's completely wrong, too."

"I'm not sure why she thought everything would be cleared up by knowing that my mother worked for Allen Morgan. If anything, it makes the whole thing more..." She hesitated. She'd been going to say *suspicious,* but that was hardly the thing to say to Trey's fiancée. "...confusing, I suppose."

Jessica nodded. "You've never heard anything from your mother in all these years?"

"No." The word had an empty sound.

"I'm sorry." Jessica touched her hand

lightly. "My mother died when I was quite young. It's so hard."

She nodded, unable to speak for a moment. There was a lump in her throat to go with the knot in her stomach.

Ridiculous. She was just exhausted, that was all. Getting that call, loading the car, rushing up to Lancaster County, and then all the turmoil of the day—no wonder she felt emotional. She needed a good night's sleep far more than she needed coffee and dessert.

She also needed to talk with Geneva at some point, to see what she actually remembered about her mother's employment by Allen Morgan. But that conversation could wait until she could catch the woman alone, without her protective sons.

Geneva came back in the room with a coffee tray, followed by the Amish teenager with another tray of dessert plates. Marisa found her gaze caught by the girl. Would her mother have looked like that, with the solid-color dress, the dark apron, the hair pulled back into a bun and covered by the white net cap? Would she have had those rosy cheeks, that shy manner? Was that what she'd run away to?

Marisa stood abruptly and then bent to retrieve her handbag from the side of the chair.

"This has been very kind of you, Mrs. Morgan, but I'm so tired I'm going to have to call it a night."

"Please, call me Geneva, remember? And you can't go without dessert. Just a little piece." She sounded as if she were coaxing a toddler to eat her peas.

"I couldn't eat another bite, really. Thank you, Geneva. It was nice to meet all of you."

"But where are you going to stay?" Geneva put the tray on a drop-leaf table and caught her hand. "We'd be so happy to have you stay here with us. The guest room is always ready. You don't want to go off looking for a motel at this time of night."

"I already have a reservation," she said quickly. "I'm staying at the Plain and Fancy Bed and Breakfast. I'm sure I'll be fine there."

"You'll be fine once you find it." Link rose from the chair by the fireplace, stretching as if he had to work out some kinks. "I'll lead you there."

"I'm sure I can find it—"

"No, no, Link is right. It's impossible to read those street signs after dark, and I'll never forgive myself if you have an accident." Geneva patted her hand. "Just follow Link, and he'll lead you right to the place. Rhoda Miller will make you very comfortable if you're sure you won't stay with us."

It sounded as if accepting Link's guidance was the only way she was going to get out of here quickly. "Thank you again."

Link was already standing in the archway. She went quickly to join him and followed him through the center hallway and out the front door.

Lights came on as soon as they stepped outside, revealing a sweep of gravel on which several cars were parked. Beyond that, the circle of light quickly petered out. The Morgan house was well out into the country, probably six or seven miles from Springville. Nothing out here but dark grass, dark trees and a chilly wind. She pulled her jacket around her.

"Cold?" Link said, walking beside her to her car.

"I'm fine. It's just been a long day."

He stood next to her while she unlocked the door and opened it. She slid in. His hand was on the door, but he didn't close it immediately.

"What my mother said about my uncle—I wouldn't pin too much on that, if I were you."

"I don't understand what you mean." She looked at him, and his face was all craggy lines and shadows in the dim light.

He seemed to shift, as if tensing for an argument. "The fact that your mother worked for my uncle doesn't lead anywhere. I don't know what you expect to find, but my mother can't help you."

"I just want—"

He stepped away. "I'll pull my car around, and you can follow me. Just remember what I said. Don't badger my mother about this." He stalked off, and the darkness swallowed him up.

# CHAPTER THREE

The narrow blacktop road spun away beyond the reach of his headlights. Link glanced in his rearview mirror to be sure Marisa was still behind him.

He probably shouldn't have said what he did to Marisa about bugging Mom on this subject. Maybe he'd just given her ideas, but he'd seen her watching Mom after the shock of her revelation faded.

It had been obvious Marisa saw his mother as a source of information. Still, if Mom was determined, she'd most likely be the one asking the questions.

Protecting their mother was Trey's

job, had been from the day of Dad's death, and he did it as well as anyone could. The best thing Link could do was get on with the renovation, get himself back to top shape and head out to California. How much was this issue going to set him back?

He could just leave. Deed the house over to Trey, let him renovate it or rent it or tear it down, for that matter. But Uncle Allen had left the place to him. Second son to second son, he'd said once, with a wry smile. Maybe he owed Allen some loyalty in return.

He pulled up at the Plain and Fancy, frowning a little. The house, a tidy Dutch colonial on one of Springville's cross streets, didn't show any signs of life except for the pole lamp by the gate. Marisa had said she had a reservation, hadn't she?

He slid out, walking quickly back to the other car. He'd help her with her luggage, maybe try to smooth any ruffled feathers.

Marisa was already pulling a suitcase from the trunk. He reached over her shoulder to grab the handle, lifting it out.

"I'll carry this. Do you want the duffel bag as well?" He paused, hand on the strap. No point in taking in anything she didn't want. And given the size of the suitcase, she hadn't planned to stay long when she left.

"I can manage." Her voice was frosty.

"I'm sure you can, but you don't need to." He hefted the duffel bag. "Besides, when I get home, Mom will ask if I helped you in with your luggage. You don't want to get me in trouble, do you?"

That earned him a faint smile, but then her gaze slid away from his as if she remembered that she was angry with him.

"Look, I shouldn't have said what I did about bugging my mother, okay?" He slammed down the trunk lid. "It's far more likely that she'll be bugging you."

"I take it both you and your brother think I should leave my mother's disappearance to the professionals." She marched toward the gate, and he followed.

"Seems like the sensible thing to do," he said mildly. "If there's anything to be found, they have the facilities. You don't."

"They didn't do so well before—" She

stopped on the porch, taking in the dark windows. "Should they be closed this early?"

"Springville rolls up the sidewalks at eight-thirty." He put his finger on the bell, hearing it jangle beyond the frosted glass of the door. "You did say you had a reservation, didn't you?"

She nodded, the movement barely visible in the dim light. "I saw the place listed on one of those tourist maps. The woman I spoke to said they had a room available."

"By the looks of it, they have plenty." He eyed the dark windows. "They wouldn't be busy on a weekday in October." He set the bags down. "Maybe we should—"

"Who is there?" The gruff voice came from the dark side lawn. An instant later Eli Miller stepped into the faint light of the pole lamp, the breeze ruffling his beard, his black pants and jacket disappearing into the darkness. "What do you want?"

Marisa took a step back, sucking in a startled breath. She was so close Link could feel the tremor that went through her at the sight of the Amish man.

"Eli, it's me, Link Morgan. I brought Ms. Angelo. She has a reservation."

"Ms. Angelo?" Eli lifted the flashlight he held, switching it on.

Marisa's face was white in the harsh beam of light. She didn't speak. What was wrong with the woman, anyway?

"She called to make a reservation," he explained.

"Ach, ja. I am so sorry. My Rhoda isn't so gut at talking on the telephone. She thought you were coming tomorrow. It's a mix-up for sure." Eli didn't sound put out at the prospect of an unexpected guest. "I'll chust go back to our side of the house for the key. I'll be right with you." He chuckled. "I'll tease Rhoda about being so ferhoodled, that's certain-sure."

He switched off the light and strode back toward the semi-detached wing where the family lived, apparently more comfortable without it.

Marisa let out an audible breath. He turned, frowning at her.

"What's going on? You've seen Amish people before, haven't you?"

Her shoulders stiffened. "I don't know what you mean."

"When you saw Eli, you reacted as if he was some kind of monster."

"I didn't." But her voice lacked conviction.

"You did. And you weren't natural with Katie, either, back at the house."

She might have told him to mind his own business, but she didn't. "I...I just haven't been around Amish people much, that's all."

"It never surprises me how prejudiced some people can be," he said deliberately. "But your mother was Amish."

"Yes. She was." Marisa glared at him. "And all I ever heard about the Amish was how they wouldn't leave her alone and how they lured my mother away from us. My grandmother said it was like a cult that wouldn't let her go."

"Cult?" He kept his voice low. Eli could be coming back at any moment. "That's ridiculous. They're as normal as anyone. More normal than most, in fact. If your father told you that—"

"Not my father. He never talked about my mother." Some of the anger seemed to go out of her. "My grandmother. All right, maybe Gran was a bit judgmental about people who are different."

"You see—"

"But I went out to Indiana a few years ago when I finally located my mother's family. I thought..." Her voice trembled and fell silent.

But he could finish the sentence. She'd thought she might find her mother.

"They stonewalled me. They wouldn't even talk to me about her. So I don't exactly have any reason to like them."

"I'm sorry." He was. No matter how inconvenient her presence was for him, he couldn't help feeling her grief.

A door closed next door, and he heard a jingling sound that might be a key ring. Eli was coming.

"Look, if you want, I'll take you to a motel. I'll make some excuse to Eli. But..." He was about to involve himself more deeply in Marisa's problem, despite his determination to stay uninvolved. "But if you really want to find out what happened twenty-three years ago, you might need to have some allies among the local Amish. Eli and Rhoda Miller could be a good place to start."

A little silence fell between them, and her reluctance was so strong he could almost feel it. Then she nodded.

"You're right. I'll stay."

Marisa woke sometime in the dark hours of the night, a cry clutching her throat. She sat upright, heart pounding. Had she cried out aloud? She didn't think so, but she cringed at the thought of Eli Miller hearing, running to her room...

But he wouldn't hear. First, because the cry had only been in her dreams. And second, because the Millers slept in their own separate section of the house next door. She was the only occupant of the Plain and Fancy.

She rubbed her forehead, willing herself to remember her dream. Something about herself as a child, waking in the night, calling out for her mother. Frightened when Mammi didn't come. Crawling out of bed, drawn toward the window, her bare feet cold on the wide wooden boards of the floor.

She could almost see it, white net curtains billowing inward from the wind. Almost.

But even as she tried to focus, the dream began slithering away from her grasp in the manner of most dreams, vanishing faster the harder she tried to grasp it.

*Forget it,* she ordered. *Go back to sleep.* But she was awake now, too awake to slip under the covers. She fumbled for the clock on the bedside table. Three o'clock. And she hadn't managed to drop off until sometime after midnight.

It was small wonder that she'd entangled herself in a bad dream, after all that had happened. That suitcase. The photo.

Her throat thickened at that. She had a copy of that picture, too, always kept carefully out of Daddy's sight because she'd thought, with a child's logic, that it would make him sad.

She swung her legs off the bed, her bare feet encountering a braided rug. She might as well get up. Try to distract herself from the endless questions that circled in her thoughts.

But that was easier said than done. She switched on the lamp on the bed-side table, and the room sprang into view. The Miller family apparently did without electricity over on their side, but provided it for their business. The logic of that escaped her.

The second floor guest room was plain and simple, with good, solid-wood furniture pieces and a comfortable padded rocking chair. The handmade quilt that covered the bed was such a work of art that she had folded it carefully and placed it atop the blanket chest before she did anything else. The room had seemed somehow familiar, as if she'd slept here before, even though she knew she hadn't.

After such an unpromising start, the Millers had done their best to make her feel welcome and comfortable. Rhoda had scurried over immediately behind her husband to show Marisa the room, and a teenage girl had followed in a few minutes with a tray containing a mug of hot chocolate and a plate of oatmeal cookies.

But despite their welcome, she still couldn't feel at ease in their presence. Her grandmother's words seemed to rattle around in the back of her mind.

*They wouldn't leave her alone. They didn't want to let her go.*

If she'd taken Link up on his offer,

she'd be pacing the floor in some anonymous motel room. But little though she liked to admit it, he'd been right. If she was going to find out what happened to her mother, part of the answer must lie with the Amish people her mother had known here.

Not *if.* She would find out. She had to. She'd spent years trying to forget, trying to live without answers the way Dad seemed able to do, and she couldn't. Not when there was a hole the size of the Grand Canyon in her psyche echoing with the same whisper, over and over. *Your mother didn't want you.*

She forced herself to stop pacing. Gran would call these middle-of-the-night fears, treating them with a hot drink, a little comforting and the assurance that things would look better in the morning.

Gran might, as Link had hinted, have been prejudiced against the Amish, but she had devoted her life to taking care of Marisa, and she'd been the most stable force in Marisa's life. She'd been gone nearly two years now, and Marisa still missed her.

This line of thought wasn't helping, either. She might as well get out her drawing pad and look through the tentative sketches she'd made. See what else she needed for the current project. Maybe, as she'd told Jessica, she'd be able to do some work while she was here.

She picked up the duffel bag Link had carried in, setting it atop the suitcase rack in front of the window, and unzipped it. The shriek of the zipper broke the silence.

The old house was quiet—too quiet. She wasn't used to this utter silence. Her townhouse in Baltimore was on a pleasant residential street, but even so, there was always noise—the distant thump of someone's boom box, the sound of cars going past, the shouts of kids playing in the park across the street. Not so here.

Pad and pencil in hand, she paused, glancing out the window. She couldn't even see any other lights. Link had been right—they did roll up the sidewalks.

She'd think that would seem natural to him. After all, he lived here, didn't he? He must...

She leaned close, shutting out the reflection from the bedside lamp with her hand. As her eyes adjusted to the faint moonlight, she could see the dark shadow beneath the huge weeping willow in the side yard. Had something moved?

A man-size shadow, moving out of the denser shadow of the willow, detaching itself as it took a step toward the house, the head seeming oddly misshapen until she realized it wore a black hat, the brim hiding the face. But he looked up, toward her window—

She bolted back, flattening herself against the wall, heart pounding as if it would leap out of her chest. The figure—a man, black clothes, black hair, a beard. Amish. Staring up at her window.

Memory stirred, someplace, sometime, she had looked out a window, had seen... The memory slid away, as elusive as the dream had been.

She shook her head, trying to clear it. Had she really seen someone out on the lawn? Or was it a figment of her imagination, stirred up by the dream?

She wouldn't be a coward about it. She went quickly to the bedside table and switched off the lamp. In the dark, she could see without being seen. She sidled to the window, grasped the edge of the curtain and peered around it cautiously.

The moon had come out from behind the clouds. It lit the side yard—faintly, but enough so that she could see. The lawn lay empty and unmarked, and nothing stood under the willow tree.

Breakfast would be served in a room at the rear of the first floor, Mrs. Miller had said. Marisa descended the stairs slowly. She had to find the approach that might make these people open up to her, but she hadn't managed to think of one.

Lack of sleep had to be part of the problem. She'd already been tired, and then hadn't been able to settle after her sighting. Or her overactive imagination, whichever it was. She'd gotten up several times to peer cautiously out the window. Nothing.

But she still couldn't quite accept that she'd produced that staring figure out of her imagination, which left her... where, exactly?

She reached the downstairs hall. There was a closed door with a sign marked "Private," which must lead to the Miller family's side of the house. The aroma of fresh baking led her in the right direction. A long, sunny room stretched across the width of the house in the back, with an open kitchen on her left, divided from a bright dining room on the right by a long counter. Rhoda Miller was pulling something from the oven while the daughter she'd met briefly last night poured juice into glasses.

"Good morning."

The pan Rhoda was lifting clattered onto the stove, as if the greeting had startled her.

"I hope I'm not too early," Marisa began, but Rhoda smiled, shaking her head.

"Ach, no, not at all. We try to have everything ready by eight and it's just that now. But I'm happy to serve breakfast earlier if need be."

"Eight o'clock is fine." She stifled a yawn. Should she mention the person she'd seen, or not?

"You didn't sleep well?" Rhoda gestured to a long wooden table flanked by spindle-back chairs. A pink geranium bloomed vibrantly in an earthenware pot in the center of the table, and African violets lined glass shelves in one of the windows.

"Not the fault of the room," she said quickly. "It was very comfortable. And this is lovely. You certainly have a gift with plants." She sat down, setting her bag on the floor and nodding when the daughter—Mary, she thought the name was—gestured with a coffeepot.

"Ach, it's nothing. I enjoy growing things already. But I am worried that you didn't sleep well. Was it...was there some noise to keep you awake?"

Rhoda looked more concerned than seemed warranted. Was it only the feeling of any hostess, or did she know something about the man in the yard last night, assuming he actually existed?

"More like the quiet," she said. "I'm used to city noises."

Was that relief on Rhoda's face? "I could never get used to that, that's certain-sure." She took a tray from her daughter. "Here is fruit cup to start and fresh-squeezed juice. The berries are ones I put up this summer, so they're near as gut as fresh."

"Thank you. It looks lovely." She lifted a spoonful of huge blueberries, bigger than any she'd seen in the store. "I did wonder..."

Rhoda, turning away, seemed to freeze. "Ja?"

"Was your husband out in the yard during the night?"

She swung back around, her face closed. "Why would you think that?"

"I thought I saw someone out in the side yard when I got up to get something. Out by the willow tree. Maybe your husband had occasion to check something there?"

"I did not."

The masculine voice startled her. Eli stood in the doorway, obviously having heard her. He moved into the kitchen, setting a pail he carried in the sink. Then he turned to face her.

"There was no one there."

She had to force herself to go on. "If you weren't there, how do you know no one else was?" Too bad she didn't have

Eileen Davies, her agent, here. Eileen would have the man turned inside out in a matter of seconds.

"There was no one." His face bore no expression at all.

"Ach, what am I thinking?" Rhoda hurried into the kitchen. "The egg casserole is done. Komm. Sit. It's time to eat."

For a moment Marisa thought the man would turn and walk out. Then he came slowly to the table and pulled out the chair at the end. Mary put a basket of rolls and bread on the table and slid into her seat. Rhoda, carrying a steaming casserole dish with a towel, hurried to her place.

Marisa was reaching for a muffin when she realized that Eli had bowed his head, the others following suit. No words were spoken. After a moment he looked up, as did his wife and daughter.

How had they known he was finished with what she assumed was a silent blessing? Telepathy?

"You will have some breakfast casserole?" Rhoda asked, but before Marisa could respond she had put a giant, steaming serving on Marisa's plate.

"Thank you. That's plenty," she added when Rhoda seemed about to give her more. "It smells wonderful."

"Chust eggs and cheese and sausage," Rhoda said.

Plates clattered as everyone was served. They began to eat, not talking. Apparently if there was going to be any conversation around the table, it would be up to her to start it. And maybe the only thing to do was to plunge right in.

"Do you know why I'm here in Springville?"

Rhoda glanced at her husband, and then she nodded. "Ja, we have heard about the suitcase Link Morgan found in his uncle's house. Barbara's, it was."

She was taken aback for a moment. She'd expected some garbled story would be going around, but clearly they knew exactly what had happened. Someone in the police department must have been talking. Or someone in the Morgan family.

"Barbara Angelo is my mother." *Or was my mother.* The not-knowing seized her in its grip, shaking her.

"Ja. We heard that, too." Rhoda studied her for a moment, her round blue eyes curious. "You look more like your father, but there is something of Barbara in your face, too."

Marisa found it difficult to tell the age of the Amish woman. With her brown hair pulled straight back from a center part and the lack of makeup, Rhoda might be as old as Marisa's mother would be now or maybe younger.

"You knew her, then."

Some silent communication passed between Rhoda and her husband, and she looked down at her plate.

"We remember," Eli said. "She came to visit the Zooks one summer." His mouth clamped shut on the words, as if he'd said all he intended.

She needed to ask another question, but there was such a huge blank in her knowledge that she wasn't sure where to begin. "Were they relatives of hers?"

"Ja," Rhoda said. "Cousins. She came from Indiana, I think."

Another silence. Clearly they weren't going to offer anything she didn't ask. A month ago she'd have said she wasn't interested in how and why her mother came to Lancaster County, but now she realized that wouldn't have been true.

"Had she been here before to visit?"

"We don't know much about it," Eli said before his wife could answer. "If you want to know, you should talk to them. Not us."

A look at his stern, closed face was enough to convince her that he wouldn't tell her anything else. With the beard reaching to his chest, Eli looked like an Old Testament prophet.

He also looked like the man she'd seen from her window. But what point could there be in his standing out there?

"I can see that you don't want to be involved," she said carefully. "I hoped maybe you'd be willing to tell me what you remembered about my mother. There's so much I don't understand."

"Poor child," Rhoda said, her voice soft. "Don't you remember her at all?" She asked the question despite the wave of disapproval emanating from Eli's end of the table.

"Not very much." Her throat tightened. "I was only five when she left. I have little bits of memory—of her making cookies, sewing a rag doll for me. Singing a little song in a language I didn't know. Pennsylvania Dutch, I guess."

The woman nodded, eyes filled with sympathy. "Of course you want to know more."

"Rhoda." There was warning in Eli's voice. "This is not our concern."

His wife answered him in the dialect, her voice filled with urgency. He seemed to argue with her. Finally he shook his head, mouth set.

Rhoda looked back at her. "Eli feels we should not interfere. That you should talk to your mother's kin. It is for them to tell Barbara's story, not us."

She saw her chance of learning anything fading away, if they were anything like the people she'd encountered in Indiana. "But I don't even know how to find them. Or if they'll talk to me."

Another quick exchange of glances. Eli pushed his chair back.

"You should talk to Bishop Amos. He can help you, if he thinks it the right thing to do. Rhoda will tell you how to find him." He rose, dropped his napkin on the table and walked out.

She glanced at Rhoda. "I'm sorry. I didn't mean to upset him."

"Ach, he is not upset. He chust isn't sure what is right, and that makes him annoyed with himself."

"Isn't it right for me to know about my mother?"

Rhoda looked down at her plate. "You'll talk to the bishop. He'll know what's best. I'll write down for you how to find him."

Door closed, it seemed. She didn't pin much hope on this bishop, whoever he was, wanting to help someone like her.

She tried to marshal an argument that might sway the woman. "You understand what I feel. I know you do. If you know something about my mother, please tell me."

She shook her head. "I can't."

Because her husband had told her not to, Marisa supposed. She wanted to argue, but obviously that wouldn't do any good. Maybe, if she approached Rhoda when they were alone, she'd have better luck.

Her cell phone rang, and she dived

into her bag to find it. Maybe her father—

But it wasn't Dad. It was the police chief, Adam Byler.

"Wonder if you might stop by my office some time this morning, Ms. Angelo? No hurry."

"Why? Have you found out something?" It was all she could do to stay in her seat, and she realized that Rhoda and her daughter were both looking at her with slightly scandalized expressions. Surely they were used to guests with ever-present cell phones, weren't they?

"No, not really." Byler sounded evasive. "There's just something I'd like to talk over with you, that's all. Come by anytime."

He rang off before she could ask him anything else, and she stared at the phone for a moment, her mind teeming with questions.

Despite his denial, she couldn't stop a feeling of optimism. Maybe, just maybe, she was about to learn something.

# CHAPTER FOUR

Link parked in front of Straus's Hardware in Springville, got out and hesitated, glancing down the street in the direction of the tiny office that housed Spring Township's police station. The village and the surrounding countryside that made up the township were served by the same small police force.

*Forget it,* he ordered himself. *Pick up the hinges you need, go back to the house, get on with the work.*

But forgetting wasn't as easy as all that. Lying in the military hospital, day after day, he'd had no choice but to accept the fact that he'd survived when the others had died. He'd made his plans. He just hadn't anticipated how hard it would be to carry them out.

First his family, so sure they could turn him back into the person he'd been before. Then there was the old house that had sheltered generations of Morgans, and even Springville itself, little changed since he'd trotted down Main Street at eight or nine with a dollar in his pocket, intent on spending it as soon as possible. All demanded he be the person he was before he left.

He could resist them. He wasn't so sure he could go on resisting the appeal of that little girl's pictured face. Or that same little girl hiding in grown-up Marisa Angelo's eyes.

He wheeled, striding down the street toward the police station. He needed to understand what was going on. Adam would level with him.

He swung open the door, and a woman seated at the counter swung around to look at him, eyes widening.

"Well, if this isn't a blast from the past.

Link Morgan. I heard you were back in town. How are you?"

"Fine, thanks, Ginger. I didn't know you were working here." Ginger Morrison had been class comedian, cheerleader and the girl most likely to cut class if anything more interesting beckoned.

"Yeah, my youngest went off to school this year, so we figured I'd better start bringing home a paycheck."

"You? A kid?" He perched on the corner of her desk. Ginger didn't look much older than she had the day they'd ditched school together and headed for a rock concert in Baltimore on his motorcycle, which had conked out thirty miles short of their destination. "You have a kid?"

"Three." She grinned. "I've been busy. You know I always—"

But he wasn't destined to hear the rest, as the door opened behind him and Ginger assumed a professional expression.

"May I help you, ma'am?"

He swung round, instinct telling him who it was even before he saw her face. "Marisa. Ginger, this is Marisa Angelo. I imagine she's here to see Adam."

"Good morning." Dismay at the sight of him was quickly masked, and Marisa focused on Ginger instead. "Chief Byler asked me to drop by."

"Sure thing, Ms. Angelo. He's on the phone right now, but it shouldn't be more than a couple minutes." Ginger raised her eyebrows at him. "You here to see Adam, too, I suppose. It'd be too much to think you stopped by to chat about old times with me."

He managed a grin, glancing at Marisa. "Ginger and I used to cut class together, back in the day."

"Not just me," Ginger said. "The wonder is that this boy ever managed to graduate, let alone get into college." She winked at Marisa. "Any girl he could talk onto the back of that junker of a motorcycle would do. I figured he'd go off the road at Horseshoe Bend one night, and that'd be the end of him." A buzzer went off on her phone. "You folks can see the chief now."

Link fell into step with Marisa. "You look as if you didn't sleep well." Purple shadows were like bruises under her eyes.

"I'm fine." The words were snapped

off so quickly they denied their meaning. She gave a quick nod back toward the desk. "Nice for you to see old friends."

He grimaced. "Especially when they go on saying the same thing they did ten or twelve years ago." He opened the door to Adam's office and let her precede him.

Adam rose when Marisa entered, then looked over her shoulder at Link with an expression that suggested he'd be better off elsewhere. Link gave him a bland smile. Adam should know better than to think he'd be discouraged by a look.

"Ms. Angelo, thanks for stopping by." Adam pulled out his only visitor's chair for her. "Link, I wasn't expecting you, as well."

"Why not?" He perched on the corner of Adam's desk. If Adam thought he'd come with Marisa, so much the better. "I'm an interested party."

Adam didn't respond. Marisa leaned forward in her chair, hands gripping the strap of her shoulder bag. "What's happened, Chief Byler? Have you found something?"

"No, nothing like that." Adam wore

that stolid mask he did so well...the look that had sometimes fooled people into calling him a "dumb Dutchman," that being the sort of sophisticated epithet folks around here came up with. Adam was not that.

And Link had known him too long not to see beyond the mask. Adam wanted something, presumably from Marisa, and it was something he felt reluctant to ask.

"You asked me to come by," Marisa said. "There must be a reason."

"Out with it," Link said. "What's going on?"

Adam shot him a glance that told him to shut up. "Ms. Angelo, would you be willing to take a DNA test? Just as a matter of routine. It—"

Marisa had gone dead white. Link couldn't help himself. He was beside her before he realized he'd moved, putting his hand on her shoulder.

"You've found a body?" Marisa's voice rose.

"No, nothing like that. It would simply be a help..." Adam let that die off, probably because both of them stared at him with disbelief.

"Come on, Adam. Level with us. Why do you want a DNA sample from Marisa?" He tightened his grasp on her shoulder, feeling the bones beneath the skin, and he felt a surge of protectiveness.

She didn't pull away, maybe because she was too shaken.

Adam lifted his hands in a gesture of resignation. "You know those dark splotches on the suitcase? They were blood."

Marisa's hand closed over Link's, gripping almost painfully. "My mother died. Is that what you think?"

Link's mind raced. Blood on the suitcase, so naturally Adam assumed it was Barbara's. The suitcase hidden in the wall of Uncle Allen's house. It was impossible to escape a link.

"Let's not jump to conclusions," Adam said. "If you remember what the stains looked like, they were relatively small patches. Certainly not enough to warrant an assumption that there was a fatal wound."

"Are you treating it as a murder case?" Link's voice sounded harsh to his ears. How would his mother cope with this, murder coming close to her family after all that had happened this year?

"Not at this time." Adam's face was his official one. "The lab says this amount could have come from a cut finger or a nosebleed. For all we know, the stains might even have been there for months or years before the suitcase was hidden. That's why it would be helpful to have Ms. Angelo's DNA for comparison."

"Will that be enough to be sure?"

Adam shrugged. "According to the lab, they'll be able to tell with a reasonable degree of certainty if the blood wasn't her mother's, and a fair degree if it was. So, if Marisa agrees...?"

"Yes. Of course." She seemed to be gathering her composure around her. "Where and when?"

"Lancaster General's lab will do it. They've already been notified, so just walk in and give them your name."

Marisa had regained some of her color, but strain still seemed to draw the skin tight against the bones. "I'll go now if you can give me directions."

"No need for that." Link heard his own

voice speak without conscious volition. "I'll take you there."

By the time they'd reached the edge of Springville, Marisa felt herself beginning to thaw. It was as if the word *blood,* coming from Chief Byler's lips, had flash-frozen her.

So much so that she hadn't objected when Link Morgan steered her toward his car, but maybe that had been the best thing that she could have done.

There were far too many questions that, as yet, the Morgan family hadn't answered. Each time the conversation had swerved in the direction of that house and its owner with Geneva Morgan, one of her sons had managed to divert it. And as for Link Morgan...

She stole a sideways glance at him. Lean, strong hands gripped the steering wheel too tightly, and he frowned at the road ahead. Link had avoided telling her anything more than what she might have learned from the police chief.

But surely he knew more. The man who owned the house had been his uncle. And Link had apparently been the favored nephew, since he'd inherited. There had to be things he could tell her, even if he wasn't old enough to remember her mother.

And after only twenty-four hours here, she'd begun to realize that the Morgan family loomed large in the power structure of this area. How hard would Adam Byler, obviously an old friend of the family, press them?

Well, no matter how big a deal the Morgans were, they weren't above suspicion as far as she was concerned.

She felt, rather than saw, Link focus on her face.

"Are you all right?" He asked the question almost grudgingly, as if he already regretted the impulse that had led him to offer to drive her.

He'd regret it even more if he knew how she expected to make use of this time.

"I'm all right. The idea of blood..." She let that trail off, not bothering to suppress the quaver in her voice. If Link thought her bowled over by this, so much the better. It might make him more talkative.

"Adam did say the amount was small." He ran one palm restlessly along the steering wheel. "It could have nothing to do with...well, with your mother's disappearance. It might not even be hers."

"I suppose they'll know that much from the DNA test. It seems to me I remember reading that the testing is more definitive when it's the female side of the family."

He shrugged. "Couldn't prove it by me, I'm afraid. That subject didn't come up in the course of illustrating children's books, did it?"

"I've looked into some odd things, but not that. That article on DNA was just random reading. I was the kind of kid who'd read the backs of cereal boxes if there was nothing else around."

"Not me. Always outside, running wild, my mother used to say." He gestured, the movement seeming to take in the patchwork quilt of cultivated farms and woodlots on either side of the road. "This was a good place to grow up for that."

"I guess it would have been. I don't remember much about Springville, or about the people we knew here. If my mother worked for your uncle, I suppose I might have met him."

That was a tactful way to bring Allen Morgan into the conversation, wasn't it?

"Could be." Link glanced in the side mirror as he merged onto a four-lane road. "Your mother might have taken you along with her to work, I guess." He spoke off-handedly, concentrating more on the traffic than the question.

"What was he like?"

"Allen?" Now he glanced at her, his attention sharpening. "Why do you want to know?"

She tensed at the direct attack. So much for being subtle. "It's natural enough, isn't it? Your uncle was my mother's employer. Her suitcase was hidden in the wall of his house."

He stared at the road again, lips tight, a muscle twitching at the corner of his mouth. "The suitcase being there might have nothing to do with my uncle."

"Really?" She let disbelief show in her voice. "How do you explain it, then?"

He yanked the wheel a bit harder than was warranted to exit at the sign for the hospital. "If your mother was working for him at the time the room was being built, she could have put suitcase there herself."

"Why would she do that?"

"Say the stories were right, and she planned to leave. She could have brought the suitcase with her to work, slid it into the unfinished wall so no one would see it and ask questions."

Much as she hated to admit it, his suggestion made a certain amount of sense. But...

"Then why was it still there? If she planned to run away from your uncle's house, why wouldn't she take the suit-case with her?"

"I don't know." He pulled into a park-ing lot marked Visitors and stopped, turning to face her. "Look, I don't know anything. I'm just trying to come up with some reasonable explanation, so you'll—"

Link stopped, but she knew what he'd been going to say.

"So I'll go away and leave you alone, is that it?" It was rare for her to lose her temper, but she was on the verge of that now. "I'm sorry my mother's disappear-ance has inconvenienced you so much."

She grabbed the door handle to get out, but he reached across to stop her hand. He was very close, and for an instant she could smell the fresh male scent of soap and shaving cream, could see the fine sun lines that fanned out from his eyes, could feel the heat that emanated from his body.

Her gaze met his, her breath catching abruptly. His brown eyes grew even darker, and the air between them seemed to thicken with something she didn't want to name.

He drew back abruptly. "Look, I didn't mean that. Yes, this is messing with my plans, but I know that's not your fault."

She took a ragged breath. "Don't you understand? The least thing, no matter how unimportant it might seem to you, could lead me to the truth. I have to know what happened to her."

"The truth." He seemed to muse for a moment, the lines in his face deepening, growing harsher. "Even supposing it's possible to find the truth, you might not like it. Have you considered that?"

"I've thought of nothing else. But I have to know." Her mind flickered to her father, and she forced herself to concentrate on this moment, on this man who might be able to help her. "I've spent my life wondering. Whatever the answer is, knowing has to be better than this."

He sucked in a breath so deep that his chest heaved. "All right." He nodded toward a bench set under the hospital's portico. "I'll wait for you there while you have the test. Then we'll talk about my uncle. I'll answer as many questions as you want. But I'm afraid it's not going to lead you anywhere at all."

Link sat on the bench, outwardly relaxed, trying to watch the world go by. Or at least, that portion of the world that had reason to be at the hospital on this sunny fall day—an extremely pregnant woman with a nervous husband in tow, an elderly woman carrying a handful of mums, an Amish couple with a young child.

People were sometimes surprised that the Amish availed themselves of modern medical facilities, but the Amish had no quarrel with the medical profession. They didn't believe in insurance, however, so if someone needed expensive care, the whole Amish community would pitch in to help.

He nodded as the couple came closer—they lived in Spring Township, although he couldn't call their names to mind at the moment. The two adults nodded back, and the little boy gave him a wide grin. Whatever brought them here today, it didn't seem to bother the child.

Unfortunately, focusing on the passersby didn't really resolve the dilemma he faced. Why had he agreed to talk to Marisa about Uncle Allen? For that matter, why had he brought her to the hospital to begin with?

The second question was easier to answer. She'd looked so flattened by Adam's revelation that Link couldn't help himself. His parents' training ran too deeply to be ignored, especially when he was here in Lancaster County.

*It is our duty to help those who need it.*

He could almost hear his father's voice saying the words. They'd come in answer to his whining about the fact that they'd stopped to help an Amish couple whose buggy had been run off the road by a speeding car, making him late for a baseball game. He could still remember the mix of fear and pride he'd felt watching Dad lead the frightened horse out of the twisted buggy shafts.

Pride. He'd always been proud of Dad, even during that terrible time when everyone thought he'd committed suicide. Link's chest tightened. Mostly he'd felt guilt then, that he hadn't been around when Dad needed him.

Even when they learned Dad had been killed by an employee who'd been ripping off the company, he'd still felt that somehow he'd failed by not being here.

His father had taken responsibility for others as a matter of course, and Trey was just like him. As for Link... He'd never forget what happened when he'd tried to follow suit.

He forced his thoughts back to Marisa. If he didn't talk to her about his uncle, she'd go to other people for her answers. He could imagine the talk that would generate, and there had been enough talk already.

So he'd answer her questions, drive her back to Springville and that would be an end to it. As for that sizzle of attraction when he'd gotten too close to her in the car...well, that was best ignored. He didn't need anything else tangling him up with Marisa Angelo's problems.

He tilted his head back, letting the slanting autumn sunlight touch his face. Gentle sunlight, a far cry from the blazing sun that dazzled the eye and made a man see things that weren't there—

A shadow bisected the light, visible even with his eyes closed.

"Link? You look as if you're going to sleep."

He hadn't seen Marisa approach, but she was there. She sat down on the bench, a careful foot away from him, which might mean that she'd felt exactly what he had in the car and was inclined to be just as cautious.

"That was fast," he said.

"It's an awfully simple process, given what's riding on it." Her eyes were shadowed for a moment, but then she focused on his face. "You haven't changed your mind, have you?"

"Nope. Ask me anything you want about Uncle Allen. I'll try to answer."

She studied him, those golden brown eyes seeming to weigh the sincerity of his words. Or maybe his motives.

"What did your uncle do? For a living, I mean."

"As little as possible," he said, his tone wry. "He always said that my father inherited the family work ethic. Allen had a teaching degree, but I don't think he ever taught."

"He could afford to do nothing, in other words." She sounded as if she didn't approve.

Come to think of it, he wasn't sure he did, either.

"Uncle Allen had a nominal title in the family corporation, and he made a token appearance at the office once in a while."

"Corporation?" Her eyebrows lifted.

He shrugged. "That makes it sound more important than it is. Morgans have been here a long time. They acquired things—land, businesses, rental properties."

"You help to run those?" She was probably trying to equate that with the manual labor she'd caught him doing.

"Trey's in charge since Dad died. I was in the military by then, so I let him." He'd taken as little responsibility as Allen had, in fact.

"I see." She was frowning, as if trying to figure him out.

He'd do better to keep this on Allen, not on himself. "Anyway, Allen's main interest was local history. He wrote some articles, did a little dealing in Pennsylvania Dutch folk art and furniture. Ostensibly that was his business, but he didn't have a shop—just bought and sold out of his home."

"He never married?"

"No. I suspect my mother tried to play matchmaker a few times, but nothing ever came of it. Allan was just...a loner, I guess. He never seemed to need anyone else's company."

She was silent, as if absorbing his impressions. Or maybe now that she had her opportunity, she didn't know what to ask.

"You don't remember my mother working for him?"

The question was the one he'd expected her to start with. "I don't think so. I didn't spend all that much time at Uncle Allen's place."

"So you don't know if she was working there the summer she disappeared." Her voice flattened on the last word.

He hesitated, but she had a right to know. "My mother says she's relatively sure she was."

"Relatively sure," she repeated.

"There's no reason my mother should remember. It wasn't her house. Or her spouse. Your father—"

"Yes, I know. It's another thing to ask Dad when he calls." Her lips tightened. "I'm sure the police chief would find this very suspicious, but just because my father doesn't like to talk about his wife leaving him, that doesn't mean anything sinister."

"I know." He lifted his hand in a placating gesture. "I mean it. There are plenty of things adults don't talk to kids about. Your questions about my uncle make me realize how little I really knew about him. It's odd, but when you're a kid, you just accept things as they are. Probably a lot of people never have reason to question those assumptions."

She nodded. "You're right. I simply accepted the fact that Dad didn't talk about my mother, and that if I wanted to know something, I had to go to Gran."

That brought up something he'd wondered about. "How did she know?"

Marisa blinked. "What do you mean?"

"She didn't live with you until after your mother left, did she? So how did she know the things she told you?"

"I suppose my dad must have talked to her." She frowned. "That's true. She didn't live with us. I remember her coming. It must have been a few days after...after I realized my mother was gone. But I suppose my dad talked to her about it. Why? Do you doubt what she said?"

He shrugged. "The idea that the Amish kept after Barbara, trying to get her to leave...well, that doesn't sound right to me. That's not the way the Amish behave toward someone who's decided to leave the church."

That soft mouth of Marisa's could look remarkably stubborn. "Are you an expert?"

"No, but I grew up with Amish neighbors. I think I know a bit more about them than you do."

"Oh, yes. You're the one who suggested enlisting the Miller family's help." Her tone was laced with sarcasm. "They admitted that they remembered my mother. But they wouldn't tell me a thing. Just said I'd have to talk to the bishop."

He had to be honest with himself, at least. He hadn't expected that response.

"Well, maybe you should start with Bishop Amos. It's possible that Rhoda and her husband felt it would be gossiping if they talked about the Zook family. I'm sure they didn't mean anything else by it."

"According to you, the Amish can do no wrong, it seems."

"I didn't say that." She'd succeeded in getting under his skin. "I just think you're misjudging them."

"Really. Like the Amish man who was out in the yard last night—" Marisa clamped her lips shut, as if she hadn't intended to say that.

He frowned. "What are you talking about? What Amish man?"

"Nothing. It doesn't matter." Her gaze evaded his.

"If you think someone is spying on you, it does matter. What happened?" He clasped her wrist firmly, determined to get an answer, and felt her pulse against his fingers.

She jerked her hand away. "I was awake sometime in the night. I looked out the window. A man was standing in the side yard. He seemed to be looking up at my window."

There were a lot of things he could say to that, including the suggestion that she'd been dreaming. Or was paranoid.

"What makes you think he was Amish?" *And are you sure someone was there?*

"The hat. The beard. The dark clothes." Color came up in her cheeks. "I know. You think I was dreaming or imagining things. I wasn't."

"Dreams can seem very real." He ought to know. He'd dreamed that explosion in Afghanistan enough times, waking up covered in sweat, a cry strangled in his throat.

"I wasn't dreaming." She rose suddenly. "Forget it. Let's get back."

He stood, not sure what to say. "Maybe you ought to tell Adam about this."

"So he can suggest I dreamt it, too?" She started toward the car.

He fell into step with her, still bothered. If Marisa was talking about something that really happened, that was troubling. And if she was imagining it, maybe that was even worse.

Marisa was wrong. She had to be. This figure in the night was a product of all the upsetting news she'd had to face in the past few days. The Amish people he knew just didn't behave that way.

The Amish couple he'd seen earlier came out of the clinic door, their little boy skipping between them. They started toward the main walk. The man looked up, his gaze going from Link to Marisa. Then he took his wife's arm, clasped his son's hand and deliberately walked back the other way.

# CHAPTER FIVE

Marisa felt quite sure that if Link knew what she was doing, he would not approve. In fact, he'd probably try to stop her.

Still, Geneva Morgan was a grown woman, well able to decide for herself what she wanted to do. All it had taken was a thank-you phone call for the dinner, a little gentle steering of the conversation, and Geneva had suggested meeting her for coffee.

Geneva had wanted Marisa to come to the house, but she'd managed to avoid that. She didn't want this conversation taking place where any of Geneva's protective family was likely to interrupt.

They were getting together at a place called Emma's Teashop at two. Marisa glanced at her watch. She was early, and she'd been walking down Springville's main street as if she were in the city. She forced her pace to slow. People didn't walk that way here. They didn't avoid eye contact.

Except, of course, for that Amish couple at the hospital, who seemed to go far out of their way to avoid coming near her. Link had noticed that. She'd been sure he had, even though he hadn't spoken of it.

There wasn't really much to Springville—one main street that became a state road at the end of town and several side streets lined with shade trees and well-kept houses. A brick bank rubbed shoulders with a Victorian house whose decorative carving was freshly painted. The township library was housed in a two-story brick building whose historic plaque indicated it had been built in 1740 as the home of a wealthy merchant.

Straus's Hardware seemed to be doing as much business as any establishment, and in addition to parking spaces for cars along the street, it had hitching rails for buggies along the alley. Three Amish buggies stood there at the moment, the horses seeming to wait patiently.

As she passed the front window, she could see several bearded men inside who were deep in conversation. One glanced at her, and she forced down the suspicion that they talked about her. That was paranoid.

Geneva had been right about the tea shop; it was virtually empty at this time of day. Even though she was early, Geneva herself was already seated at a small glass-topped table in the back of the room, shielded from view of the street by a white latticework screen. She waved, a silver bangle sliding on her arm, and Marisa went quickly to join her.

"This is a lovely place to chat." Geneva smiled as warmly as if meeting Marisa was exactly what she'd most wanted to do with herself this afternoon. "I've ordered tea and sticky buns, because that's Emma's specialty, but if you'd rather have coffee..."

Marisa slipped into the chair across from her, hanging her bag from the back. "Not at all. That sounds lovely." She'd have happily consumed whatever Geneva wanted to order for the chance to talk with her.

Geneva had been a contemporary of Allen Morgan—his sister-in-law—living in the same small area. She must surely know more about him than Link did. There had to be some fact, no matter how small, that would lead Marisa to understanding.

"You look tired, dear." Geneva spoke as if Marisa were one of her children. "Link told me you had a bad night last night."

She hadn't expected that, and it took a moment to regroup. "He probably told you I have a too-vivid imagination."

"Don't mind him. Both my boys focus too much on what can be proved and not enough on intuition. Just because Link couldn't imagine someone watching your room, that doesn't mean it didn't happen." Geneva's eyes sparkled at the thought, and her silver and turquoise earrings seemed to sparkle, too.

Marisa felt a momentary qualm. Geneva looked a little too enthusiastic, bright blue eyes snapping, cheeks rosy with excitement. All she wanted from the woman was information, not a partner.

"I could have been wrong, I guess. That's part of being an illustrator—responding to everything in visual terms. Sometimes my imagination gives me images that aren't real."

Like the recurring image of her mother that haunted her dreams, walking away from her, disappearing into the dark woods where Marisa couldn't reach her.

"Well, naturally. You're an artist. I'm sure it must be fascinating to illustrate children's books. Some of them are so beautiful that I can't resist buying them even though I don't have any children in the house any longer."

Geneva wore such a wistful expression at the thought that Marisa found herself hoping Jessica and Trey planned to provide grandchildren for her. Geneva would throw herself into that role with enthusiasm.

"The books are lovely, aren't they? I buy them, too, and then rationalize that I have to keep up with what's happening in my—"

Marisa broke off as a woman came through what must be the door to the kitchen. Round and smiling, she carried an enormous tray laden with teapot and cups and a platter piled high with baked goods. She was also, to judge by her clothing, Amish.

"Ach, here we are." The woman set the tray on the edge of the table and began to unload it. "I brought some apple kuchen fresh from the oven, as well as the sticky buns. You'll want a taste of that, for sure."

Geneva smiled. "If we have a taste of everything, you'll have to roll us out of here. Emma, this is a friend, Marisa Angelo. Marisa, Emma Weaver, best baker in the township."

"Ach, I am not that." Emma responded to Geneva warmly, but there was a reservation in her face as she glanced toward Marisa and as quickly looked away again.

So, Emma already knew who she was, obviously. And probably, like Rhoda Miller, she would be unwilling to talk.

"You will tell me if you need anything else." She spoke to Geneva, turned and scuttled back to the kitchen.

Geneva looked after her, seeming perplexed at the woman's rapid retreat.

"I'm afraid it's me," Marisa said, answering her expression. "That's the effect I have on the local Amish. Nobody wants to talk to me."

Geneva transferred her gaze to Marisa. "Are you sure? That seems odd."

Marisa shrugged, pouring tea from the pot into her cup. "I tried to talk to Rhoda Miller, but her husband clearly didn't want her to discuss my mother." She seemed to hear again that rapid-fire patter of dialect that she couldn't understand. "All they could say was that I should go to my mother's cousins. Or to the bishop."

"That's the answer." Geneva's face cleared. "Bishop Amos is a dear man. He'll know just what the problem is and how to deal with it. He's so wise and kind."

Maybe, like his parishioners, he'd want her to go away and stop asking questions. "I'm not sure that's a good idea."

"Of course it is. If you like, I'll set up a meeting for you."

She hesitated, but it was an obvious answer. She could search out the man on her own, using Rhoda Miller's directions, but Geneva's intercession might be the one thing that would ensure he talked with her.

"I'd be very grateful."

"Not at all. It's the least I can do." Geneva paused for a moment, staring down at the tea she was stirring. The spoon made a delicate clinking noise, the only sound in the room. Finally she sighed.

"I know Link talked to you about Allen, but you want to hear it from me, don't you?"

She nodded. "Yes." She smiled slightly. "But I was going to try and find some tactful way of bringing it up."

"No need for that. It's obvious why you want to know." Geneva seemed prepared to talk, but the vertical lines between her brows suggested that the subject troubled her. "Allen was a difficult man. I'm not sure anyone really understood him."

"Not your husband?" She asked tentatively, having gathered that Geneva was a widow.

"Blake least of all. It's that way with brothers, sometimes. We tried to guard against that with Trey and Link, but I'm not sure we entirely succeeded."

She'd love to know why, but that was not her business, and she wasn't going to betray interest in Link to his mother, of all people.

"I didn't have siblings, so I don't really understand, I'm afraid."

"Fight like cats and dogs in private, but present a united front to the world." Geneva's face cleared, as if she were remembering something pleasant. "That was always Trey and Link, anyway. As for Allen..." She let that trail off, shaking her head. "I think perhaps he envied Blake, although he'd never admit that."

"Link said he was a loner," she prompted.

"He lived all by himself in that house,

with just a housekeeper coming in a few days a week to do for him." Geneva broke off a piece of the sinfully rich sticky bun. "Your mother wasn't the only person who worked for him in that capacity, but she stayed the longest, I think. Four years, if memory serves."

That startled her. "Four years? Then she must have gone to work for him when I was little more than a baby."

"She took you with her, for the most part. I remember dropping some dinner off for Allen one day, and you were playing with some plastic measuring cups on the kitchen floor, good as gold while she cleaned the cabinets."

She had another image now to add to the small store she had of her mother, and she tucked it away to think about later. "Did you know my mother well?"

Geneva considered. "Not well, but to talk to. She was a very sweet person. You could tell that by her expression." She tilted her head, studying Marisa's face. You have that, too. But I thought..."

"Yes? What did you think?" She couldn't let Geneva stop short.

"That there was a little sadness in her

eyes, too. My imagination, maybe. Certainly her face always lit up when she looked at you."

There was a question to be asked, and she wasn't sure how to put it. Maybe best just to blurt it out. "What about her relationship with your brother-in-law? Did you ever think..." Her nerve failed her then, and she couldn't manage the rest of it.

Geneva reached across the glass-topped table to clasp her hand. "Never. There was never anything between them but a business relationship."

She wanted to believe that, but could she? "How can you be sure of that? They wouldn't advertise it, if there was."

"Barbara wouldn't have taken her child to the house if there'd been anything untoward going on." Geneva's voice rang with assurance. "I may not have been close friends with her, but I knew her well enough to be sure of that."

Tension that had been stretched tight seemed to ease. "I'm glad to hear you say that."

"You poor child." Geneva patted her hand. "I understand how worrying this all is for you. But whatever caused Barbara to pack that suitcase, I'm quite sure it wasn't Allen." Her lips quirked. "I doubt that Allan got his nose out of his dusty old history books long enough even to notice that she was a woman."

"Was she..." *Happy,* she wanted to say, but who could ever really know that about another person? "You know that she had been Amish, don't you?"

"Oh, yes. As I recall, she was a relative of the Zook family, and she came to visit them. That's how she met your father."

She nodded. "I did know that. My grandmother must have told me, because my dad hardly ever talked about her."

"Too upset, probably. It had to have hurt him terribly, the idea that she would just walk away to go back to her people."

Marisa shoved aside that image of her mother walking away from her. "For a long time I imagined that she would come back. She'd explain what happened, why she hadn't been in touch with us, and we'd all be happy again."

She shrugged. "It's a typical fantasy for a child whose parent has deserted them."

Geneva's bright eyes sparkled with tears. "I know. It had to be terrible for you. I remember stopping by the house to see if I could do anything. You were just sitting on the stairs, looking lost. For her to disappear like that, without a word…"

"She intended to leave." Marisa forced herself to admit the ugly truth. "The suitcase proves that. But if she left, why didn't she take it with her? And if she didn't, what happened to her?"

"I wish I had the answer for you." Geneva leaned toward her, clasping her hand in a warm grip. "I promise we'll help you all we can. I'll set up a meeting with Bishop Amos, and I'll see if any of my Amish friends will talk to me about it, as well."

"I'm so grateful. Thank you." At least Geneva's response wasn't hampered by official reticence, like the chief's was, or complicated by emotion she didn't understand, like Link's.

"It's the least I can do." Geneva sat back, seeming satisfied. "In the meantime, you mustn't brood about it. But you said that you'd brought some of your work with you to do."

"The illustrations, yes." She hadn't been in touch with her agent in days, and she should do that. "I should get working on them. I've never missed a deadline in my career, and I'm not going to start now."

"Good for you." Obviously a doer herself, Geneva seemed to approve. "Now, what can we do to help?"

"Nothing that I can think of, but thanks. The setting involves a farm." The image of Link cutting wood flashed into her mind. "And some scenes in the woods. It's a simple little story, about a baby chick that gets lost in the woods, and the forest creatures try to help him find a place to live." She could feel the desire to work on it rising in her. Working would shut out her fears as nothing else could. "The images are a little old-fashioned in style, done in pastels."

"It sounds charming, and I know just the place. Our neighbors have a working farm, and I'm sure they'd be delighted to let you work there. As for the woods, nothing could be easier. There are acres of woods behind our place. I'll have Link show you around and help you find just the right spot."

Link, and that inexplicable flash of attraction between them that she'd been trying to deny since it happened.

"That's very generous of you, but you don't need to bother Link with it. I'm sure I can find something suitable without his help."

"You could. But it would be a blessing if you'd do this for me."

Marisa was so startled she couldn't speak, but Geneva plunged on.

"He's been so preoccupied ever since he got out of the army hospital. He doesn't think about anything but finishing that house and going away." Geneva blinked rapidly, as if to hold back tears. "He used to be so outgoing, charming and laughing and never serious for more than a minute at a time. Now he doesn't talk, doesn't laugh, doesn't seem interested in anything."

"I'm sorry." Her throat tightened. She'd guessed there had been something wrong with him. Now she knew. "Was he injured?"

Geneva nodded. A tear spilled over, and she dashed it away. "In Afghanistan. Link was with an engineering unit. They were rebuilding a school that had been destroyed, and there was a terrible accident. Well, not an accident. It was blown up." Geneva blotted tears again and gave a shaky laugh. "If he could hear me now, he'd be furious with me. But you know, as sad as it is, finding that suitcase seems to have brought him back to life. I don't want him to slip away again. You understand, don't you?"

Marisa nodded. "I do. I'm sorry. But I don't see how—"

"How a walk in the woods will help?" Geneva finished for her, smile flashing through her tears. "Believe me, I'm thankful for every little thing that pulls my son out of his shell. Even a walk in the woods."

Marisa couldn't imagine that her presence and her problems were any antidote for Link's ills, which sounded very serious indeed. But she could hardly refuse.

"Of course I'll do it, but Link may not agree."

"Don't worry about that," Geneva said. "I'll handle him."

Somehow she didn't doubt that she would. She was beginning to feel that Geneva Morgan, in spite of her charming, insubstantial manner, was a force to be reckoned with.

By the time Link had dropped Marisa off, it had been time for lunch, so he'd stopped at home, mainly because it seemed to please his mother to feed him. Then he took off on his deferred errands at the hardware store and the lumber yard.

He glanced at his watch when he got back to what had been Uncle Allen's house and was now his. Late afternoon, and most of the workday gone, thanks to his getting involved in Marisa Angelo's troubles. Too late to start anything time-consuming now, but he could unload and organize his work for the next day.

He pulled around to the back and began lugging supplies onto the back porch. He'd barely made a dent in the job when Trey's truck pulled up behind him and Trey slid out.

"Looks like you could use a hand." Trey grabbed the end of a two-by-four as Link swung it out. "Is all this for the family room?"

"Most of it. Thanks." He hated admitting weakness, but the truth was, by this time of the day it was all he could do not to resort to the pain pills the doctor insisted on giving him. "I need to fix a couple of the upstairs windows. The sills are nearly rotted through."

"I figured as much." Trey helped him carry a sheet of paneling. "Toward the end, Uncle Allen didn't seem to care much about anything, including the house. Just shut himself up in his study with his books."

Link nodded, leaning against the porch rail for a moment's respite. "He always was kind of that way, wasn't he? Liked his own company better than anyone else's."

"Yeah, but this was even more so." Trey took off his ball cap, wiped his forehead and put it back on again. "You were away, what with school and the army, so you probably didn't notice it, but he really turned... Well, Mom calls it *eccentric.*" He grinned. "Odd was more like it. Didn't want anyone in the house. I had to twist his arm to let me send someone over to mow the yard."

The worry that lurked at the back of Link's mind poked out. "Is there anything in that to make you think he could have been involved in the Angelo woman's disappearance?"

Trey's answer didn't come as quickly as he'd like. Trey actually seemed to be considering that as a possibility.

"I wish I knew," he said slowly. "I'd like to say that was ridiculous, but I can't. For Mom's sake, I hope he wasn't. She's been through enough the past couple of years."

A weight settled on Link's heart. Dad's death, thought to be suicide, something that seemed impossible to believe. And then the revelation that someone they'd known all their lives had killed him.

And only a few weeks later, Link had managed to get himself nearly blown to pieces. No, Mom hadn't had an easy time of it lately.

"Marisa's not going to give up until she knows the truth." Link spoke with a sureness that surprised himself. He hadn't realized he felt that convinced of what Marisa would and wouldn't do. "If Allen was involved... Well, I don't think we can keep it quiet."

"It wouldn't be right, anyway. Come on, let's get this stuff unloaded."

That was Trey, always determined to do what was right, even when it hurt. Just like Dad. Together they carried the rest of Link's purchases to the porch.

"Thanks for the help." Link hesitated, but Trey would have to know. "About this situation with Marisa Angelo... I stopped by the station this morning to see if Adam had come up with anything. She came in while I was there."

"Why?" Trey fired the word, frowning.

"Adam had called her. He wanted her to take a DNA test. It seems the blotches on the suitcase were blood."

Trey looked as if he'd like to cut loose with some colorful language, but he didn't. "That's torn it. It'll turn into a murder investigation for sure."

"Not necessarily. Adam says the amount was fairly small—not enough to indicate a fatal wound. But naturally they've got to find out if it was Barbara Angelo's."

"Yeah." Trey rubbed the nape of his neck. "I can't see Adam letting anything slide. He'll be thinking the police did a lousy job of it twenty-three years ago."

"Anyway, I drove Marisa to the hospital in Lancaster to have the test done. She told me something I found hard to believe."

Too bad that just mentioning her name made him think of those moments when he'd been too close to her, the scent of her in his nostrils, the silky hair that had brushed his arm...

Trey lifted an eyebrow. "You going to tell me?"

Good thing Trey had pulled him back from that line of thought. "She's got the idea someone was watching her room last night. A man, out in the yard at the guest house in the middle of the night. An Amish man."

"That's nonsense." Trey's first instinct was to reject it, just as Link's had been. "She must have been dreaming."

"That's what I said, but she seemed pretty certain. She also said that the Millers wouldn't talk to her about her mother. She seemed to think the Amish are hiding something."

"Then she wasn't just dreaming, she's paranoid," Trey said flatly.

It was what he'd thought himself, but it annoyed him to hear Trey say it.

"Maybe so. Except that when we were walking to the parking lot at the hospital, I happened to see Josiah Esch with his wife and little boy. And Josiah took one look at Marisa and very deliberately went the other way."

Trey was still for a moment, weighing that. "You sure *your* imagination isn't working overtime?"

His temper flared. "Listen, I'd like nothing better than to find out this is all some misunderstanding, but that won't wash. Something's going on, and like it or not, it involves us."

"I don't like it." Trey held up his hand to forestall an angry comment. "But you're right. Even if we could steer clear of the whole thing, you know as well as I do that Mom won't."

Link nodded, his momentary anger fizzling away. He and Trey were alike in this. They both wanted to protect their mother from any more hurt. "Any ideas as to how we keep Mom from getting involved?"

Trey looked harassed. "I've been trying to figure that one out since Dad died, without much success. But she does seem to assume you're keeping an eye on Marisa. Maybe that'll help."

*Keep an eye on Marisa. Stay close to her.* "I've got a house to renovate, remember?"

"You're the one who found that suitcase, remember?" Trey turned his question right back on him.

"I should have thrown it in the trash without opening it."

"You really believe that?" Trey gave him a questioning look.

"No." He bit off the word, thinking of that photograph of Marisa and her mother. "But maybe we'll all be wishing that before this is over." He nodded toward the door. "I could use something cold to drink. You?"

"Sounds good." Trey followed him toward the door, still frowning, his mind obviously on the problematic possibilities. "You know Mom feels responsible. I wouldn't put it past her to be scurrying around trying to find things out about Allen, and stirring up a lot of gossip while she does."

"She's got your wedding to look forward to," Link said. "And don't think Libby and I aren't grateful for that." He grinned, thinking of his twin. "Maybe it'll distract Mom from both playing detective and our single state."

"I wouldn't count on that." Trey smiled, his eyes softening at the mention of his and Jessica's wedding. "Once Mom smells orange blossoms, she'll try to get the whole lot of us married off."

Link shoved the door open. Just inside he stopped, senses alert. He put out a hand to keep Trey from moving.

"What?" Trey said, his voice quiet.

"Somebody's been in here."

Trey looked around the barren room. "Are you sure?"

He nodded. "The box on the work-bench has been emptied out. I didn't leave it that way." He might be careless about some things, but not his equip-ment. "And there's insulation pulled loose from that wall." He pointed to the section next to the fireplace.

"We'd better have a look around." Trey picked up a length of wood from the workbench, hefting it like a bat. "I'll check upstairs."

It was a matter of minutes to check the house, empty except for a few pieces of furniture Link had been meaning to have a dealer come to evaluate and Un-cle Allen's books, which would have to be sorted. No one was in the house, but some books had been pulled from their shelves and a marble-topped table moved across a bedroom.

"Nothing missing?" Trey asked when they reached the family room again.

"Not that I can tell." He shrugged, an-noyed with himself. "I guess I should have locked up when I left to run to the hardware store this morning, but I fig-ured I'd only be gone a half hour or so."

Trey frowned absently at the fireplace.

"Could have been somebody who was just curious. Talk's been going around, probably getting exaggerated as it goes."

"Maybe." That was as likely as anything, so why did he have so much trouble buying it? "I suppose I still should tell Adam."

"Yes." Trey growled the word.

Link understood his feelings. No matter how much either of them wanted to be clear of this situation, they couldn't ignore it. Barbara Angelo's presence, whatever her relationship to his uncle, would certainly have been less complicated than her disappearance.

# CHAPTER SIX

"I don't suppose I could convince you to go home and let the police handle this situation." Eileen Davies, Marisa's agent, had become a good friend over the years, and she didn't sound optimistic about Marisa's plans.

"I can't do that." Marisa moved to the window of her room, her gaze lingering on the willow tree and the floating shadows it cast even in mid-morning. "If there's anything I can find out about what happened to my mother... Well, I have to try."

"I know. I just don't want to see you get hurt by this."

Eileen's often brusque voice softened with sympathy. Marisa could picture her leaning across her always-cluttered desk, a pencil skewered through her wiry dark curls. Eileen was one of the few people who'd heard the whole story of Marisa's mother, sitting over a late-night dessert during a children's-book expo.

"Nothing could hurt more than not knowing." She believed that, despite the nameless dread that filled her when she let her guard down.

"Just be careful, okay? Don't trust people too readily. This Morgan family, for instance. They might have a very good reason for not wanting the truth to come out."

True enough. Despite Geneva's warmth, despite Link's apparent openness when they'd talked the previous day, she couldn't take their honesty for granted.

"I'll be cautious about believing any-one."

"About the project... Do you want me

to talk to the editor and try to get you some extra time?"

"No, I can finish it." Marisa touched the portfolio that held her sketches. She'd ignored the work for too long. "I'm getting back on the illustrations this afternoon. I can use the distraction."

"Good. You're a pro." There was relief in Eileen's voice. She'd go to bat for an extension, but she hated to have to do it.

"Yes, well, I'd like to stay an employed pro, so I meet my deadlines." A gentle tap on the door punctuated her words. "I have to go, Eileen. I'll check in with you in a few days."

She clicked off and opened the door. Mary stood there, her hand raised as if to knock again.

"There is someone to see you downstairs. In the parlor, ja?"

Link? Geneva? Well, she wouldn't find out standing here. "Thank you. I'll be right down."

She took a quick glance in the mirror. She'd put on jeans and a loose shirt in anticipation of working, but it would have to do. Closing the door, she ran lightly down the stairs.

When she reached the parlor door, she came to an abrupt stop. Not one of the Morgans at all, but Adam Byler and another man...middle-aged, slightly balding, with a florid face and a barrel chest that strained at the dress shirt he wore with a lightweight tan suit. Unusual attire for Springville, she realized, and a whisper of unease touched her.

"Ms. Angelo." Chief Byler stood as she entered, and after a second the other man did the same. "Sorry to bother you so early."

"The DNA tests—you don't have results already, surely." That was impossible, wasn't it?

"No, no, not yet." There was something behind Adam Byler's phlegmatic expression, some emotion she couldn't identify. "This is our district attorney, Preston Connelly. He'd like to talk with you."

District attorney. The flicker of apprehension turned to alarm. Why was the district attorney involved in this?

She turned to acknowledge the introduction, to find that the man had moved to close the parlor door. He must have seen her expression, because he smiled slightly.

"Just to make sure we're not over-heard," he said. "How do you do, Ms. Angelo."

Marisa nodded, glancing back at Adam. "District attorney? I thought my mother's disappearance wasn't consid-ered a criminal case." *Yet,* she almost said.

"That's why I'm here." Connelly an-swered for him. "Just to ask a few ques-tions and be sure we're handling the situation properly. I assume you'll want to cooperate with us in learning the truth."

Connelly's words were pleasant enough, but his eyes were cold. Watch-ful.

"Of course. That's why I'm here. To know the truth."

"Good, good." He rubbed his hands together…large, well-kept hands, with a gold and ruby ring on the right ring finger. "We're on the same page, then. Let's sit down."

Marisa took her time about pulling up a rocking chair, her mind busy with the possible implications of this visit. Admittedly she didn't know much about the duties of a district attorney, but was it usual for him to involve himself with a situation that might not even be a criminal matter?

"Now, then." Connelly planted his hands on his knees, clearly taking the lead in this conversation. "I understand you were surprised when Chief Byler contacted you about finding your mother's suitcase."

"Yes." Strange to think that had only been a few days ago. "Of course I was surprised."

"You didn't expect any information about your mother's disappearance would show up after all this time?" He made that sound vaguely sinister.

"I suppose I thought…hoped…that my mother would contact me one day. As for disappearing, we thought that she had gone back to her family."

"We?" His eyebrows lifted.

"My father. My grandmother. Apparently she'd said something about doing so."

*I don't belong here.* A far-off voice seemed to echo in her mind. *I don't belong anywhere.*

She clasped her hands together, forcing the thought away. Where had that come from, anyway?

"Is that something you remember yourself, or something you were told?"

"Well, I—" The voice seemed to echo in her mind again, thinly, fading. "I'm not sure. After all, I was only five at the time."

"Five isn't that young. A five-year-old might know a great deal about what's going on in the family, for instance. But I see from the case records that the police didn't even talk to you at the time."

Chief Byler stirred slightly. "I'm sure they didn't feel there was any need to upset a child. It all seemed very straightforward."

"You don't need to cover for your predecessor, Byler," Connolly said. "It's obvious he didn't take the situation seriously."

Marisa took advantage of the byplay

between the two men to consider Connelly's comments. Should a five-year-old know more than she seemed to about that time? Her memories, except for fragments of images, didn't seem to encompass much before the house in Baltimore.

Connelly turned back to her before she found an answer. "Now, Ms. Angelo, just tell us what you remember about the day your mother went away."

She looked at him blankly. "Nothing."

"Nothing?" His returning stare expressed disbelief. "Come now. You were there. According to the file, you attended kindergarten. Was your mother there when you returned home?"

"I don't... I'm not sure."

She tried to grope her way back through the years. She'd ridden the bus to kindergarten, she knew that. She'd come home on the bus every day, too. She'd scurry down the high step of the bus, clutching her papers from the day, eager to show off a star or a sticker.

"You must remember that day. After all, your whole life changed then, didn't it?" His voice sharpened.

She was suddenly resentful of this stranger and his questions, probing into something that was hers, her private memories of Mammi waiting at the lamp-post in the front yard, reaching out to sweep her into a hug.

Her breath caught. She hadn't thought of that in years, but suddenly it seemed she could see her mother, see the long denim skirt she always wore with a plain blouse, see the way her face lit with pleasure at the sight of her small daughter.

"I don't know." She spoke sharply, intent on that inner vision, unwilling to share it. "I don't remember. I'm sure, if I'd thought anything was wrong, I'd have told my father at the time."

"Your father." He leaned back, something speculative in his dark eyes. "What did he say when you told him about the suitcase?"

She blinked. "I haven't told him. I haven't talked to him."

"Come, Ms. Angelo. Do you really expect us to believe that he's been out of touch this long?"

The man was a hair away from being

openly antagonistic. From the corner of her eye she caught a glimpse of Adam Byler leaning forward in his chair, frowning at Connelly as if about to speak. The room, with its solid Pennsylvania Dutch wood furniture, braided rug and simple muslin curtains seemed an odd place for an interrogation.

"Well?" Connelly snapped the word when she didn't answer.

She took a breath and tried to find a reservoir of calm. "I'm not sure what you believe, Mr. Connolly, but it happens to be the truth. My father is on a Western trip in his camper. It's something he always planned to do when he retired."

"Without a cell phone?" The question dripped with doubt.

"He has a cell phone. But if he's camping someplace up in the mountains or in the desert, it's entirely possible that he's not getting service. I've left messages. He'll call when he gets them."

He would call.

"That could well be," Byler said. "I've lost cell service camping in places like that, no matter what the cell-phone companies claim."

Connelly didn't seem willing to admit that. "Hard to believe, his being out of touch with his only daughter for this long."

He thought her father had something to do with her mother's disappearance. Marisa clasped cold hands together. That was what he was really saying.

"I'm not a child, Mr. Connelly. My father and I are on good terms, but we don't live in each other's pockets. My father will call me, and when he does, I'll tell him what's happened."

"What did you tell him when he came home the night your mother left?" Connelly's question snapped at her out of nowhere, leaving her floundering for a moment.

"I don't know. I've already told you I don't remember." Her hands were as icy as her heart, but she managed to keep her voice calm. She couldn't do much more of this. "If that's everything…" She pushed herself to her feet, pressing the backs of her legs against the chair for support.

Connelly looked as if he'd dispute that, but Byler stood.

"That's all we need for now, Ms. Angelo. We'll let you know if we have any further questions."

She held her breath, waiting for Connelly to overrule him. But he didn't, and in a moment they were gone, leaving the house empty and still.

Marisa discovered that her legs didn't want to hold her up any longer. She sank into the rocker, clasping the curved arms until the wood bit into her fingers.

Why now? What had brought the district attorney into the picture? Why was he so antagonistic?

Unfortunately, she could think of plenty of answers. *Because he thinks the police are being too low-key. Because he thinks my dad had something to do with my mother's disappearance.*

She might as well stop skirting around it. If they believed her father had something to do with it, then they didn't think this was a matter of a disappearance. They thought Barbara Angelo was dead.

*Please, God, no.* The words formed without conscious thought. *No.*

Was that what she'd been dreading? That her mother was dead and her father had killed her?

A shudder of revulsion shook her. That wasn't true. It couldn't be.

She'd been there, Connelly had said. If there was anything to know, her five-year-old self might have known it. So why didn't she remember?

"Better douse yourself thoroughly with this stuff." Link handed the insect-repellent spray to Marisa.

She looked at it, her expression reluctant. "Is that really necessary? I hate using things like this."

"It is if you don't want to risk a tick bite. And maybe Lyme disease." He was probably overstating the case, but if he had to be responsible for Marisa's trek through the woods, he didn't want anything happening to her.

Seeming to accept the lesser of the evils, she began spraying the legs of her jeans. At least she was dressed suitably, wearing a long-sleeve shirt over a T-shirt with the jeans.

He waited, trying to contain his impatience. He'd gotten in a good start on work at the house this morning, but when he'd stopped at home for lunch, Mom had informed him she'd made plans for his afternoon. Marisa was coming over, and Mom expected him to help her find places to sketch.

He'd have objected, but if he didn't do this, his mother would have. Trey had been right in his assessment of Mom's propensity for landing herself in the middle of things.

Marisa set the spray on the back porch step and swiftly pulled her hair back into a loose ponytail. He supposed the small backpack she wore contained her drawing supplies.

"I'm ready." She smiled as she said the words.

But there was something not quite right about the way Marisa looked today. Surely she wasn't still obsessing about the DNA test, was she? Something had put new lines of tension around her mouth and shadowed her eyes.

*Not your business,* he reminded himself. *You're not responsible for her.*

"Okay, let's go." Mom had insisted he take a thermos of lemonade, and he slung it by its strap from his shoulder. They weren't going to deepest Africa, just for a walk in the woods, but it was easier to take it than to argue.

He started off at a quick pace across the yard toward the barn. Beyond it, the trees in the orchard were heavy with apples. And beyond the orchard was the easiest path through the woods.

They walked in silence until they reached the orchard.

"Is this all yours?" Marisa looked up at the laden apple trees with wonderment in her voice. Fallen apples crunched underfoot, and their aroma filled the air with the scent of fall.

"Every last tree, unfortunately. When we were kids, we all had a quota of baskets to pick and lug into the storeroom." That had usually led to a certain amount of wrangling, as he recalled.

"Do you still do that?" She was a few feet behind him, making him realize how fast he was walking...as if he could walk away from feeling he was saddled with taking care of her.

"Not so much anymore. We keep reminding Mom that it's not necessary to use every single apple with so few of us to eat them." Come to think of it, that probably wasn't very tactful of them. "But Mom still likes to can applesauce and make apple butter, and she'll give away what we can't use."

"That's very...thrifty." She sounded a little surprised.

"My parents didn't believe in waste. And they thought we should learn the importance of work at an early age." He shrugged. "It's the way things are in the country. I guess we took it for granted."

They were nearing the woods now, and he pointed. "See the path? Trey keeps it cut for Mom. She insists on walking, and he says at least this way he knows where to start looking for her. You can take this on your own any time you want."

They stepped into the shadow of the pine trees, and the temperature seemed to drop ten degrees. Marisa shivered, looking around with what he thought was apprehension.

"You okay?"

"Yes, fine." Her smile just deepened the impression of strain. "I was surprised that it's so dark here."

"Once we're past this stand of pines and hemlock, there'll be more sunlight coming through the trees." He looked a little more closely at her face. "You're not afraid, are you?"

"I grew up in a suburb. Parks and playgrounds, but no real woods. I wouldn't want to get lost out here."

"You can't," he said. "Just stay on the path, and you'll be fine. And even if you got off the trail, all you'd have to do is walk downhill. Sooner or later you'd get to the road."

There was more to her tension than that, he thought, but he didn't intend to pry. Everything he learned about her just brought them closer, and that was the last thing he wanted.

The pines thinned out, replaced by the mixed deciduous trees that had grown up when this land had been timbered generations ago. Last season's leaves covered the path, and sunlight slanted through the trees.

Marisa sucked in a breath. "This is

lovely. So much better than the setting I'd intended to use."

"Which was?" They'd reached the low stone wall that was all that was left of the railroad embankment, and he put out a hand to help her up.

"Oh, a park." She laughed...at herself, he thought. "My editor will thank you. This is going to be much more realistic." The color had come back to her cheeks, and her eyes lit with enthusiasm, the tension he'd seen earlier ebbing. "That fallen tree is perfect for one of the illustrations. Look at the way the branches arc, and the color of the moss where the sun comes through."

"If you say so. I just see a fallen tree that should have been cut for firewood."

"You're used to it, that's all."

"True." And he'd longed for it when he was overseas, dreamed he was walking this path instead of a dusty road that might well be mined. "This was our backyard when we were kids. Trey and Adam had a fort right over there, and they wouldn't let us in, so Libby and I built a treehouse that looked down on them."

"Libby?"

"My sister. Twin, actually. You'd have a lot in common with her. She's a photojournalist, working on the West Coast right now."

"Does she look like you?" Marisa seemed to be assessing his claim to have a twin.

"She's much prettier, as she always reminds me." He put out a hand to halt her. "Look."

Twenty yards away a doe stood, her head lifted to nibble the tender shoots on a bush. The delicate curved line of the creature's neck moved him... Maybe Marisa had him noticing things.

And then he realized it wasn't just noticing. The deer reminded him of Marisa: the same timid grace, the same wariness in wide brown eyes.

He must have made some involuntary movement, because the doe turned her head, ears coming forward. In an instant she was gone, the white tuft of her tail visible as she fled up the hill toward deeper woods.

"Beautiful." Marisa said the word on a sigh, as if she'd been holding her breath.

*Like you.* "I'm afraid we can't get her to pose for you."

"Seeing her was enough." She seemed to realize she was clutching his hand and let go.

"It's just as well we stopped. I wanted to point out one thing. See that place up ahead where it looks like a trail cuts off through that thick stand of rhodo-dendrons?"

She nodded.

"You can go as far as you want on this path—it's the old railroad bed, and it runs clear around the hill. But don't take that trail. It leads to an old quarry. Been abandoned for years, and it's a steep drop."

"Dangerous?"

"Dangerous enough if you came to the edge suddenly and didn't realize it was there. It was strictly forbidden when we were kids."

She eyed him. "Something tells me you might have considered that a chal-lenge."

"You figured that out, did you? Yeah, I broke the rules a time or two. Decided I was going to climb down. There's a path of sorts, and the hillside is riddled with little crevices and caves. I figured I'd get clear to the bottom and have something to crow about."

"What happened?"

"About what you'd think. I got stuck halfway down, Libby had to run for help and Trey pulled me out. He lambasted me all the way home. Made me feel about six inches high. He never told Mom and Dad, though."

"Of course not. You two are loyal to each other."

It startled him, coming from Marisa. She didn't have siblings. How much did she understand of that complex relationship? He didn't answer, because anything he said might show her too much of himself, but she didn't seem to expect it.

She'd turned, looking back the way they'd come. "Would you mind if I made a few sketches of that hollow log? You can go on back, if you want. I'm sure I can find my way."

She didn't sound all that sure. "It's fine. I'll wait for you."

They walked back along the trail. As

they reached the log, a volley of shots sounded in the distance. Marisa made an involuntary movement.

"Do people hunt here? I wouldn't want someone to mistake me for a deer."

"No danger. Rabbit season doesn't start for a while yet, and deer season not until after Thanksgiving. Our land is posted, anyway."

"But someone was shooting." She dropped the backpack to the ground and pulled out a sketchpad and pencils.

"It's probably someone sighting in a gun or target shooting." Would she even know what that meant? "Sighting in means trying the gun out before hunting season, making sure the aim is true. That was far away...maybe even the other side of the valley. The sound car-ries, that's all."

She seemed to accept that. Sitting down on the backpack, she began to draw. It didn't take a minute until she was completely absorbed, the pencil fly-ing across the page. He propped his back against a tree and prepared to wait.

He expected to feel impatient, but he didn't. It was oddly restful, listening to

the soft rustling of the leaves, the faraway hum of a car. He could even hear
the movement of Marisa's pencil on the
page. Sometimes he thought he hadn't
really relaxed since he'd left the hospital.

He studied Marisa, liking her total ab-
sorption in what she was doing. The
tension had left her face, replaced by a
sort of inward look that told him she
didn't see anything except the scene
she transferred to the page.

But somehow he didn't think she'd
lost the tension. It was simply in abey-
ance while she worked.

He found his mind drifting back to
that incident with Trey and the quarry.
Funny that the day should be so clear in
his mind. He remembered everything
about it, from the heat of the sun on his
back to the cool of the rocks under his
hands. He seemed to smell the tiny
plants that grew between the rocks, releasing their aroma where his body
brushed against them.

He remembered the fear, too. And the
relief when Trey had come. As soon as
he'd heard Trey's voice, he'd known he

was going to be all right, although he'd never admit that to his brother.

Marisa leaned back abruptly. She studied the page for a moment, then closed the pad and looked up at him.

"Good enough. That'll let me rough it out. I hope I didn't keep you too long."

"No problem." He put out a hand to help her up. Still clasping her fingers, he found himself asking the question he hadn't intended to. "Something happened since yesterday, didn't it? Something that upset you."

Her eyes were as wide and startled as the deer's. "How did you know?"

He shrugged, not willing to put it into words. "What was it?"

"Adam Byler came to see me this morning." She pressed her lips together for an instant. "He brought someone. A man named Preston Connelly. The district attorney."

It hit him like a blow to the gut. "The DA. That means they're treating it as a criminal case." And their probing would be bound to lead to Uncle Allen.

"He said not necessarily, but I didn't

believe him. I think they suspect my father."

He wasn't surprised, but he could hardly say that. "I'm sorry." But was he? Would he rather see Marisa's father a suspect than his uncle?

"He—Connelly, that is—seemed to think it's odd that I remember so little from that time. I don't think he believed me when I said I didn't know anything."

She was looking for reassurance now, and he wasn't sure he could give it. "What do you remember?"

"Next to nothing. I was only five, after all." Defensiveness threaded her voice. "Do you remember things from when you were that age?"

He considered. "I remember things from kindergarten pretty well...kids I played with, trips we took. I'm not sure I could pin down what happened when I was five compared to when I was six. But you—" He stopped.

Her eyes sparked as she must have finished his sentence in her mind. "You mean I should remember because that's when my mother went away. That's when my life changed. That's what Connelly said."

He wouldn't know Connelly if he fell over him, but he had to agree. "That's true, isn't it? I mean, your life did change. You must remember when your grandmother came to live with you."

He was probably pushing too hard, but wouldn't she remember? He'd think anyone would have such a pivotal moment burned into her mind.

"I don't remember." Her face closed, shutting him out. "There's no point in saying that I must, because I don't." Her voice rose on the last word, and it was punctuated again by shots off in the distance.

# CHAPTER SEVEN

Marisa looked down at her clothes when she got out of the car the next day, wiping her palms on the gray slacks. She had an appointment with the spiritual leader of the district's Amish, Bishop Amos Long. She wasn't sure what one wore to talk with a bishop, but since they were meeting in a barn where he was apparently shoeing horses, she'd decided slacks and a jacket would do.

Geneva had set up the meeting at the Esch farm, just down the road from her house. The directions were to park in the lane and walk back to the barn behind the house, where Bishop Amos would be working. That was the correct way to address him, Geneva had assured her.

Clutching the strap of her shoulder bag, Marisa strode toward the barn, whose doors stood open, disclosing a shadowy interior. The lane led past a garden, obviously still producing. Rampant green vines wove over and around pumpkins and squash, and the tomato plants still bore a few heavy red tomatoes. Someone, probably Mrs. Esch, must can all that produce for her family's use. Even as she thought that, she glimpsed a white prayer cap where a woman bent over a plant, basket in hand.

She reached the barn door and stepped inside. The interior was dark after the bright sunshine outside, and she paused, letting her eyes adjust. A horse stood in the center aisle, tied to a post, and a man bent over the massive hoof he held in his hands. He straightened at the sound of her footsteps.

"Ach, you must be Ms. Angelo. Komm. I am Bishop Amos."

He regarded her gravely. Did he see her mother in her face?

"Yes, I'm Marisa Angelo. It's good of you to see me, Bishop Amos."

Apparently he'd finished his inspection, because he gave a short nod and turned back to the horse. "You will not mind if I work while we talk. I have said all week I would get here today."

"That's fine." In fact, she felt a little calmer now that he wasn't looking at her with that assessing impression in his shrewd blue eyes.

She wasn't sure what she'd expected of an Amish bishop, but he wore the same sturdy work clothes she'd seen on other Amish men, with the addition of a heavy apron. His beard was almost completely gray, and it came nearly to mid-chest.

"I didn't realize you did another job in addition to being a bishop," she said, moving a step closer so that she could see the hoof he held braced against the leather apron over his knees.

"I am a farrier, like my father and his father before him. For the Amish, to serve the community as a minister or bishop is not a job. We work for our keep, like Paul in the Bible."

If there was a challenge in the comment, she knew the answer. "Making tents, you mean."

"Ja." A quick smile warmed the austere features. "So you are Barbara Zook's daughter, komm back here at last. I remember you as a little child."

That startled her. "You do? But after my mother left the church..."

"She was no longer a part of us by her choice." His words held a tinge of sorrow. "But still I saw her from time to time in Springville. You had a look of her then. You still do, I think. Something about your eyes."

"I don't remember her very well."

She glanced around the barn, not sure she wanted him to see what was in her face when she made that admission. Stalls ran along both sides of the aisle, several of them occupied by horses probably waiting their turn. The loft above them was filled almost to overflowing with bales of hay.

"That is a shame." Bishop Amos seemed to measure a horseshoe against the shape of the hoof. "She was a gut mother, I think, from all I heard. But a little sad, maybe, at all she gave up. Still, you would know that better than I, ain't so?"

She was beginning to become accustomed to the almost singsong quality of his speech, to the upward inflection that turned a statement into a question inviting agreement.

"I don't know." She took a steadying breath. This was what she had to say to the man...the chance that Geneva's influence had given her. "I know almost nothing about my mother's life. My father never talks about her. And now that her suitcase has been found, it raises so many questions."

"Ja." He frowned a little, putting the hoof down. In a quick movement he braced the shoe against a toolbox, hitting it several times with a hammer, she supposed to reshape it. The metal rang in the still air, and the horse threw its head up.

Bishop Amos straightened, meeting her eyes. "Some folks think it would be better if it had never turned up. You don't feel that way."

She met his gaze steadily. "I have to know what happened to her. The truth is better, even if it hurts."

"Ja." The word was heavy with regret. "I can see why you feel that."

"None of the Amish people want to talk to me about her. Geneva Morgan said that you might help me."

"Geneva is a friend to us. To the Esch family, whose farm this is. Did you know that she provided a defense for their son when he was accused of a crime?"

"No." Although...had something been said that night at dinner, about Geneva bringing Jessica here to defend a case?

"She did. It was such a difficult time. I think people want to forget, but it is not so easy. There are still those who think that the Amish were involved, and others who are embarrassed by what happened."

"You mean that people fear this business about my mother will rake all that unpleasantness up again?"

He studied her face again. "You think that is strange, but to us, any publicity is bad. We try to live quietly, separate from the world." He made a small movement with his shoulders. "Sometimes the world won't allow that."

Her heart sank. He was going to turn her down. "So you won't help me."

"I did not say that. I would like to do what Geneva Morgan asks, both for her sake and for the sake of that little girl I remember." He smiled, kindness in his face. "I will try. But I cannot make people talk to you. If they don't want to..." He gave an expressive shrug.

She could breathe again, relief easing tense muscles. "I understand that. I'd appreciate anything you can do."

"You want to ask me something more, ain't so?"

He was perceptive. That was probably a good quality for a bishop.

"I hoped you could tell me what you knew about my mother. About why she came here in the first place. About what happened."

He nodded. "Let me finish this last shoe, and I will tell you what I know. Will you hold Blackie's head? He is a bit nervous when the shoe goes on."

She was a bit nervous about the idea of holding so large an animal, but it was the least she could do since the man seemed willing to cooperate. She took hold of the halter gingerly with one hand

and stroked the silky neck with the other. The horse's skin moved under her hand.

"Gut." Bishop Amos fitted the shoe to the hoof and positioned a nail against it. "Chust talk to him."

What did one say to a horse? "There, now." The hammer rang against the nail, and his eyes rolled. "It's all right. You're getting a new pair of shoes, aren't you? You'll like that when they're all finished."

The animal trembled a little but seemed to calm under her stream of nonsense. In a moment Bishop Amos had finished pounding. He clinched the nails down with another tool, his movements sure and steady.

"Ach, gut, all done." He straightened, hand on his back. "Farriers end up bent over, that's for sure." He untied the horse, led him to a stall and ushered him in. Then he came back to her.

"A straw bale makes as gut a seat as any. We will talk."

She sat where he indicated, next to him on a bale of straw, glad she hadn't worn a skirt. He leaned back against the side of a stall, seeming lost in thought for a moment.

"It was a long time ago, ja? Thirty years since the summer Barbara Zook came here to spend a couple of months with her cousins. The Zook family has a farm over on Liberty Road, the other side of Springville. Nate Zook was brothers with Barbara's father."

She pulled out a notebook, jotting down the name. It was already more than she'd known before. "Was there any special reason she came that summer?"

He shrugged a little. "The way I remember it, she had been writing to Ezra Weis, a neighbor of the Zooks. They were both eighteen, thinking about finding a mate, and she came to stay so as to get to know Ezra better, to see if they'd make a match of it."

Eighteen seemed young to be thinking of marriage to her, but probably not to an Amish person.

"Also Nate had a daughter and son about Barbara's age, so that was a gut enough reason."

"Does the Zook family still live around here?"

"Ach, ja. Amish don't usually move around much once they're settled. William Zook runs his father's farm now. Elizabeth, she married Thomas Bell, from over on the Paradise road."

She added their names to her list. "The man she was interested in, Ezra Weis. Is he still here, as well?"

Bishop Amos seemed to take a long time to answer that—long enough to make her wonder. "He is. He has a cabinet-making business in Springville."

"I think I've seen it. Right on the main street?" A flicker of anticipation went through her. He, at least, would be easy to find.

"Ja." Again that hesitation. "Ezra... Well, he took it hard when your mother didn't feel the same way about him as he did about her. He may not want to talk about it."

She had a sense of something held back. "What do you mean by taking it hard? Did he threaten her?"

"Ach, no. Ezra would not do that. But he thought she loved him. He talked about marrying her, and then she went off to be with your father. His heart was sore, maybe his pride hurt, as well. It was a couple of years before he even thought again of marrying."

"But he's married now?"

Bishop Amos nodded. "Ja, he married...a sister of Eli Miller, who has the guest house where you are staying."

"I see." That no doubt explained why Eli didn't want his family talking to her. "How did she meet my father?"

Bishop Amos shook his head. "That I don't know. It wondered me at the time, but sometimes the young people went to parties with Englischers. I'm thinking that Nate and his wife got suspicious that Barbara wasn't where she was supposed to be. They confronted her, and it all came out. She declared she loved Russell Angelo and was going to marry him, and she left the house that night."

She tried to picture it. Her memories of her mother were of a soft-spoken, gentle woman. Hard to believe she'd been able to stand up to everyone for a stranger.

"You...the Amish, I mean, must have tried to dissuade her."

"Ja. The family talked to her. I talked to her. Her mother came on the bus all the way from Indiana to try to change her mind, but no one could. She left the church and married your father, and that was the end of it."

The end. It sounded so final. "You shunned her." The words came out more accusingly than she'd intended.

He sighed. "It is not what anyone wanted. But she left. We would have welcomed her back at any time, but she did not come. And her cousins... I think, after the first shock they would have wanted to stay in touch with her. That is possible, you see, even when someone is under the bann. Maybe she didn't want to. She had made her choice."

"I don't understand how she and my father could stay here." She tried to imagine that and failed. "I'd think they'd want to go away where no one knew them."

Again he shrugged. "His work was here. He owned a little house in Springville, and they lived there until—" He stopped abruptly.

"Until she disappeared," she finished for him. "My father and my grandmother believed she had gone back to her family in Indiana. Did you?"

He shook his head. "No. I would have heard if that were so." There was a certainty in his voice that didn't allow argument.

"Then why didn't you go to the police, if you thought that wasn't true?" *If you thought something had happened to her.*

"It is not our way to turn to the law. And Barbara was no longer Amish."

She was speechless for a moment. "But if you were sure…"

He shook his head. "You do not understand, I know. But that is part of what it means to us to live separate."

"No. I don't understand." She took a breath, reminding herself that she still needed this man's cooperation. "I appreciate all you've been willing to tell me. It helps to understand that much." But there was so much more she didn't understand.

"You want more." He seemed to read her thoughts. "I will ask my people to talk with you. If they are willing…" He left that open.

"Thank you." She rose, not sure whether she felt better or worse for what she had learned. "I'd be very grateful."

He nodded, the lines in his face seeming to deepen. "I hope that this search does not lead you into sorrow."

She didn't doubt he hoped that. But it was clear from his tone that he felt she was headed straight into trouble.

Marisa drove along Springville's main street on her way back to the bed-and-breakfast, her mind still occupied with her conversation with Bishop Amose. She'd learned more from him about her mother in one short talk than she had in twenty-three years with her father.

Dad found it too painful to talk about her mother. That was the answer she'd always come up with. Any man might feel that way about a woman who'd left him and their daughter.

But what if she hadn't? What if Dad knew—

She stopped, not willing to let her thoughts go in that direction.

There was Springville's minuscule police station, a reminder of that confrontation with Adam Byler and the district attorney, if you could call it a confrontation when one party could only say that she didn't remember. She should have stood up for her father. She shouldn't have let herself be bullied.

To do him justice, Adam hadn't bullied her. If anything, she'd sensed that he hadn't liked the DA's tactics but had been powerless to stop him.

Her mind winced away from the man's thinly veiled accusations. *Dad, where are you? Why don't you call?*

The furniture maker's shop was in the middle of the block. Impulsively, Marisa drew to the curb a few spaces down from it. She sat for a moment, letting her gaze wander over what there was of Springville.

She had been six when they left here. This street would have been familiar to her. Maybe she'd walked down it with her mother. She ought to remember.

She'd tried to dismiss the district attorney's doubts about her convenient lack of memory, but they kept creeping back in when she wasn't looking. Link had been doubtful, too, although he'd been more polite about it.

She frowned, narrowing her eyes as she focused on Market Square, a simple crossing of the two largest streets. An informal curb market appeared to be in progress, with several trucks and wagons pulled up to the curb and tables set out filled with produce.

She could walk down and take a look, strolling past Ezra Weis's furniture shop as she did. She could go inside, for that matter. It was a store, wasn't it?

She got out of the car quickly, before she could change her mind, and set off down the sidewalk, her steps slowing as she came level with the shop. Plate-glass windows allowed her to see the interior.

Several chairs, a large chest and a set of cabinets bore witness to the furniture maker's craft. One side of the shop had shelves with a variety of small items, probably the sort of thing a tourist might buy. A couple who must be tourists, to judge by the cameras slung around their necks, were being waited on by a teenager in Amish dress. No one else was visible. She opened the door, hearing the tinny jingle of a bell, and stepped inside.

"Wilkom," the girl called out. "Chust look around. I'll be with you in a few minutes."

Marisa nodded, bending to study the

carving on a three-drawer chest. The piece of furniture was solid, the wood—maple, she thought—polished to a high sheen.

She gave a sidelong glance toward the Amish teenager. Not Weis's wife, obviously. Maybe a daughter. Her light brown hair was pulled back under her kapp, of course, as demurely as any Amish woman she'd seen. But the girl's green dress and apron matched her eyes exactly, probably not a coincidence. Apparently even Amish teenagers cared about how they dressed.

The young woman took a step to the side to show the couple something, and Marisa suppressed a smile. With her dark stockings, the girl wore the latest in running shoes.

Marisa ran her fingers along the top of a chest that was painted with a colorful stylized design of birds and hearts. If her mother had married her Amish sweetheart, would this be Marisa's life now? She glanced again at the girl. Would the young Barbara have looked like that, with rosy cheeks and laughing eyes?

"Well, you have just the most precious

things I ever saw." The female tourist's voice rose. "I can't decide what else to buy." She gestured with the camera in her hand. "You stand over there by those shelves, and I'll take your picture, okay?"

The young woman smiled. "You can take pictures, but not of me, please."

The woman bridled. "All I want is one little picture. That's not too much to ask, is it?"

"I'm sorry, but that is against our beliefs." Judging by the young woman's calm response, she'd dealt with this before.

"I don't see what harm," the woman began.

Marisa couldn't help herself—she had to intercede. "Why don't you and your husband pose over here by the display, and I'll snap a picture of the two of you?" she suggested.

"Well, I really wanted..."

"Right over here." Marisa gestured, taking the camera from the woman's hands. "You want a photo of both of you to remember your trip, don't you?"

The woman giggled. "That'll be cute.

Harvey, you hold one of these dolls, and I'll point to you."

Once they were arranged to the woman's satisfaction, Marisa snapped the picture. The Amish girl slipped behind the counter and began wrapping their purchases. By the time the camera had been returned to its owner, she was handing them a package and wishing them a pleasant day.

The door closed behind them with a final jingle, and Marisa exchanged smiles with the young woman. "Some people make me embarrassed to be a tourist."

"Ach, they don't know any better, ain't so? They don't understand why we don't want our pictures taken."

"I'm afraid I don't, either, but it was obvious you didn't care for it." Was the girl Ezra Weis's daughter? She could hardly ask.

"The Bible teaches us not to make any graven images, that's why." She busied herself putting away the items the couple had been handling.

So if Marisa's mother hadn't left the church, she wouldn't even have a photo to remember her by.

"Is there something special you are interested in?"

Obviously she was going to have to buy something to justify being here. Marisa pointed to a pair of wooden bookends, painted with the same design she'd seen on the chest. "Could I have a closer look at those, please?"

"Ja, for sure." The girl lifted them down, putting them on the counter.

Marisa ran her finger over a painted heart. "These must be traditional designs, are they?"

"Ja, they are Pennsylvania Dutch. You will see them on everything from wood to metal. Straus's Hardware has some nice metal trays with the design, too."

A soft thud made Marisa glance toward the door behind the young woman. It apparently led to a back room, and it stood open, revealing a workbench and what seemed to be a rocking chair in progress. The sound she'd heard had come from a man who bent over the chair, seeming intent on his work. Before she could get a good look at him, he'd moved out of her line of vision.

The Amish girl waited, probably used

to people having trouble making up their minds.

"Are these handmade?" Marisa asked, touching the bookends again. She couldn't see into the back room without being obvious, but for some reason she needed to look at this man her mother had almost married.

"Ja, everything in the shop is made by my father. Well, my brothers help some, but they are only twelve and thirteen."

"I'll take these, then." There was no use prolonging this visit. The man was apparently not going to come back where she could see him. She could ask, but it would be best to let Bishop Amos use his influence first.

"Gut. I will wrap them for you." The girl pulled butcher paper from a roll and began wrapping them. "Are you staying in Springville or just passing through?"

"I'll be here for a few more days, at least. I'm staying at the Plain and Fancy Bed and Breakfast."

Was it her imagination, or did the girl's hands pause momentarily in their work?

"That's nice, ain't so? I'm sure the Millers make you comfortable."

"Yes, very."

Marisa handed over the money and took the package. As she did, a step in the back room brought her gaze back to the door.

She'd wanted the man to move back where she could see him. Now that she had her wish, she wasn't so sure.

He stood in the doorway, his hands braced on the sides, staring at her, black brows drawing down over his eyes, even his black beard seeming to bristle.

This was the man her mother had planned to marry, but no fond remembrance showed in his face. He looked at her as if he hated the sight of her.

Link stood on the front steps of the Plain and Fancy. He'd come to see Marisa, primed to face her about her memories. Or rather, her lack of them. The more he'd thought about that, the more her inability to recall the events of that time didn't make sense.

Or, looked at one way, maybe it did. If she'd seen something or heard something that made her believe her father had been responsible for her mother's disappearance, she might well block that out.

Not that he had any possible excuse for thinking like a psychiatrist, but there were plenty of things he'd like to block out. Like lying trapped in the rubble of the school, hearing groans and knowing they were his wondering who else was alive, and for how long.

He was trying to shake that off when he saw Marisa's car pulling up at the gate. She got out, her movement checking at the sight of him. Then she continued on, arranging her face in a smile that didn't quite disguise the worry beneath.

"Were you looking for me?"

He managed his own smile. "Nice as they are, I didn't stop by to visit with the Millers. I should have called first."

"No problem. I was out at the Esch farm, talking with Bishop Amos. Your mother set it up."

"Was that a help?"

She nodded, her eyes shadowed, making him wonder what insights the bishop had.

"Look, can we talk for a few minutes?" *Or however long it takes to get you to level with me.*

"Of course. There's a garden seat around the side of the house."

He followed her along the flagstone path, appreciating her foresight. She'd talk, all right, but in a spot where she could get up and walk away from him if his questions got too personal.

The bench was placed so that one could sit and admire the yellow and rust mums that sprawled against the fence separating the guest house from the neighboring yard. Link recognized the workmanship—this was one of Ezra Weis's creations. His mother had one very similar. He waited until Marisa settled and sat down next to her.

"Was Bishop Amos willing to talk to the Zook family for you?" Obviously her relationship with her mother's family would be a lot smoother if the bishop interceded for her.

"He said he would talk with them, as well as any of the other Amish who might know something." She sent him a sidelong glance. "Like Ezra Weis."

"Ezra?" He put his hand on the back of the bench Ezra had made, turning to face her more fully. "What does he have to do with this?"

"He's the reason my mother came here the summer she met my father. They were...courting, I suppose the word is." She darted a look at him. "I wondered if you knew."

Apparently she was satisfied with his surprise. "I didn't. I'd have told you." He frowned absently at the weeping willow that overhung the yard. "What else did Bishop Amos say about him?"

"That he took it very hard. He didn't marry for a long time after that." Marisa was studying a cluster of bright golden mums as if they held a secret. "He might have been jealous."

He saw where she was going with that, but he didn't find it very convincing. "I suppose he must have been at the time, but your mother didn't disappear until several years later. You think it likely he'd hold a grudge that long?"

"I don't know." She flung her hands up in a gesture of futility. "I don't know enough about anything. Including your uncle."

He stiffened. "We've been honest with you about him." Had he, though? He hadn't told her what Trey said about Uncle Allen's eccentric behavior in his later years.

That didn't need to have anything to do with Barbara's disappearance, he assured himself. And what about Allen's place being searched, the voice of his conscience asked. Maybe Allan wasn't involved. But his house certainly was.

Marisa pulled open her bag and burrowed in it, coming up with a pad and pencil. "Do you mind?" she asked, holding the pencil up. "I think better when my hands are busy."

"Not at all. I'm the same way, but I can't very well hammer anything here."

"I wasn't accusing you of withholding information about your uncle." Her pencil began to move on the pad almost without her attention. It was like watching automatic writing. Or drawing, in this case. The thick clumps of mums began to take shape on the page. "But there may be things about his relationship with my mother that you don't know."

He couldn't argue with that. "True. But I don't see how we'll find out at this point. One thing, though. We were able to confirm that the addition was being built at the time your mother vanished. Trey is going through the old records, trying to find out who did the work."

"That's kind of him. And you." A horse began to take shape on the page, with Bishop Amos delineated bending over its hoof in a few swift lines.

"We're involved," he said shortly. Whether he wanted to be or not. "The house belongs to us."

And that set him thinking about the break-in. Except he couldn't really call it that, since whoever it was had walked right in. He didn't like that. Neither had Adam, when he and Trey had reported it. Chances were that it was just a curiosity seeker, but if not...

He found he was looking at the area behind the guest house from a different perspective, maybe getting the wind up since that incident. There were neighboring houses on either side, but at the back, the yard ended in a patch of woods. Easy enough for anyone to approach the guest house without being seen, and Marisa was alone here at night.

"You look like a thundercloud." Abandoning Bishop Amos and the horse, she'd begun sketching the willow tree. "What's wrong?"

*Don't tell anyone about the house being searched,* Adam had said. *Not until we know a bit more.* But how could he justify that, remembering Marisa's story of someone standing under the willow, watching her window?

"Adam told me to keep my mouth shut about this," he said abruptly, before he could change his mind. "But when I went back to the house the other day, I realized someone had been in there while I was gone. The place had been searched."

Her pencil dropped, and she looked at him, eyes wide. "Did they...? Was anything taken?"

"Not that we could see. Trey was with me, and we checked it out as best we could." He shrugged, frustrated. "There's not much there to search. A few pieces of furniture, Uncle Allen's books."

"And the house itself," she added, obviously thinking of the wall that had yielded her mother's suitcase.

"That's not as easy as it sounds. The old part of the house is solid double-plank construction." Seeing her lost look, he demonstrated. "They built the walls using two layers of boards put in perpendicular to each other, with a layer of horsehair plaster finishing it. With age, those boards draw together so much that you can't even fit an electric wire between them."

"There's still the floors," she suggested. "A loose floorboard, maybe." She paused, looking for a moment as if that started a train of thought. "Or something in a piece of furniture or a book."

Next she'd be planning an all-out search. "I'll have a look through everything. It all has to be sorted to be sold or trashed anyway."

"I'll help you," she said quickly.

"That's not necessary." Maybe he said that with a little too much emphasis.

She gave him a steady look. "You mean you don't want me."

"You have better things to do with your time. Your illustrations, for instance." He was grasping at straws and he knew it, but he just didn't like the idea of Marisa looking through Uncle Allen's belongings, looking for...well, looking for evidence that he'd been involved with her mother, he supposed.

"That almost sounds as if you're afraid I'll find something that compromises your uncle."

That was exactly what he feared, but she didn't need to point that out.

"Fine. You can help me search. We can start right now, if you're so determined—" His temper ran out as he glanced at the drawing pad.

There was the willow tree. But that wasn't all. Under the tree she'd drawn a figure...the man in Amish dress she claimed to have seen.

But the man wasn't the unidentifiable blur she'd talked about. The face was clear. It was that of Ezra Weis.

# CHAPTER EIGHT

Geneva had shown up at Allen's house midway through the afternoon and joined their search, for which Marisa was thankful. The tension between her and Link had done nothing but grow when they were alone together.

It wasn't her fault, Marisa kept assuring herself as she removed drawers from an old chest, looking for anything that had been left behind. Only dust and mouse droppings. Link ought to understand her need to know whether this old house had any other secrets to offer concerning her mother. Instead, he only seemed to care about his family's good name. Small wonder that tension existed between them.

As for the other type of tension that seemed to vibrate between them whenever they got too close—well, if she didn't acknowledge it, maybe it would go away.

She slid the last drawer back into place and glanced across the room. Geneva, generously covered in dust, sat on the floor, where she'd been tapping floorboards.

"Now, Link, be sure you check all those closet walls. There might easily be a cubbyhole behind one."

Link tapped a closet wall, looking more than a little frustrated. "Mom, I'm telling you, there can't be anything here. Look, you can see that this closet was built into the corner years and years after the house itself. The walls aren't thick enough—"

"Try anyway, dear." Geneva gave her most beguiling smile. "Please."

Looking like a man whose patience had been tried to the utmost, Link began to tap on walls.

Marisa's lips twitched. Geneva's mastery of her two tall sons was something to behold. How was she with her daughter? That would be an interesting relationship, she'd imagine.

Her smile slipped a little. Whatever their relationship was, it was better than what she'd had with her mother. She thought again of the girl in the shop, trying to picture her mother there.

"That drawing you made of Ezra Weis as the man under the tree," Geneva said, as if continuing a conversation already begun. "How did you feel when you were drawing it?"

Link had told Geneva about it almost as soon as she arrived, obviously hoping to enlist her support in his contention that Marisa had let her imagination run away with her. But Geneva had refused to commit.

"I'm not sure I felt anything." It was never easy to explain the workings of her subconscious mind. "We were talking about something else, and my hand just seemed to move automatically."

"You connected the incident of the man under the tree with having seen Ezra." Link ducked his head out of the closet to deliver his opinion once again. "Your imagination did the rest."

"You could be right." She had to admit it, even though her instincts didn't agree.

"I am." Link's tone was firm. With one hand braced against the door frame, he gave an impression of wiry strength restrained but ready to spring lose in a moment.

"But then why did he look at me as if he hates me?" A shiver touched the nape of her neck despite the stale, dusty warmth of the room. "I didn't imagine that."

"You shouldn't have gone into the shop alone." He frowned, the hand on the door frame tightening until the muscles stood out on his arm.

"Why not?" Her temper flared, her gaze clashing with his. "Because I might learn something?"

"Because you shouldn't go around antagonizing people." A muscle twitched in Link's jaw. "I don't believe for a minute that Ezra would harm you. Anyway, you said at the time that you just saw a blur. That you couldn't identify the man. So why pitch on Ezra?"

"Instinct," Geneva said promptly. "Just because she didn't consciously know who it was at the time, that doesn't mean her instincts are wrong. Usually a woman's instincts are right."

Geneva looked so serious, sitting on the floor in her faded jeans, her white hair tousled, laying down the law to her son, that Marisa had to grin.

"There you have it, Link. Your mother believes me."

Link's only answer was a muted snort as he went back into the closet.

"It still might have been very innocent," Geneva said. "Ezra is a bit of a prickly personality, but I shouldn't think he could do violence."

Link reappeared, cobwebs in his hair. "Explain to me how Ezra could innocently be in the inn's yard at three in the morning."

"Well, it is his brother-in-law's place," Geneva said. "Aaron Miller could have told him who was staying here. Ezra loved Barbara, after all. Learning her daughter was actually there might have upset him. He could have gone out for a walk and just been drawn there." Geneva made an amorphous gesture, apparently intended to convey an irresistible urge.

"At three in the morning?" Link said again. "I still say Marisa imagined the whole thing."

"Thanks," she said, letting her sarcasm show. "I suppose that's better than saying I'm paranoid."

Link's gaze met hers across the room again, and for an instant the air seemed to sizzle with heat. "I don't think you're paranoid," he said.

The trouble was that Geneva wanted everyone to be innocent...that was her nature. And Link just wanted to be clear of the whole thing. She could hardly blame him for that.

"Have we finished everything on this floor?" she asked, trying to regain the balance that had been disturbed by his look.

"I think so." Link ran both hands through his hair as if to dislodge any cobwebs. "The books downstairs will take some time."

"Don't forget the attic," Geneva said, standing and dusting off the seat of her jeans. "That's still full, I'd guess."

Link groaned, obviously not having thought of that. "You're kidding me. Far as I can tell, nobody who lived in this house ever threw anything away. It'll all have to be gone through before it's sold."

"It's a shame. This was a happy house once," Geneva said wistfully. "It could be again. I hate to see you sell."

"I have a job in California," Link reminded her, his tone gentle. "I don't need a house here."

Geneva made a noncommittal sound that might or might not have been agreement. She glanced at her watch.

"Goodness, look at the time. Now, Marisa, you and Link come right to the house for supper. You don't need to go shower or change—it'll just be a light meal for the three of us. I have chicken stew in the slow cooker."

"I don't think..." *I don't think Link would like any more of my company* was what she wanted to say, but she couldn't.

"No arguments," Geneva said, as if Marisa were one of her kids. "We all need comfort food after this job. Don't you be more than twenty minutes behind me, you hear? I just have to put biscuits on." She trotted out of the room, and her light footsteps sounded on the stairs.

Marisa leaned against the chest, her gaze on Link. "I could go back to the B and B. You can make some excuse to your mother..."

She stopped, because he approached, bracing his hand against the bureau next to her so that he pinned her in place. Her pulse gave an extra little thud.

"No way," he said firmly. "If I show up at home without you, I'll never hear the end of it."

He was exaggerating, no doubt, but she smiled, wanting to keep the moment light. "Right. It's easy to see that your mother rules the roost."

"She'd never admit to that, but she generally gets her way with me and Trey."

"Not about you staying here." The words were out before she realized she was inviting a confidence he might not want to make.

"No." Lines deepened in his face. "I'd like to make her happy, but I can't do that."

"You have to live your own life." She focused her eyes on his chest. Looking up into his face would be a mistake. A cobweb had attached itself to the collar of his polo shirt. She reached up to brush it off.

He captured her hand in his, pressing it against his chest, and she couldn't breathe.

"Thanks. For understanding." His voice had gone low, and his heart thudded against her palm.

"It's all right." She was breathless, not sure she was even making any sense. "But I..." She let that trail off. He was so close she could feel his breath move against her cheek, feel the heat that emanated from him, wrapping around her.

"But you...?" he repeated, the words rumbling in his throat.

"I know what she's feeling, too." It wasn't easy to concentrate on the words when she was so aware of his closeness. "Especially after your injury."

He didn't move, but it seemed the air cooled between them and the space widened. "My mother told you about that?"

"Yes." And obviously he didn't like

that. "I didn't ask her anything. She just mentioned it."

"Yeah. Well, I'm fine now." He released her hand, stepping back, not looking at her. "Good as new."

"Are you?" She didn't think so, but she was powerless to do anything about it.

He didn't deign to answer that. Instead, he turned toward the door. "We'd better get going, or Mom's biscuits will burn."

Marisa turned off the side street toward the Plain and Fancy, her low beams piercing the dark. It had rained while she was at Geneva's and now a mist hung over the valley, distorting everything.

She shouldn't have stayed so late. She wouldn't have, but Geneva had begun talking about Allen, despite Link's occasional efforts to divert her.

Geneva seemed determined to talk about her late brother-in-law. Maybe having been in the house that afternoon had brought back memories. She'd told story after story.

Marisa frowned. Geneva had given her a picture of the man...a person whose intelligence had set him apart but maybe also made him look down on his neighbors. He'd apparently had a malicious tongue that alienated people.

Geneva, always seeming to see the good in others, had struggled to be fair. She'd insisted Allen was lonely, even lonelier as he grew older.

Looking at it from an outsider's perspective, Marisa couldn't help but wonder if there had been any guilt involved in Allen's eccentric behavior. Certainly Link hadn't liked her hearing all that, probably because he guessed the interpretation she'd put on it.

She parked in her usual spot just past the gate. Rhoda had left the porch light on, and it made a welcoming yellow circle in the gloom. Beyond the main entrance to the bed-and-breakfast the Millers' wing was dark. They must have gone to bed already.

She got out of the car, the sound of the door closing echoing like a shot in the still night. Fortunately she'd had a sweater in the car, because it had gotten chilly after the rain.

She walked toward the gate, her feet

making little sound on the wet grass. As she reached for the handle, the lilac bush next to the gate seemed to shiver in the breeze.

Except that there was no breeze. The night was still; the air heavy with moisture.

Marisa caught her breath, trying to quell her fear. It was nothing. Some small animal, maybe.

Her hand tightened on the gate. She could get back into the car. Go to the police, tell whoever was on duty that she was afraid to go into the Plain and Fancy.

*Wimp,* she jeered at herself. *No one is there. March up to the door and let yourself in.*

Quickly, before she could talk herself out of it, she opened the gate and strode up the flagstone walk. Was that a sound behind her? She hurried, reaching the pool of light with a sense of relief. She thrust her key in the lock, turned it and hurried inside.

With the door safely locked, she looked out at the lawn. It was still and empty.

Rhoda had left a plate of cookies and

a thermos of cocoa on the counter for her. Marisa wasn't really hungry after the meal Geneva had served, but it seemed impolite not to touch them. She sipped a scant half cup of the cocoa and nibbled on a cookie, then carried another cookie upstairs with her in case of a sudden attack of the munchies.

It was only after she'd showered and changed into a robe and pajamas that she realized someone had been in her room that day. Not just in her room. Someone had searched it.

She stood still at the dresser, staring down at the clothes that had been rearranged. Rhoda? Mary? Maybe just curious about her things and having a look while they were cleaning?

Or Eli? He had access to the room, as well. A shiver went through her.

It could be simple curiosity, but that was what they'd said about Allen's house being searched. How could this be a coincidence?

Nothing had been taken, but the incident shattered whatever illusion she'd had of safety. How could she possibly sleep in this room tonight?

Get a grip, she scolded herself. Even if an outsider had gotten in here today, which seemed unlikely, they could hardly still be here. The wing where the Miller family slept was on the other side of the house, but if she screamed, they would certainly hear her.

This was hardly a call-the-police emergency, but she would definitely stop at the station in the morning and report it, no matter how many skeptical looks that got. And she'd make some excuse to ask for a different room—maybe one facing the street on the side closest to the Miller's, she'd feel safer there.

When she crawled into bed, her nerves were still so jangled that she was convinced she'd lie awake for hours. Instead, she fell almost immediately into a deep, exhausted sleep.

She woke sometime later, disoriented, heart pounding, her throat choked with tears. She was clutching the pillow to her face, and she shoved it away with shaking hands, sitting upright in bed.

Not a nightmare, no, but certainly a bad dream. Even once she stood, the remnants of it clung to her. Angry voices, still ringing in her ears so that she almost thought there was someone in the house.

But there wasn't. She knew that. The voices came from her past, from the memories of a small child huddled in bed, holding a pillow over her ears to shut out the sound of angry adult voices.

What had they been saying? She tried to grasp the dream, but it slid away, squirting through her fingers like a wet bar of soap. Gone before she could even be sure whose voices they were.

She crossed to her backpack and pulled out a water bottle, drinking deeply. Setting the bottle down on the dresser, she glanced out the window and froze.

He was there again. The man in the yard. Not standing under the tree this time but moving, an indistinct dark figure crossing the yard from the direction of the woods.

Instead of the fear she expected, a wave of anger swept over her. Searching her room, watching her window while she slept—it was outrageous. She would not let them get away with it.

Without stopping to identify who that

amorphous "them" was, she snatched her robe from the foot of the bed and ran for the stairs. She didn't stop to think until she'd switched on the outside light and opened the door.

The chill air hit her, bringing with it a sense of caution. Did she really want to do this? Could she do this? Still, what could the man do? If it was Ezra Weis, just knowing she'd identified him would surely make him stop this silent persecution.

And if not—well, she could scream, couldn't she? Rouse the sleeping street if she had to. She would not huddle in her room afraid.

Crossing the porch, she stared into the darkness. The figure had been crossing the side yard. Headed for the front door? Or for the street?

Even as she thought it, she spotted him, walking down the street away from the B and B. Quickly, before she could change her mind, she darted down the walk, through the gate and down the grassy verge. When he reached the circle of illumination from the streetlamp, she caught him by the arm.

He swung around, face startled. It was Ezra Weis.

She experienced a moment's hope that Geneva had been right about the man. "What were you doing out in the yard, watching my window? Well?" Her voice sounded braver than she felt.

He looked down at her, his arm stiff as iron under her hand. "I do not know what you mean."

"You were in the yard just now. And before...a few nights ago. I saw you, watching my window."

"You are mistaken." He spoke with a flat assurance that was almost convincing.

"No. I'm not. You were there. You were my mother's friend, but she married my father. You hated her for it."

How stupid was she, blurting that out to a man who might be her mother's killer? But how could she go on, stumbling in a maze and learning nothing?

For a long moment Ezra Weis said nothing. Then he gave a stiff nod. "I thought your mother and I would marry. She went with the Englischer instead, and I was angry. But I would not hurt her. Or you."

"What are you doing here in the middle of the night then?" Her certainty ebbed, leaving her aware that she was cold and her bare feet wet from the grass.

"When I have trouble sleeping I walk," he said. He pulled loose from her grasp, but then took her arm.

"What are you doing?" Fear shimmered through her.

"You are afraid of someone being in the yard. I am seeing you to the door."

"I don't need—"

But he hustled her along, ignoring her protest. In the gate, up the walk. When they reached the porch he released her and stepped back.

"You didn't need to do that." She tried to hang on to her dignity, but it was a little hard in pajamas and bare feet.

"It is what I would wish for someone else to do for my daughter." He paused, emotion moving in the stoic face. "And for Barbara's daughter."

Before she could respond, he turned

and walked quickly away, disappearing into the dark.

Finishing the baseboard in the family room was a back-breaking job, Link decided. Maybe he should have followed Trey's suggestion to hire out some of the renovation work. It certainly would have been faster.

If he had, this whole business with Barbara Angelo's disappearance would have been avoided. A hired crew might easily have tossed the suitcase out with the rest of the building debris.

Then he wouldn't be involved. And he'd never have met Marisa.

Good or bad? He didn't know.

Still, when he heard a vehicle pull into the driveway, his heart lifted. Marisa, maybe, come to continue the search. But when he moved to the window, he saw that it was Trey.

"Hey, big brother." He took a second look at Trey's expression. "What's wrong?"

Trey shrugged. "Nothing. Just a few more answers that raise even more questions."

He held the door. "There's coffee on the counter."

"Maybe I will." Trey went into the kitchen, which was next on the renovation list.

Link followed. Right now the kitchen still contained the old glass-fronted cabinets and the gas range that he'd never dared turn on for fear of blowing the whole place up.

He waited until Trey had filled a cup. "So? What did you find out?"

"I went back through the old records at the office, trying to find an account. Seemed likely that Uncle Allen would have used Morgan Construction for building the addition, but knowing Allen, you could never be sure."

"And?" Link leaned against the counter, forcing himself to be patient. Trey liked to tell things in his own methodical way.

"The work was done in September that year, which jibes with Barbara Angelo's disappearance. She supposedly went missing on the fifteenth of the month, a Friday."

Link nodded. At the moment he didn't

see how that would be helpful, but every little bit contributed. "That fits with what we thought. Adam says according to the police report, the mother wasn't there when Marisa got off the school bus from kindergarten that day. Her father claimed he gave it the weekend, just in case Barbara had gone someplace to cool down after an argument. When Barbara hadn't shown up by Monday, he reported it."

"Allen did use Morgan Construction, so that simplifies things." Trey blew on his coffee. "Unfortunately, the job records aren't very complete. They should have been working that day, but you know how it goes. The boss could have called the crew off for an emergency job."

"Who was running construction then?"

"Tom Sylvester, same as he is now."

Link remembered Tom—a bluff, hearty, red-faced man who always had a joke and a laugh for the boss's kid. "He must be getting up there."

"About ready to retire. Claims he's going to head down to Florida and spend all his time fishing. His wife says she gives him two weeks before he's fixed everything in the house and started on the neighbors."

Somehow it didn't surprise Link that Trey knew all that about someone who worked for Morgan Enterprises. Trey was like Dad in that respect, always taking responsibility for everyone else.

Unlike him. His mind winced away from that reminder. "Somebody should talk to Tom about it. He may be able to fill in the blanks. Will you?"

Trey shook his head. "Don't you think it would come better from you? Marisa is sure to want in on it, and she seems to rely on you."

His jaw hardened until it seemed it would crack. He didn't want Marisa or anyone else relying on him. But Trey was right—she would definitely want in on this.

"Okay, I'll do it. Maybe it will distract Marisa from searching this house."

"To say nothing of Mom." Trey grinned. "She's now convinced that there's a secret hidden somewhere in the book room."

"If there is, it'll be a bit hard to find, since we don't know what we're looking for." That was worse than useless, in his opinion. Still, someone else had searched, so maybe Mom had a point.

Trey shoved himself away from the counter and set his coffee mug in the scarred sink. "Don't tell Mom that. It would ruin the story she's inventing. At least this might keep her out of worse trouble."

Link doubted it, but let Trey keep his illusions for the moment.

"Guess I'll leave you to it." Trey went toward the door. "Let me know what else you need."

"Thanks, Trey." He followed him to the door.

"By the way..." Trey stopped, hand on the screen door. "Tom is retiring in a couple of months, like I said. I was thinking you might want to take his place."

While Link was still gaping at him, Trey hurried on with what sounded like a prepared speech. "You know the business, and you're more than capable of running the operation."

"And besides, it would keep me here so Mom would be happy," Link finished for him. "Thanks, Trey, but that's not for me."

"Think about it." Trey rested his hand on Link's shoulder for a moment. "We sure like having you around, little brother."

The gesture touched him, but he shook his head. "I don't think so."

"The offer's open." Trey went on out of the house, then stopped on the porch and looked back at him. "Sleep on it. Morgans belong here."

He stepped off the porch and headed for his pickup. Link watched him go, choking down the tightness in his throat.

It was a nice offer. If the job were anywhere else, with anyone else, he might consider it.

But despite what Trey thought, this particular Morgan didn't belong here. The only way he'd ever be able to forget the past was to go someplace where no one knew him. Or would expect anything from him that he couldn't deliver.

# CHAPTER NINE

As Marisa approached the turn to Allen's house, a pickup truck spurted out the driveway. Trey, at the wheel, waved and continued toward town.

It was just as well he was leaving, not arriving. Not that she didn't like Trey, but she'd prefer not to have two Morgans to contend with this morning. Her head was already splitting from loss of sleep.

She tapped on the back door and walked in at a call from the family room. Link was on the floor, tacking a strip of molding in place, but he rose when he saw her. "Morning. I thought you'd be along soon."

"I hope it's not too early. I want to get in some painting later this afternoon."

"No problem," he said easily. "The book room is waiting."

She had a twinge of conscience at how much of his time she was taking. "You can get on with your work. I'll be glad to go through the books alone."

He stretched, hand on his lower back. "That's okay. I'll join you."

"Are you sure?" Or did he just not trust her to search alone for fear of what she might find? "I know you're getting behind on your remodeling."

But he was already leading the way into one of the other ground-floor rooms. Shelves lined three sides, all of them crammed with books. Arched windows looked out on an overgrown garden that might once have been lovely. The fourth wall was entirely taken up with a massive fireplace, its bricks blackened from years of wood fires.

"This was Uncle Allen's favorite room. He'd close himself up in here for hours, working on some obscure item of county history or meeting with a few friends who were obsessed as he was."

She could almost picture the man, sitting here alone for hour after hour. Maybe year after year. Had he been thinking about Barbara?

"It's a lot of books. I guess we'd better get started." She scooped up an armload of books and promptly sneezed at the dust. No furniture was left in the room, so she piled them on the floor and sat down beside them. "Would it help you if we sorted as we went?"

"I suppose, although how to go about it is beyond me." Link grimaced before pulling his own stack of books off a shelf and sitting down beside her.

She leafed through an account of the area's early landowners. "Maybe sort them by topic. Or age. I'd think the older books would be worth more."

"Or I could just donate the lot to the county historical society. They could call it the Allen Morgan Memorial Collection."

"It would be a fitting memorial, given what I've heard about him." She kept her voice even. She couldn't let her suspicions contaminate her thoughts when she didn't know if they were true.

"A lonely, unproductive life," Link said dryly. "Maybe so."

She just looked at him, shaken by the bitterness in his voice. Did he even realize how he sounded?

He seemed to feel her gaze, because he looked back, his eyes meeting hers. He studied her face and frowned.

"You look as if you haven't slept in a week."

"Thanks." She tried to turn it off lightly.

"Come on. What's wrong?"

She'd evade the question, but what was the point? Adam would no doubt tell him what she'd reported anyway.

"When I got back last night, I found that my room had been searched."

Link dropped the book he was holding, sending up a puff of dust. "What? How could anyone get in there with the Millers around?"

"It seems unlikely," she admitted. "I suppose it's possible that Rhoda or Mary disturbed things when they were cleaning the room, but that seems unlike them. Still, nothing was missing."

Link's frown deepened. "This place is searched—now your room. A person would have to stretch coincidence pretty far to think the two events aren't related."

"I reported it to Adam. I don't see what else I could do."

"Right." He didn't look satisfied. "There's something more, isn't there?"

She nodded, taking a deep breath. She still wasn't sure how to explain her uncharacteristic action last night.

"I was having bad dreams." She paused, wishing she hadn't said that. She certainly didn't want to tell him what those dreams were. "I woke up—around three again, I guess. When I glanced out the window, I saw someone moving across the yard."

She looked for skepticism in his face but didn't find it. Instead, he leaned toward her.

"Was he watching your window again?"

"No." In a way, she was glad of that. "He seemed to be crossing the yard from the back to the front. He could have been going either toward the street or toward the front door."

"You called the police."

"No. I...I went after him."

For a full second he stared at her. Then he grasped her shoulders in his hands, his fingers so tight they must be leaving prints on her skin.

"Are you crazy? Why would you do such a thing? The danger—" He cut off, his eyes blazing into hers.

But not just with anger. With passion, longing... She found herself leaning toward him, their faces so close she could feel his breath on her lips.

Something inside her...a longing she hadn't even been aware of, seemed to yearn toward him in return. If only this could be so simple; if they could hold each other and every other issue would fade away...

He pulled back, his face tightening to a rigid mask. His hands dropped from her shoulders.

"Sorry." Face averted, he sucked in an audible breath. "I didn't mean to hurt you. But you should have better sense."

"I know that." Was it relief she felt or disappointment? "I can't explain it. I was so upset already that I lost it when I saw him. I just wanted to know who it was. If I'd waited until the police got there, he'd have been long gone."

"You're lucky you weren't long gone." He muttered the words. "Did you? See who it was, I mean."

"Yes. I caught up with him on the walk." Her nerves jumped at the memory. "It was Ezra Weis."

"Ezra again." His jaw tightened. "You caught up with him. I don't suppose it occurred to you that it would have been safer not to let him see you."

The sarcasm was better than his anger had been. It helped her get her balance again. "It occurred to me, yes. About the time I accused him of watching my window."

He ran a hand through his hair, looking as if he'd like to yank on it. "Not the smartest thing to do."

"Well, I know that." Did he think she was a complete idiot? Probably. "He denied it, of course. Said he couldn't sleep and decided to take a walk."

Link considered that. "Would there have been time for the intruder to slip away while you were coming downstairs?"

"I guess. Although why would he, if he didn't know I'd seen him?"

"I don't know, but my point is that there's at least a chance Ezra was telling the truth." Link looked as if he weren't sure and didn't like the feeling.

"Yes." Her hands went slack in her lap. She didn't want to search through old books or ask people questions. She just wanted to crawl into a corner and close her eyes. "He insisted on walking me back to the door. He said it was what he'd want someone to do for his daughter. Or for Barbara's daughter."

Link rubbed the back of his neck. "I don't know Ezra well enough to guess at his motives. I'd love to hear Bishop Amos's honest opinion of the man, but I don't suppose he'd give it."

Bishop Amos would want to protect his own people, she supposed. "The bishop still hasn't gotten back to me about setting up a meeting with my mother's cousins. I'm beginning to think it won't happen."

She must have sounded bereft, because he reached across to clasp her hand firmly for a moment.

"Don't give up on him. It's just been a couple of days. And the Amish view of time isn't as structured as ours. If he said he'd talk to them, he will."

She nodded, too dispirited to argue.

Link picked up another book and shook it, sending more dust into the air, heedless of the binding. She grabbed it.

"You can't treat what might be a rare book like that. The historical society will tar and feather you."

He grinned. "They might try. If they're all like Uncle Allen, they'd have to debate and write a few papers about it first."

"I'm sure they're not all like your uncle."

"Maybe not." He didn't sound convinced. "I guess we'd better get on with this if you plan to paint this afternoon. Is the deadline pressing?"

"A bit. I overnighted a few sketches to my agent, and she called this morning, very enthusiastic. She said these were far better than the others. I had to admit that's probably because they were done in real woodland, not a manicured park."

"There, you see?"

"She also asked me to do a few drawings of the Amish while I'm here. It seems there are a couple of children's books about the Amish coming out, and she wants to send my portfolio around to a few publishers."

He arched an eyebrow, probably not understanding her lack of enthusiasm. "That's good, isn't it?"

"If I can't even get access to my mother's people, what are the chances I'll get any Amish to let me make sketches of them? I can't do Amish illustrations without models."

He seemed to be considering that seriously. "Well, they probably wouldn't let you draw their faces in any event, but I'm sure we could find a family who'd let you hang around and do some sketches, as long as you didn't show the faces."

One barrier fallen, it seemed, at the cost of simply telling Link about it. "That would be enormously helpful. I'm not very good at intruding on people at the best of times, and with the Amish—well, my experience so far hasn't been encouraging."

"My mother roped me into taking her to the Amish auction on Saturday. You could go along, if you want. You'll see plenty of Amish, maybe get some ideas. And the Zook family will probably be there. Maybe we can contrive a meeting."

She had to admit that it was better than just thinking about the problem. "It would be an interesting experience, anyway."

"I can promise you that. Going anywhere around here with my mother always is. She knows every person in the township, and she'll want to introduce you to them all, down to the last toddler and great-grandfather."

"I think that's nice." She picked up another book.

"It is if you're not the one on display," he said. "She's been trying to parade me around ever since I got home."

"That's natural, isn't it? She's just so glad you're back safely that she wants to share it with everyone she knows." It wasn't hard to put herself in Geneva's place. How she must have worried over him.

"I guess." Link grabbed another book and then opened it carefully, mindful of her eyes on him.

"That's better," she said. She opened

the cover of the book she held, to discover that it wasn't a printed volume at
all. The pages were covered with fine,
dense writing.

She turned to the inside cover and
drew in a breath. Allen Morgan's journal.
The date was after her mother's disappearance, but still...

Her excitement must have shown in
her face, because Link stopped what he
was doing. "What's that?"

She actually considered a lie before
she came to her senses. "It seems to
be a journal your uncle kept. It's from
the year after my mother vanished, but
there might be some mention. I could
go through it."

"It's family," Link said flatly. He held
out his hand.

She'd argue, but what would be the
point? It belonged to Link, presumably,
along with the house. All she could do
was trust he'd share anything he found.
She put the book in his hand.

Link managed to stay busy until mid-
afternoon, but eventually he had to go
home. And all the while those moments

with Marisa clung to his thoughts, entangling him in feelings he didn't want to have. He couldn't get involved—that was a given. He couldn't put himself in a position where people relied on him and he let them down.

But Marisa's face filled his mind...the way it had looked when he'd almost kissed her. And the way it had changed when he'd pulled away so abruptly.

He couldn't get involved, but that didn't mean he had the right to hurt someone in the process. Was it better to explain or to take the coward's way out and ignore the feelings that hummed between them?

He was still arguing the point when he walked through the orchard and started up the path into the woods.

The sumacs were starting to change color, and already the sun slanted golden across the field, touching the wild blue asters that drifted like smoke through the tall grass. Signs of autumn, and he'd hoped to be gone by Christmas. That grew less and less likely the longer this mystery about Barbara Angelo dragged on.

Would it peter out eventually, with no real answers ever found? That might be best for everyone, with the exception of Marisa, who'd try to live with not knowing. And there was the little matter of justice. Oddly enough, he still cared about that.

The ground began to slope upward, and Link's pace slowed. He pressed his hand to his side, trying not to limp. He'd been pushing hard the past few days. His body was complaining.

The green shirt Marisa wore blended so thoroughly into the background that he didn't spot her until he reached the abandoned railroad bed. She was working in the same place she'd sketched the other day, but this time she'd brought a camp chair and a small easel.

She obviously didn't hear him coming, and he slowed, watching her. Her light brown hair was pulled back in a ponytail, but strands had escaped to curl against the column of her neck. Her movements were swift and sure as she worked. If she doubted herself in any other area, she didn't do so where her work was concerned.

A dry twig snapped under his foot, and she looked up, a startled expression giving way to a smile.

"Link. I didn't expect to see you this afternoon. I thought you'd be trying to catch up on the work I interrupted."

"I ran over to the house to pass that journal along to my mother. I thought she ought to have the first look at it. She said you were up here working." Which didn't really explain why he'd come to find her.

She nodded, gesturing toward the scene that had appeared under her hand—the colors the lightest of pastels, the lines delicate. "As you see."

"That's beautiful." The illustration was so much like its creator.

"Thanks." She ducked her head slightly on the word, as if embarrassed by the praise. "Do you want to join me? I only have the one chair."

"I'll make do with the ground." He lowered himself, leaning against a handy tree, but couldn't help wincing when he hit the ground.

She saw, of course. "I know you don't want me to comment," she said carefully. "But I can't help thinking you're overdoing it."

"I'll try not to bite your head off for noticing." Come to think of it, he'd probably been a bit irritable on that subject.

She smiled, but her eyes held concern. "You've been working pretty hard on the house. And—" her hand sketched a circle in the air "—everything else."

"Trey keeps after me to hire someone to do some of the renovating."

"Why don't you?"

He didn't answer for a moment. Somehow he couldn't turn Marisa off with the easy half-truths he used on other people. She was different. She got under his protective screen for a reason he didn't really understand. He just knew he had to be honest with her.

"When I got out of the hospital I needed something to focus on. This project with the renovation—well, it gave me a goal. And I figured the work was just what I needed to get my strength back, and more interesting than going to the gym to work out on a machine."

"I can see that," she said. "But if you

push too hard, won't it send you in the opposite direction?"

He shrugged. "You're more tactful about it than my brother, but you're saying the same thing. Maybe you're both right. No need to do every single piece of the work myself. If I'm going to have the job done by Christmas, I'll have to get some help in."

"Why Christmas?" She studied him as if assessing whether or not he was telling her the truth.

"Trey and Jessica are getting married then, so I have to stay here that long anyway. I'd like to get the house finished, sell it and move on. A buddy of mine is keeping a job open for me in California."

"California's a long way."

He shrugged. "That's where the job is."

"Do you know anyone there, besides your friend?"

"No." The word sounded rude, all by itself. "That can be an advantage when you want to make a new start. There's no one to notice how much the army changed me."

Her lashes came down, veiling her eyes. "I only know what your mother told me, but I can understand that you'd want to forget what happened there."

He was still for a moment, arms linked around his knees, staring at the sunlight filtering through the trees. In her illustration, Marisa had captured the golden glow that autumn sunlight brought to the woods.

But he wasn't seeing the quiet woodland. He was seeing sun-dried brick and sand and light so fierce it nearly blinded you.

"Did she tell you about my team?" The question came out harshly.

"No, she didn't. She said you were injured when someone blew up the school you were rebuilding."

His jaw clenched almost too tightly for speech, but he managed to get the words out. "They wanted to destroy the school. That was part of terrorizing the villagers to keep them in line." He stopped, swallowed hard. "There were six of us working on it that day. Four were killed. One lost a leg. I'm the lucky one."

"Are you?" Tears trembled on her lashes. "You don't sound as if you feel very lucky."

He clenched his fists and then released them. Clench and release. Clench
and release.

"We were trapped in the rubble for
hours. The villagers couldn't get us out
until dark because of the gunmen watching. Celebrating."

"I'm sorry." Marisa's voice was choked
with tears. He hadn't even noticed her
move, but she knelt beside him, touching his hand. "I'm so sorry."

He said the thing he didn't want to
say. "I was in charge. They counted on
me." His lips twisted. "Should've known
that was a mistake."

"Don't, Link." One hand clasped his,
and she touched his cheek with the
other. "Don't blame yourself this way. It
wasn't your fault."

"You don't know anything about it."
He snatched at anger, because if he
didn't, he was going to turn to her for
comfort, and that would be a mistake.

"I know that the people who planted
the bombs are the guilty ones, not you."
Her palm brushed against his cheek in
a gesture of comfort.

He couldn't help it. He turned his

head, bringing his lips to her palm, pressing a kiss there.

He heard the quick intake of her breath, felt the skin warm under his lips. And then he drew her close and kissed her. She was soft and sweet, and as long as he held her he could keep the guilt at bay.

Her arms went around him, hands touching his back gently, as if to soothe away the pain. He buried his face in the curve of her neck, inhaling the scent of her. Wanting more.

But that wasn't fair. He should—

A shot cracked the air, loud as a clap of thunder. For an instant he froze, disbelieving, thinking he was flashing back to the past. Then another shot, and he heard the thunk as the bullet hit a tree not six feet from them.

He reacted, rolling Marisa under him, behind the scant shelter offered by the tree he'd been leaning against, his arms over her head, his mind racing.

Not Afghanistan, where people shot at you because of the uniform you wore. This was home, his own woods, the safest place possible. Except now it wasn't.

"…shooting at us," Marisa murmured.

"Maybe not," he said, as much to reassure her as because he believed it. "Some idiot hunting out of season, not realizing we're here."

Their land was posted, but that didn't necessarily deter people. And he'd rather think it was that than figure somebody was trying to kill them.

He pushed Marisa down, flat into the dry leaves where the ground dipped slightly. Not great protection, but he'd learned the hard way that any safeguard was better than none. Survival could depend on that.

"Stay there," he ordered. He stood, careful to stay behind the tree.

"Hey!" he shouted, his voice ringing through the trees and echoing back faintly. "Stop the shooting!"

Nothing. No sound at all. Even the birds were still.

"You hear me?"

Nothing. Still, if it was someone hunting out of season, or some kid cutting school and out with his gun, they wouldn't want to identify themselves.

Belatedly he realized he had his cell

phone in his pocket, and he pulled it out. "I'm calling the police," he shouted.

Silence again. Then the sound of the call going through. He heard Adam's voice, and his legs seemed suddenly boneless. He slid down the tree trunk to sit on the ground while he explained.

"I'll be right there," Adam snapped. "Stay on the line."

"Right." But he let the phone drop in his lap as he eased Marisa to a sitting position behind the shelter of the tree. "You okay?"

She nodded, eyes wide. "Was it...? Were they aiming at us?"

"I doubt it," he said quickly, trying to wipe the fear from her face. "Probably somebody trying out a new gun and not realizing how far it carries."

He pulled her close beside him, not moving until he heard the wail of the police siren in the field below.

# CHAPTER TEN

Marisa wrapped her hands around the mug of hot tea Geneva had pressed on her. Geneva had also insisted on sugar, and on Marisa eating one of the oatmeal cookies she put on the kitchen table, for all the world as if this were a tea party.

"Sugar is good for shock," Geneva said, seeming to read her mind.

At the end of the table, Adam put down his mug. It made a soft thump on the wooden tabletop. The long table looked as if it had seen worse—probably generations of family breakfasts and lunches, countless pies and cakes made on its surface.

"It may be nothing more than an accident," Adam said.

"Still a shock," Geneva countered briskly.

"Right." For an instant Adam looked like an overgrown kid being corrected by an adult. "Just take it easy, Marisa. I don't have to ask you anything else right now."

She nodded and then took a gulp of the tea. Hot and sweet, it seemed to move through her, warming her.

Link sat with his elbows on the table, hands clasped around the cup into which he stared. She found herself watching his hands...strong, a little scarred from the work he did. Hands that had pulled her to safety. Link had shielded her with his own body when the shots came. She'd never forget that as long as she lived.

Any more than she would easily forget that kiss. At the moment, Link's face might be carved in stone for all the expression it showed, but she had a vivid image in her mind of how he'd looked in that moment before he kissed her... alight with caring and passion.

"You really buy the theory that it was an out-of-season hunter?" Link glared at Adam.

Adam shrugged. "Could be. I'd definitely write it off as that if not for the... the current situation."

"Nice way of putting it." Link's hands tightened, the muscles standing out. "Marisa told you about Ezra Weis, didn't she?"

"She did." Adam's tone was mild. "But I find it hard to believe Ezra was out in the woods taking potshots at you today. Why would he?"

"Ezra wouldn't—" Geneva began, but Link spoke over her.

"Why would anyone? But it happened."

"Well, if it was deliberate, let's consider that." Adam sounded as if his patience was fraying. "Even if we assume a worst-case scenario that Marisa's mother was killed and her suitcase hidden in the wall, why would the killer have you in his sights twenty-five years later?"

"Me?" Link's eyebrows lifted.

"Or Marisa," Adam added. "But if it was deliberate, the shooter could have been aiming at you."

Link frowned. "Not unless he was a lousy shot. I was sitting on the ground, while she had been in a chair. The bullet hit a tree at about the three- to four-foot mark."

"Either way. What would be the point?" Adam looked from Link to Marisa. "Unless one of you knows something that would incriminate him that you haven't told to the police."

"That's ridiculous," Geneva said sharply. She put her hand on Marisa's shoulder.

"This is all supposition," Adam said, sounding a bit dogged. "My point is that while Ezra Weis might be curious enough about Barbara's daughter to do a little trespassing, no one, even our hypothetical killer, has a reason to stage an attack. Unless, like I said, you know something to point the finger at him."

"I don't know anything. Neither does Marisa. But somebody must think one of us does, because that gunfire wasn't hypothetical." Link's fingers clenched so hard it was a wonder the mug didn't break. "Even after twenty-five years, murder is still murder. And if the person who fired those shots did kill Marisa's mother, he'd have to be someone who's still around after all these years."

Marisa could feel his tension from across the table. It was as if she'd become ultrasensitive to his every movement, every breath.

Adam was saying something soothing, but she stopped listening. Instead, her mind replayed the story Link had told her...the school, his team, the explosion.

His reactions of grief and guilt were all too clear. Survivor's guilt, that was what it was. He felt responsible, and he was dealing with that by rejecting any chance of taking responsibility for other people.

That was why he was going to California. Not for a job. He was running away from home and family, afraid that if he stayed, he might let them down. Her heart twisted in pain for him.

"All I can say is that we'll investigate," Adam was saying. "I'll check on Ezra's whereabouts this afternoon, as well." He glanced at Geneva. "Sitting around your kitchen table talking about crime is getting to be a habit. Seems like the Morgan men have been attracting trouble lately."

Marisa blinked. "What...?"

"You wouldn't know about that, dear," Geneva said. "Link's heard, but he wasn't here at the time. We had some trouble back in June, when Jessica came to represent a local boy accused of a crime."

"I guess I did hear something about that. Is that when she and Trey got together?"

Geneva smiled, nodding. "I knew they were meant for each other the moment I saw them together." Her smile slipped away. "But we went through some bad times before it was over."

"It's over now, Mom." Link reached out to pat his mother's arm.

Geneva nodded, but regret touched her face. "I wonder if it will ever really be over. Those weeks in jail were terrible for Thomas. He still goes around looking as if he's afraid of his own shadow.

And people still talk. About him. About us, too, but we can handle it better."

Obviously there was more involved than Marisa had heard. But it wasn't her business. She wasn't part of the Morgan family.

Adam rose, pocketing his notebook. "I'll be going. On the off chance this was a deliberate act, I'd suggest you take some reasonable precautions about your own safety." He looked at Marisa. "Like not going in the woods alone. Or chasing after prowlers in the dark."

"I'll be careful," she said, knowing her cheeks were probably red.

"I think Marisa should go back to Baltimore," Link said abruptly. "She can't do anything useful here, and if she is a target, she—"

"I can decide for myself what I'm going to do," she said, cutting him off before he could hit his stride. "If you want to tell me to go, at least don't talk about me in the third person as if I weren't even here."

Now it was Link's turn to flush. "I didn't mean—"

"Think I'll let you two argue that one,"

Adam said. He nodded to Geneva and went out the back door.

Geneva, murmuring something about the garden, followed him outside.

Link stood, frowning at Marisa. "Look, are you deliberately trying to put yourself in danger?"

She returned his look steadily. "Are you sure that's what this is about?"

He just stared at her, his face a mask. Then he turned and walked out of the room.

Marisa put her face in her hands. She knew exactly what was going on with him. He'd confided in her, and he'd opened himself up to the attraction between them. And then the gunfire started. She'd been in danger. He'd protected her.

But he didn't want to be responsible, and his reaction was to backpedal as fast as he could away from her.

If Link could have found any possible way of getting out of going to the Amish auction with his mother and Marisa, he'd have done it. But he couldn't, so here he was, committed to spending the better part of the day in Marisa's company.

He slowed, getting into the line of cars, pickups and buggies that moved into the field next to the township fire hall. Marisa saw too much. Understood too much. He never should have told her about the bombing.

And he certainly never should have kissed her. In most circumstances, a kiss was...well, just a kiss. But neither he nor Marisa was in what anybody would call a normal emotional state right now. A sensible man didn't throw gasoline on a fire.

"They have this auction twice a year," Mom explained. "Spring and fall. It's the major fundraiser for the three Amish schools in the area, so everyone turns out to support it. After all, the Amish have to pay school taxes just like everybody else and then pay for their own schools, as well."

"I didn't realize that," Marisa said. "I guess I should buy something, then, even if I don't need it."

"If you're like my mother, you'll probably come home with far more than you intended," he said.

"I'm just terrible about bidding on things." Mom's laugh gurgled. "Blake used to sit beside me at auctions and hold my hands to keep me from bidding on stuff I didn't even want. And still, I came home with a quilt frame that was so big we couldn't fit it through the front door."

"It can't be that bad, can it?" Marisa smiled, but she was looking at the buggies—row after row of them pulled up in the shade at the edge of the field. Amish boys darted along the line, their task to handle the horses and buggies, while a high-school-age English kid directed the cars to parking spaces.

"The bidding goes pretty fast," he said, pulling into the space the boy indicated. "If you don't want to own a butter churn or a snow shovel, don't wave to your friends."

"Since I don't know very many people here, that shouldn't be an issue." She slid out, joining his mother. "Except you and the Millers and Bishop Amos, of course. He stopped by to see me yesterday."

"You didn't tell me that." The words sounded as if he expected her to confide in him, and he could have bitten his tongue.

"I haven't seen much of you," Marisa said.

True enough. He'd managed to find a reason not to be at the house yesterday morning when she'd continued the search in the book room. Given what happened when they were alone, that seemed safer.

"Was Bishop Amos able to help?" Mom touched Marisa's arm lightly.

"He said he'd introduce me to a few people today who might remember my mother. Unfortunately, my mother's cousin, William Zook, doesn't want to meet me."

He thought she was trying not to sound bitter and not entirely succeeding. He'd say something encouraging, but he couldn't come up with anything.

"You must be disappointed." Mom's voice was warm with sympathy. "I'm afraid they were hurt when she left that way. They'd have felt responsible, too, since she was their guest."

"I'd think they could have gotten over that by now." Marisa slung the strap of her bag over her shoulder. He spotted the ever-present sketch pad peeping out of it.

"Family disagreements can be the most painful and long-lasting." His mother seemed to be gazing into the past. "I suppose William might feel it better not to open it up again."

"I suppose." Marisa didn't look especially satisfied with that, but she didn't say anything more as they joined the crowd moving toward the fire hall and the tents and stands that were set up around it.

His mother slipped her arm through his as they crossed the rough ground at the edge of the field, and he wondered if he was supposed to be helping her or the other way around. Nothing would convince Mom that he didn't need babying.

"Oh, Link, did you tell Marisa about meeting with Tom Sylvester tomorrow afternoon?"

"Sylvester?" Marisa echoed the name.

"The person in charge of the construction project on Allen's house when your mother..." Mom let that trail off.

"Not yet." Actually, he'd been wondering if he could avoid telling her so he could talk to the man alone.

Judging by Marisa's expression, she knew exactly what was in his mind. "That's good. I've been hoping we'd be able to talk to him soon." There was a faint underline on the word *we.*

"I'm not sure how much he'll be able to tell us, but he says he has some old job notes in a file at home. He promised to look through them before then."

"Good." She clamped her lips shut, as if to hold back something she'd rather have said. She glanced up, and he saw her face turn pale.

"Preston Connelly." Mom didn't sound especially welcoming at the sight of the district attorney. She'd had a grudge against the man since he'd prosecuted Thomas Esch.

"Geneva, how nice to see you." Connelly, florid and hearty, either didn't notice or chose to ignore the lack of welcome in her face. "And Link." He shook hands. "Glad to see you back safe and sound."

Link muttered something noncommittal. Marisa's tension was strong enough to feel even though they weren't touching.

"And Ms. Angelo." Was it Link's imagination, or did Connelly's gaze sharpen when it rested on Marisa? "I take it you haven't heard anything from your father yet?"

"No." Marisa's lips moved just enough to let out the one word.

So that was Connelly's interest in her. She didn't like it, obviously, but it was only natural, wasn't it? Why hadn't her father been in touch yet? For Marisa's sake, he had to hope there was some logical explanation.

"Too bad." Connelly's words sounded speculative. The way his gaze lingered on her face seemed an invitation to her to say more.

But she didn't. She just stood, a meaningless smile on her face, like a rabbit freezing into immobility at the sight of a hawk's shadow.

"It was nice to see you, Preston." His mother's social sense came to the rescue. "We must get on to the auction, or the pieces I'm interested in will be gone."

"Yes, of course." Connelly nodded politely and walked away, greeting another one of his constituents with a practiced air.

"Jessica says he was only doing his job." His mother sounded disbelieving. "But I still haven't forgiven him for the things he said about Thomas."

"He's up for reelection in November," he reminded her. "He can't afford to offend the electorate."

"That doesn't give him an excuse..." Mom's voice trailed off as she spotted one of her friends. "There's Edna Pollard. I really have to talk to her about helping with the fall rummage sale at the church."

His mother scurried off before her victim could escape, and he caught Marisa's arm before she could follow.

"Don't let Connelly upset you."

"I'm not upset about him." Her level gaze met his. "Let's talk about the construction boss."

He might have known she'd seize on that. "Look, I intended to tell you about talking with Tom."

"You mean you intended to do so after the fact."

His jaw tightened. "I thought he might be more forthcoming without you there."

"Did you? Or are you trying to control what I find out?"

They'd been plunged into the middle of a quarrel in the worst possible place. The trouble was that he couldn't entirely deny her accusation.

"Do you blame me? When this is over, you're going to go back to Baltimore with whatever answers you have. But my mother, my brother...they'll go on living here. I don't want them to end up dealing with a lot of talk over something that's not their fault."

"I'm not out to cause trouble or start rumors." Her face had paled, but her determination didn't falter. "I'm after the truth, plain and simple. And I won't be satisfied with less."

She turned and walked away, leaving him standing there wondering how much of Spring Township had just overheard her.

She shouldn't have let Link's response get to her. Marisa paused, not sure where she was going, except away from him. Geneva seemed deep in conversation with several other women, so she moved to the nearest booth, staring blankly at a display of crocheted pot holders.

Link's first loyalty was to his family. She couldn't let herself forget that, no matter how she felt about him.

She'd been looking too long at the pot holders...the Amish woman behind the counter would be expecting her to buy. Marisa smiled at her and moved on.

The firehouse itself was an uncompromising cement-block rectangle, the bay doors open to reveal two fire trucks. Next to the building a huge white canopy stretched over folding chairs. The patter of an auctioneer, amplified by a loudspeaker, floated out. Obviously the auction had begun.

People, many in Amish dress, wandered through the rows of items spread out across the field next to the tent. They must be picking out the objects they wanted to bid on. She noticed a couple of men jotting down information in notebooks. Dealers, maybe, out for a good buy that they could resell.

Booths of various sizes, shapes and construction circled the auction tent... everything from a commercial-type trailer selling cotton candy to a card table with yet more pot holders, sheltered from the sun by a beach umbrella whose bright stripes were a startling contrast to the dark dresses of the women fingering the pot holders.

She moved toward the next booth. An eddy in the crowds whirled around her, and she found she was in the midst of a throng of Amish. For a second their dark clothing seemed vaguely menacing on such a bright day, and she was carried along with them, all talking in a language she couldn't understand.

About her? Some sidelong glimpses made her wonder if that might be true.

She stopped, letting them flow past her. Two men stopped by the next booth...heads together, glancing at her as they carried on a low-voiced conversation. She recognized one of them. It was Ezra Weis. He spoke, vehemently it seemed, to the other man. They both turned to stare at her, their faces bleak.

She might be imagining some things, but she didn't imagine that. She turned away. If she could just find Geneva... She'd even settle for Link right now. At least she understood his occasional antagonism.

Instead, Bishop Amos's smiling face bobbed up from the crowd.

"Marisa, I have been looking for you. I saw Link and Geneva, so I knew you must be here someplace."

"I was checking out some of the stands." She didn't glance back toward Ezra and the other man. Were they still watching? If so, they'd see her on good terms with their bishop.

"Ach, today we have anything you could want. And probably much that you don't." He chuckled. "But here is someone I want you to meet." He gestured to a nearby stand stocked with dozens of jars of jam and preserves, their colors sparkling like gems in the sunshine, and led her to the counter. "This is Doris Yost. Doris, here is Barbara Zook's daughter, Marisa, come back after all this time."

*"Wie bist du heit."* The woman nodded, a smile creasing her broad cheeks. "You have a look of Barbara about you, ain't so?"

"Ach, that is what I said, too." Bishop Amos's eyes twinkled. "Doris and your mamm were girls together once, Marisa. I will leave you two to talk for now."

He moved away, his attention claimed almost immediately by a cluster of small children chattering in Pennsylvania Dutch.

"The kinder all love Bishop Amos," Doris said, watching him fondly.

Marisa could see why. Kindliness radiated from his face. "So, you knew my mother?"

"Ach, for sure. We were running-around friends when she came to visit the Zooks...me and Barbara and Barbara's cousin, Elizabeth. I lived next door to the Zooks back then."

"I'm so glad you're willing to talk with me."

"Ja, for sure." Doris's face sobered a

bit. "I hear tell that William Zook doesn't want his cousin mentioned, but that is foolishness, it is. Barbara has been gone a long time." A shadow of sorrow crossed her eyes.

"You think my mother is dead, don't you?" The question was out before she realized that probably wasn't the best way to start.

Concern set wrinkles between her brows. "I suppose...well, ja, I do. I'm sorry. Maybe I shouldn't say that to you."

"I'd rather hear the truth." She would, wouldn't she? "Bishop Amos said the same. I don't understand, though. My father, the police—they don't seem convinced of that. I was always told that my mother ran away."

Doris was already shaking her head. "That I don't believe. Even if she had reason to go away, Barbara would not leave you behind."

Those were the words she'd always longed to hear. But could she believe them?

"If she went back to her family in Indiana..."

"No, that she did not. If she had, we

would have heard." Doris sounded sure. And looking at her plain, sincere face, it was impossible to believe she would lie about it.

She could still be wrong, of course. Barbara might have gone somewhere else.

Without her suitcase? The voice of reason would not be silent.

Marisa took a breath, trying to steady herself. This was her opportunity to find out more about her mother. She couldn't let it slip away.

"Will you tell me about her? What she was like? I don't remember her very well."

Doris clasped her hand where it lay on the countertop. "Ach, for sure. She was like sunshine, Barbara was. Always lively and happy. She loved coming here to visit, especially that last summer. She and Ezra Weis were courting." She paused. "You maybe knew that?"

"Yes. Bishop Amos told me. And I've talked to Mr. Weis." Unsuccessfully. An image of that futile conversation in the middle of the night came back to her.

"Well, to tell the truth, I always thought she was too lively for Ezra." Doris looked reminiscently back through the years, a small smile playing about her lips. "Maybe that's why she loved to come here. From what she said about her folks back in Indiana, they were pretty conservative."

It took a stretch to imagine anyone more conservative than the Amish she'd met. "I see."

Doris chuckled. "No, you are thinking that I'm a fine one to talk about someone else being conservative, but it's true, all the same. Some Amish are much stricter than others. Here, she could go to singings with our gang, or even to Englisch parties if she wanted, so long as her aunt and uncle didn't know about it. And William, he was ripe for any mischief."

Now William was so strict that he wouldn't even talk to her. The two things didn't seem to fit together.

"Is that how my mother met my father? Going to an Englisch party?" She repeated the woman's expression, wondering if that meant a beer bash, thrown by the local teenagers.

"She didn't tell me about your daadi.

If she had, maybe I'd have talked her out of seeing him. So maybe that's why she didn't tell me." Doris shrugged. "No sense in thinking about what didn't happen, and I can't tell you about your mamm and daad because I never knew about them being together, not until it was too late and she'd left the church."

"Did you see her afterward? I mean, they settled right in Springville."

"Once in a while I'd see her. We'd speak. I remember seeing her pushing you in a buggy. She stopped, and we had a chat, comparing babies, you know. She was so proud of you."

Marisa wanted to hang on to the image of her mother showing off her baby.

"Did she seem happy with the decision she'd made?"

Doris hesitated. "Happy? Well, she had regrets about her parents. They were so strict, like I said. She said she wrote to them, to tell them about you, but they never answered."

That rejection must have been an arrow in her heart. "I don't see how they could do that to their own daughter."

Doris shook her head. "It's hard to

explain. The bann is meant to show a person that he or she is wrong. Turn them back to the church. If that doesn't happen...well, most folks adjust after a while. They can still stay close to relatives who left. Maybe her parents would have come around in time."

But time was one thing her mother hadn't had. "What about her cousins? Did they adjust?"

Doris frowned. "I'm not so sure I can answer that. Elizabeth married, and she went to live over toward Paradise, so she wasn't here, but I seem to remember she and Barbara wrote. As for William..." She shrugged. "William keeps his own counsel. And Barbara never mentioned him to me, the times we talked." Doris glanced over her shoulder. "Ach, we were just speaking of you. Marisa, here is your cousin, Elizabeth Yoder. Elizabeth Zook, she was, before she married."

The woman who stood smiling at her looked so like Marisa's memory of her mother that for a moment her heart seemed to stop. Elizabeth Yoder's light brown hair was pulled smoothly back under her kapp, of course, so it was impossible to tell if it had the slight curl her mother's hair had had. But she had the same golden brown eyes, the same pointed chin that Marisa remembered.

"You look so much like my mother." She'd been staring, she realized.

"People always did say we looked more like sisters than cousins." Elizabeth's smile showed a dimple at the corner of her mouth. She had to be in her mid-forties, but her skin was as clear and unlined as a girl's. "Ach, we loved being together." A shadow touched her eyes, and she reached out impulsively to take Marisa's hand. "I am so sorry I didn't get to see you grow up."

Marisa nodded, her throat tight. Here at least was someone who mourned for Barbara and was glad to see Barbara's daughter.

"I'd love to talk to you about my mother. Maybe not here..."

"No, not here." She spoke quickly. "This is not the place or time." She pushed a paper into Marisa's hand. "That is my address. It's not hard to find. Come any day next week."

Marisa nodded, a little perplexed by the urgency in her voice. "I'll come. Thank you."

"I must go—"

Someone spoke suddenly behind her, a quick, harsh rattle of Pennsylvania Dutch.

Doris, with the air of someone hoping to keep the peace, touched Marisa's arm. "Marisa, here is your cousin, William Zook. William, this is your cousin, Marisa."

Marisa swung around. Somehow she wasn't surprised that her mother's cousin was the man she'd seen talking to Ezra Weis.

He didn't acknowledge Doris and didn't seem to notice when his sister slipped away with a regretful glance at Marisa. Instead he stared at Marisa, his face a stern mask above his dark beard.

She managed a smile that she hoped didn't look as false as it felt. "I'm pleased to meet you. I was hoping to talk to you about my mother."

"No." The word was flat, harsh with some emotion she couldn't identify.

Doris made a faint murmur of dismay. "William, you can't—

"I have only one thing to say to you." He swept on as if he hadn't heard Doris. "You must go. Go home. You can do no good here. Listen to me. Leave Springville now or you will be sorry."

# CHAPTER ELEVEN

If Marisa had driven herself, she would have gone straight back to the inn after that encounter with her cousin, but that just showed what a coward she was, she'd decided. As it was, she had to endure several more hours of the auction, smiling and nodding to all the people Geneva wanted her to meet, until finally, the trunk loaded with her purchases, Geneva had been ready to go home.

Turning down a dinner invitation on the grounds that she had work to do, Marisa had made it back to her new room at last. A shower helped to wipe away the remaining unpleasantness that had lingered throughout the day.

Or maybe it hadn't. Propped up in bed with her drawing pad on her lap, she ought to be able to dismiss the encounter with William Zook from her mind. But she couldn't. His frowning face seemed to appear on the blank page in front of her.

She was being stupid. She'd already known he didn't want to talk with her. If he wouldn't respond to Bishop Amos, he certainly wouldn't to her. But it had been different, hearing that directly from him.

His words echoed in her mind. *Go home, or something bad might happen to you*. That had been the message. *Like your mother* had been unspoken but implied.

It had been a warning. That didn't mean it was a threat. But why? What had been the point, when he'd already said he wouldn't speak with her?

Maybe because he'd seen her with his sister and perhaps known that she would not be as silent as he on the subject of Barbara. If he couldn't get his sister to fall in with his opinion, scaring Marisa away would accomplish the same thing.

She would not let herself fall victim to fear. She'd go to see Elizabeth on Monday. With a little luck, William's sister would know a bit more about what had been going on with Barbara that fall when she'd vanished. Meanwhile, she'd distract her thoughts with some work.

She'd barely picked up a drawing pencil before a knock at the bedroom door sent it moving in a jagged line. Nerves, she scolded herself, and swung off the bed. It was probably Rhoda, who seemed convinced Marisa wouldn't sleep without a nightly mug of hot chocolate. Or wondering if the new room had everything she needed.

But it wasn't Rhoda. It was Geneva.

"Geneva. I didn't expect to see you."

"I know." Geneva's blue eyes were filled with sympathy. "Link told me you had an upsetting experience with your cousin William."

"Really." And how exactly did Link know that? "I didn't mention it to him."

"I understand Doris Yost said something about it." Geneva wrinkled her nose. "You have to understand how word gets around in a small place like this." She nodded toward the room. "May I come in?"

"Of course." Marisa stepped back, holding the door wide. She could plead the excuse of work, but she couldn't shut the door on kindness. Geneva cared. She could stand a little caring about now.

"Link said I should leave you alone, but I just couldn't." Geneva glanced appreciatively around the cozy room and then sat down in the rocking chair. "It never seems to occur to a man that women sometimes need to talk."

Marisa sat on the bed again, since that was the only other place to sit. "I shouldn't let it upset me. I knew already that William didn't want to see me. I just didn't expect him to be so vehement about it. He actually warned me that I should leave here."

Geneva shook her head, forehead wrinkling in distress. "I just can't understand that. I don't know the Zook family well, I confess, but frankly, it seems out of character for an Amish person. Especially when the bishop asked for coop-

eration. Bishop Amos is universally ad-
mired."

"It's odd that William still feels so
strongly, isn't it? I mean, that happened
years ago. In a way, I could understand
Ezra Weis's attitude more easily. If he
was in love with my mother, he might
resent having the whole subject brought
up again."

"I've often noticed that the Amish don't
have the same concept of time that most
English do." Geneva rocked absently.
"Our days are crowded with different
things, while theirs move at a slower
tempo. And anything to do with family
has a deep effect, because they're so
close. I suppose William must have felt
responsible, in a way, for Ezra's pain."

"Why would he? It was my mother
who fell in love with someone else. William was hardly responsible for that."

"No, but he and Ezra were best friends
in those days. I'd guess William encour-
aged that relationship and then felt terrible when it turned out badly. But neither of them should blame Barbara for
falling in love. The heart doesn't listen to
common sense." Her smile carried a

tinge of sorrow, reminding Marisa that it hadn't been all that long since Geneva's husband died.

"So many people seem to have been hurt in one way or another by my mother's decision." She stopped, not sure she wanted to go further.

"You wonder if she had regrets, don't you?"

Geneva saw too much. Marisa nodded. "I suppose I do. I remember..."

"What do you remember?" Geneva asked gently.

"Something I heard my mother say once. I don't know when, or even who she was talking to. Just the words." She hesitated, but the urge to tell someone was too strong. "'I don't belong anywhere.' That's what she said. 'I don't belong anywhere.'" The weight of unutterable sadness seemed to accompany the words.

"I'm sorry." Geneva reached across the space between them to put her hand over Marisa's. "That's not something a child should hear."

"I didn't understand, then. I just knew she was unhappy, and it frightened me."

"Of course it would. Every child needs to feel that his or her parents are the solid center of their world."

She tried to manage a smile. "You and your husband obviously achieved that with your children."

"We tried." Geneva sighed. "But we made other mistakes. Having children is such a reminder of our frailty. If anything will bring a person to their knees, it's having children. When the boys were small, I used to pray every night for more patience. And God just kept giving me more occasions to learn patience."

She smiled, as she was sure Geneva intended. "From what I've heard of Link as a boy, I'm sure he gave you plenty of practice."

"He went from one scrape to another, always trying to keep up with his brother or do something Trey hadn't done. No matter what was going on, there would be Link in the thick of it, always popping up grinning, whatever happened." She paused. "Maybe that's why it's been so difficult, seeing him as withdrawn as he's been since he came home. And he's past the age at which I can kiss the hurt and make it better."

Marisa nodded, not sure what to say. Geneva was showing a bit of her heart. "I'm sorry. It has to be so hard to watch him struggle." She moved slightly, and the sketch pad slid from the bed, fluttering to the floor next to Geneva's feet.

Geneva bent to pick it up, pausing to look at the drawing on the page. Marisa sucked in a breath. That picture revealed too much.

Geneva gave her a questioning look. "Is this something you saw?"

"No. I don't...I don't think so." She moved her hand over the image of a woman in Amish dress, walking away toward a misty wood. "It's just the picture that's in my mind. Sometimes in my dreams. My mother, going away from me. Not hearing when I call her. Not turning back."

"Oh, my dear." Geneva's eyes filled with tears. "I'm so sorry."

"I guess that's the picture I formed when I was a kid, piecing it together from what I heard about my mother." Her father hadn't done her any favors by trying to protect her from the truth, always assuming he had known it. What her imagination had conjured up had been worse.

"But now you know that—" Geneva stopped, clearly thinking she was about to say the wrong thing.

"I know that nothing I believed was true, but I still don't know what is." Pain gripped her. "Is it better to think that my mother ran away and didn't take me with her or that she was murdered?"

She hadn't said that out loud before, but now she knew that was the question that haunted her. And would continue to haunt her until she knew the truth. "What if I never know?"

"You mustn't think that way." Geneva gripped her hands as if to give her strength. "The truth will come out. Sometimes it happens when you least expect it."

"I'd like to believe that." But she thought Geneva was being overly optimistic.

"You can." Geneva hesitated. "I know it's easy for people to say they understand. But I do. Because it happened to me."

"To you?" She tried not to sound skeptical.

Geneva leaned back, clasping her hands together as if in prayer. "Thirty-four years. That's how long Blake and I were married." She let out a long breath. "He went in for a regular checkup. That was all, just a checkup. And they found the cancer."

"I'm so sorry." That was tragic, but hardly the same.

"We were coping, I thought. It wasn't hopeless, according to the doctors. Serious, but there was a chance. But two days later, Blake went out to the hunting cabin. He said he had something to take care of. Trey found him the next day. It looked as if he'd killed himself."

Geneva's pain was so tangible that it seized Marisa's heart. "Geneva, you don't have to tell me."

"Yes, I do. Because I thought I had to believe that my love wasn't enough for him. That he'd choose to kill himself rather than fight to stay with us."

Marisa's heart twisted, and she made a murmur of distress.

"But that wasn't the end of it. It was nearly a year later that we learned the truth. Blake hadn't killed himself. He'd been murdered by someone we knew and trusted." She leaned forward, face intent. "Terrible as that was, it was better to know the truth. I don't suppose I'll ever stop grieving for my husband, but I know he didn't choose to leave us. So you see, I do understand."

"I guess you do." Her voice was husky with tears.

Geneva rose and bent to hug her. "I'll pray for you."

With Geneva's soft cheek pressed against hers, Marisa could almost feel herself in her mother's arms again, and her heart was too full to speak.

Link gripped the steering wheel a little tighter, trying not to glance across the front seat at Marisa. She'd been cool, to say the least, since he'd picked her up at the bed-and-breakfast for their appointment with Tom Sylvester. She obviously hadn't yet forgotten their sharp exchange at the auction yesterday.

Well, what had she expected of him? She could hardly think he'd be happy at the can of worms opened by finding that suitcase.

Mom hadn't said what happened between her and Marisa after she got home the previous night, and he'd had to respect her feelings. But she'd looked strained, and he didn't like that. Mom had been through enough in recent years. She didn't need any further grief.

Then this morning Mom had been fussing because she hadn't invited Marisa to attend church and have brunch with them. He'd assured her that Marisa would be more comfortable not being overwhelmed with invitations, and Trey had jumped in to agree with him. Link could tell that Trey was thinking the same thing he was...that if anything unpleasant came out about Uncle Allen, Mom was going to be hurt, and developing a friendship with Marisa would just make that even worse.

He glanced at Marisa. She stared out the window at the houses they were passing—pleasant newer houses built along a tree-shaded street sometime in the '50s, probably. Her face was set.

"I suppose you'd rather be going to talk to Tom Sylvester alone," he said, more in response to her expression than anything else.

"Whether I would or not, that's not going to happen, is it?"

It took an effort to reply evenly. "If you went alone, you might not get very far. Tom has worked for Morgan Enterprises all his life. He'll talk more freely if I'm there."

"He's loyal to the Morgan family, in other words. Like a lot of people around here."

"Are you accusing us of something?" He ground out the words.

She turned to him with what seemed honest surprise. "I'm not accusing. I'm stating what seems to be a fact. Going anywhere at all with your mother makes that clear. Everyone knows her. Everyone likes her."

"Is that so surprising?" He caught hold of his temper and tried to look at the situation as an outsider would. "Look,

Morgans have been here since year one. The old-timers remind me that they knew my grandfather, watched my dad grow up, watched me grow up, too. That's not exactly an unmixed blessing."

"I wouldn't know. I didn't have the sort of family background you did."

And what exactly was she implying? He pulled into the driveway at Tom's split-level and stopped. "This is it. It might be better if you let me take the lead in this conversation."

Her lips tightened. "I realize that."

A few minutes later they were following Tom Sylvester onto the patio at the back of the house. Tom, heavyset and jovial as always, ushered them out the sliding glass doors.

"The wife says this might be the last nice Sunday afternoon this fall, so she wants to cook out. I keep telling her that in a month we'll be in Florida, able to cook out every day of the year, but she doesn't hear me."

"Don't let us slow you down. If you're supposed to be starting the grill, you'd best get on with it."

Tom grinned. "Already done. If I tell

her I have to watch the fire, I can stay out of her way in the kitchen." He prodded at the coals with a long fork. "The neighbors all have those fancy gas grills, but as far as I'm concerned, nothing beats the flavor you get with charcoal."

"Right." That was enough chit-chat. "Well, you know why Ms. Angelo and I are here. You've probably heard about the suitcase I found in the wall of the addition."

"Everybody in the township has heard about that by now. Especially since Ms. Angelo arrived. You know how news travels around here."

He nodded. He did, unfortunately.

"Adam Byler stopped by with some questions, but I couldn't help much."

Link thought he recognized the caution in Tom's voice. Loyalty. He'd have to defuse that, make it clear that Tom should talk.

"Now that you've had a chance to think about it, I'm hoping you remember more."

There was a pause as Tom gave him a long look, probably to see if he meant that. "Well, yeah, I guess I might. I looked through my old files, too, like you asked."

"Good. I appreciate it. So, what can you tell us about that project?"

Tom waved them to a pair of Adirondack chairs, taking a seat facing them. "Wasn't much that special about the job, except I have to say, Allen wanted stuff done on the cheap. Didn't make much sense to me, but he was the boss."

Link nodded. "That was Allen, all right. Always pinched every penny, unless he was spending on old books."

"Yeah, he had plenty of those. So, anyway, I had a crew of maybe four or five on the job most days. The room went up pretty fast."

"What about that Friday I asked you about? September 20?" Link could feel the tension in Marisa as he asked the question.

"Well, remembering one specific day after twenty-some years..." Tom shrugged, as if to indicate the hopelessness of such a task.

"You had job notes," Link reminded him.

"Right. According to my records, we

started putting up drywall that week. That Friday morning, I had a call about another job we had going...they'd run into problems, needed help. So I went over there, took part of the crew." He frowned. "Funny how it comes back to me now that we're talking about it. I left two guys to work on the drywall. They must've knocked off early, because when I got there on Monday, it had been left half done. I chewed them out over that, you can bet."

"So a suitcase could have been shoved into the wall that day after they left."

Tom shrugged. "Or anytime over the weekend. We wouldn't have noticed it when we came back on Monday—just slapped the rest of the drywall up. We were behind schedule, and your uncle was always on our backs."

"Why was that?" Marisa spoke for the first time.

"He wanted it done, that's all." Tom looked at Marisa as if he'd forgotten she was there. "He complained about the dust, said it would damage his books. Complained about the noise. I remember he said he was hosting some meeting or something one day that week, wanted us to clean up everything we'd been working on. What difference did it make? It was a construction site, not a tea party."

"Was Allen there that Friday?" Link asked. Much as he hated to admit it, Allen was the most likely person, aside from Barbara herself, to have put the suitcase behind that drywall.

"I don't know. I was busy, concentrating on a couple different jobs." Tom rose, poking at the fire again. "He didn't like the noise, like I said. Didn't want the guys having a radio on while they worked, even. Sometimes he'd go off. That day…" He shrugged. "I can't remember."

Link glanced at Marisa. This was unsatisfactory, and he didn't know what to ask that would elicit anything else helpful. He could see the frustration on her face that probably mirrored his own.

"Do you remember my mother?" Marisa asked suddenly.

Tom looked startled. "I…well, sure, I'd see her sometimes, when we were there working."

"Did you ever talk to her?" Marisa persisted.

"I don't know." His jaw set, as if she'd accused him of something. "I suppose we might have said hello, talked about the weather. That's all."

"Was she there that Friday?"

"I don't know." His face reddened. "Look, I don't know what you expect me say. I don't know how that suitcase got inside the wall. Maybe she put it there herself after my guys knocked off work."

Pressing him on that was obviously not going to pay off. "Can you give me the names of the two men you left there that Friday?"

"Sure. One was Len Barnhart... He passed away a couple years ago. Heart attack right on the job. Shame, that was."

"I heard that. He was a good man."

Tom nodded, pausing a moment as if in tribute to Len. "I had him working with a younger guy...Brad Metzger. Brad wasn't with us all that long. He got a job at the inn, and he's still there. Assistant manager now."

"I know Brad." At least he was available. It could well have been someone who'd moved away a long time ago. "What about the people you said were coming for a meeting that week? Did you happen to see them?"

Tom seemed to freeze, his hand hovering over the grill top. "No." He almost snarled the word. "Why would I? You think I had nothing better to do than take notice of who was coming to that house?" He slammed the rack down on the grill and then paused, his back to them. "Think this fire is about ready."

"We'll let you get on with your supper. Thanks for your help."

Tom turned around, smiled, held out his hand. Perfectly normal. Just as he should be.

But Link knew he wasn't imagining things. Tom hadn't been particularly happy about being asked to remember that time. And he'd been downright upset at the mention of whoever it was who'd come to Allen's house that week.

Marisa stepped off the porch of the bed-and-breakfast, waving to Rhoda, who had walked to the door with her. Rhoda had been almost solicitous this morning, and Marisa couldn't help wondering if she'd heard something about what happened at the auction. Perhaps Marisa had been the main topic of conversation at Amish worship yesterday. That gave her a prickling at the nape of her neck, as if she were being watched by unseen eyes.

Enough. She was letting herself get rattled, and she couldn't allow that. The directions to her mother's cousin's house were tucked in her bag. It shouldn't take more than a half hour at most to find the house.

Elizabeth had said to come anytime, but she might not have anticipated Marisa's appearance this soon. Still, the sooner the better. She didn't want to give William time to influence his sister against her.

Marisa had just reached her car when a township police car pulled up, stopping directly in front of her. She stiffened automatically. Even an innocent person might tense at the sight of an officer in uniform headed toward her with a purposeful air. He wasn't anyone she'd met before—brush-cut blond hair and a round, youthful face. He didn't look old enough to be a cop.

"Ms. Angelo?" He didn't pause for her affirmative answer. "Chief Byler wants to see you at headquarters."

"Now? I was just leaving."

"Now. He's waiting."

"I have an appointment this morning." Well, that was almost true. Elizabeth didn't know she was coming, but she'd said anytime. "Can't I stop by when I get back?"

He took a step toward her and reached for her arm. "Get in the patrol car, please."

Apprehension slithered through her. He acted as if she were a criminal. And she had no doubt at all that people were watching from behind the muslin or lace curtains along the quiet street.

She straightened. She would not be intimidated. "I'll drive my own car, thank you. You can follow me, if you feel compelled to be sure I get there."

Before he could argue, she turned and yanked her car door open. Somehow she doubted that Adam Byler had ordered that she be picked up by the patrol car, and she wasn't going to give the neighbors anything else to talk about.

Her guess must have been right, because the cop didn't attempt to stop her. He marched stiffly to the patrol car, got in and slammed the door. And he did follow her all the three blocks to the township police station. When she got out, he was there at her elbow to escort her inside, hustling her past Link's high-school friend at the desk and on into Adam Byler's office.

Byler wasn't there. Preston Connelly, the district attorney, waited, standing with his back to the window so that he was, for the most part, a bulky shadow against the light.

"Good morning." She heard the door close behind her and knew the young patrolman had left. "I understand Chief Byler wants to see me."

"Sit down, Ms. Angelo." Connelly moved, going behind the chief's desk, nodding to the visitor's chair. "The chief was called out on another matter. I have a few questions for you."

She sat, her uneasiness increasing instead of ebbing. "I hoped that he had some news for me about the investigation."

Connelly frowned down at the scarred top of the wooden desk, seeming absorbed in its battered surface. It was as if he didn't hear her.

When he looked up, he focused on her, eyes intent. "I understand you've been conducting your own investigation, Ms. Angelo."

"Conducting—no, of course not. I've been hoping to find someone willing to talk to me about my mother, that's all."

Connelly sat down, his face creasing in a smile, and the atmosphere in the room seemed to ease. "That's difficult, isn't it? I certainly sympathize, but I'm afraid the Amish tend to be very clannish. It's unlikely they'd want to talk to an outsider about something they view as a bit shameful."

She stiffened. "I don't see anything shameful about my mother falling in love with my father."

"Naturally not. Most people wouldn't think such a thing, but the Amish are different." His voice had warmed with sympathy, and she was suddenly glad

that Byler wasn't there. He would probably be frowning with disapproval.

"So I've noticed. Several people have
refused to talk to me at all. They act as
if it's possible to simply close a person
out of their lives and never think of them
again."

"Your mother was banned. They're not
going to want to talk about her. I know
it's hard to accept, but I'm afraid you
won't be able to learn anything here."

"It's not quite that bad." She had to
be fair, much as William Zook's attitude
rankled. "Bishop Amos has been very
helpful, and a few other people have
been willing to talk."

"That surprises me." He leaned back,
so that he was again silhouetted against
the window behind him. "If you've learned
anything useful, you know it's your duty
to pass it on to the police."

"Nothing about my mother's disappearance. Just—well, some memories of
her." Memories that were precious to her,
even if not helpful to the police. "My
mother's cousin, Elizabeth Yoder, has also
agreed to talk with me. She may know
more. I've heard they were very close."

"Well, I hope you're successful. And you will keep us informed of anything we should know, won't you?"

If there was a warning in that, it was well-hidden. "Yes, of course I will."

"Good. Now, about your father."

She leaned forward. "Have you heard from him?"

"Why would you think we'd hear from him? Surely it would be more likely for him to contact you."

"It would, but I did give him Chief Byler's number in the messages I've left for him."

"Are you certain he hasn't been in touch with you, Ms. Angelo?" His voice had hardened. "A text, an email, a phone call?"

"Nothing." Did she really have to go through this again? "I'm sure he's camping someplace where he doesn't have cell service. He's not that good about using his cell phone even when he's not out in the wilds, and as for email or texting... Well, he wouldn't know where to begin. He's avoided that technology like the plague."

"Hmm." The sound expressed skepticism. "So you didn't talk to him, say, about two or three days ago?"

"I did not." The pleasant atmosphere had disappeared from the office, reminding her that this was a police station. And she was, if not a suspect, still a person involved in a case.

"So you'd be surprised if I told you that two days ago, your father crossed the border into Canada."

She couldn't speak for a moment. She took a breath. That was a perfectly innocent action on Dad's part, but she could just imagine how it looked to the police.

"I didn't know that, no, but I'm not surprised. He enjoys the fishing in Canada."

"You expect us to believe that your father would just head to another country on the spur of the moment without letting you know? Frankly, Ms. Angelo, I find that about as hard to believe as your singular lack of memories of the time when your mother disappeared. Particularly since both of those things might easily be designed to protect your father."

"I don't know what you mean." Her lips were stiff.

"Don't you?" He rose, coming around the desk so that he loomed over her, trapping her in the chair. "Let me explain it, then. You might conveniently forget hearing your parents argue during that time before your mother disappeared. You might even manage to forget your father hitting her."

"No."

He swept on, ignoring her protest. "And now that some clues have turned up as to what happened to your mother, your father is conveniently missing. And you don't know where he is. As I say, convenient. For him."

"It happens to be true." Her heart was pounding at the contempt in his voice, and his presence was so intimidating that she could barely catch her breath.

"You're doing him no good, you know. This just makes him look even guiltier. An innocent man would be eager to come forward and explain himself in a situation like this."

"My father doesn't know anything about it. If he knew, I'm sure he would be here." He wouldn't let her be facing this alone. *You wouldn't, would you, Dad?*

"Well, we only have your word for that, don't we?"

"I'm telling you the truth."

"For your sake, I hope that's true, Ms. Angelo." He leaned back against the desk, easing the pressure ever so slightly. "As for your investigations... Well, I do understand, but I think it might be better for everyone if you left that to the professionals. You'd be wiser to go back home, redouble your efforts to find your father and hire a good attorney for him."

Her throat was so tight she wasn't sure she could speak, but she had to. "I don't see why my father needs an attorney at all. You have no proof a crime was even committed." She stood, forcing him back a step. "Until then—"

"Didn't I mention it?" His tone was silky. "The DNA results came back. The blood on the suitcase may not be enough to guarantee that anyone was murdered. But one thing is sure. That blood came from your mother."

# CHAPTER TWELVE

By the time she reached Elizabeth Yoder's place, Marisa had stopped shaking inside, which was just as well. She had to put all the questions the DA had raised out of her mind and focus on what she was going to ask Elizabeth. This might be her only chance.

She already had gathered a general picture of her mother's life as an Amish person. What she needed was someone who had remained in touch during the years from Barbara's marriage to her disappearance. That field was pathetically small. Elizabeth was probably her best, maybe her only, hope.

Marisa drove down a narrow gravel lane to the white farmhouse, and then past it to the rear, looking for a place to leave the car where she wouldn't block the lane. As the area behind the house came into view, she pulled off onto the grass verge and stopped, staring.

She was looking at the perfect image of an Amish farm. Neatly tended flower beds, filled with mums and asters, stretched across the back of the house. A few apple trees, their limbs bending with the weight of their fruit, lined a massive vegetable garden. Elizabeth and another woman, aided by several children, seemed to be busy in the garden. Beyond that, a crew of Amish men unloaded something from a wagon in front of the barn.

Sliding out, she started toward the garden. As she neared, she realized what she was looking at. Elizabeth and her helpers were picking pumpkins and squash, loading them into several wagons parked along the side of the garden.

Marisa waved. Straightening, Elizabeth put one hand on her back, stretching, and waved back.

"Marisa. Ach, I am so glad you have komm. Just what I hoped." She waved a hand. "This is my daughter, Mary Ann, your cousin." The other woman, who must be about Marisa's own age, smiled.

"Wilkom, Cousin Marisa. Here are my children." She gestured toward the four youngsters who were loading pumpkins into wagons—the youngest must surely be not much more than four, her chubby arms clasped around a pumpkin that was half as big as she was. "Aaron, Katie, Anna and the little one is Mary Beth."

"Hello. It's nice to meet all of you."

The children looked back at her with solemn blue eyes, all so alike that she'd probably not be able to tell them apart once they were no longer standing in a row. Their clothes were a miniature version of the adult Amish clothing—the boy wearing black pants, a blue shirt, suspenders and a straw hat, while the girls wore the dress-and-apron combination the older women wore, in solid colors ranging from purple to rose to blue.

Elizabeth brushed her hands on her

apron. "I want to sit and visit, but we must get these pumpkins picked today, and Mary Ann and the children have come to help...."

"That's fine. I'll be glad to wait for you." She smiled. "I'd like to help, if—"

"Ach, no, you are not dressed for this. Sit on the bench, then, if you don't mind waiting. We won't be much longer."

Marisa sat where she was directed, aware that her fingers were already itching for the pad and pencils that were always in her bag. "Cousin Elizabeth, would it be all right if I made some drawings? I wouldn't show anyone's face, I promise."

"Ja, no harm in that." She was frankly curious. "I have heard that you make the pictures that are in story books, like those we have for the children."

"That's right." She hesitated, but since Elizabeth had indicated that the children read storybooks, surely it was all right to offer. "I have some back at the bed-and-breakfast that I've done. I could bring them for your grandchildren, if that's all right?" She ended on a questioning note, hoping she hadn't erred.

But Elizabeth beamed. "That would be

wonderful gut. They would like to have those, that's certain-sure."

"I'll drop them off sometime soon," she said, feeling irrationally pleased.

Elizabeth and her helpers returned to their work, and she did the same, pencil flying across the page as the scene took shape. The lushness of the garden and the bright colors of the vegetables gleamed in the afternoon sunlight, contrasting with the sober dress of the workers.

But there was nothing sober about their manner, she realized. A flow of cheerful chatter in Pennsylvania Dutch accompanied the work, punctuated by laughter and what was probably some gentle teasing. Everyone seemed happy, and each person had a job suited to his or her size. The older children were quick to offer a hand to the younger ones. It was work, probably valuable work since she imagined the vegetables were headed for market, but they certainly seemed to have a good time while doing it.

This would have been her mother's life when she was a child—growing up on the farm in Indiana, working with her

family, probably enjoying it just as Mary
Ann's children seemed to. Would this
have been her life, as well, if Barbara
had never met Russ Angelo and fallen
in love?

But that was useless speculation. If
she'd had a different father, she'd be a
different person. But at least she might
have had her mother for longer than five
years.

She forced her focus back to the
drawing, losing herself in the scene as
she so often did. When she finally looked
up, she realized she had an audience.
The women and the two oldest kids
were hauling the wagons to the lane,
but the two youngest stood next to her,
gazes glued to the drawing.

She smiled at them, almost afraid to
speak for fear of scaring them away,
turning it so they could see more easily.
Would they even understand her? She
wasn't sure when Amish children learned
English.

They edged a little closer to each
other, smiling back shyly.

She put the pencil down, realizing that
the stress of that interview with the DA

had faded away. Perhaps that was the effect of the scene she'd been drawing. There was something so unhurried about the whole process. The family had been working, accomplishing something that must be done, but the rhythm was one of smooth, easy grace, without any sense that they watched the clock or needed to move on to something else. Maybe people who lived close to the land fell naturally into its rhythms.

"Now we can talk," Elizabeth said, approaching. She put her hands on the children's shoulders and looked over their heads at the sketchpad. "Ach, that is fine work, for sure. I can see the garden the way you do." She didn't wait for any response, just patted the children's heads and started to the house. "Komm, we'd all like something cold to drink."

Marisa followed her into the house, trying not to appear too curious as she looked around. At first glance, the kitchen looked like any modern kitchen, but a second look showed her the differences. The appliances all seemed to be run on gas, and the lighting fixture over the long kitchen table wasn't the usual electric lamp. No pictures hung on the walls, but the windowsills were crowded with pink and red geraniums.

"Sit now." Elizabeth waved her to a chair. Mary Ann was already getting out glasses and what seemed to be jugs of lemonade and iced tea. In moments the two women had poured drinks and set out plates of cookies and some sort of round chocolate palm-size cakes.

Mary Ann saw her looking at them. "Whoopie pies. Try one."

"They look wonderful." And fattening, she thought, but picked one up and bit in. The vanilla filling spurted out, sweet as the chocolate. "Delicious."

The children, in response to something their grandmother said, took snacks and drinks and headed out to the porch.

"Now." Elizabeth sat down across from Marisa. "What can I tell you about your mammi?"

"Anything you tell me would be more than I know now," Marisa admitted. "I'm really hoping you know something about her life those last few years, after she married my father."

Elizabeth's face grew serious. "That is

the one thing I can't say much about. You see, I married soon after she did and moved here. If I'd stayed closer, maybe things would have been different."

Her eyes filled with regret, and Marisa could feel her pain. So many people had been hurt in such different ways by the decisions her parents had made.

"Or maybe not. We won't ever know."

"It is as God wills," Elizabeth said. "Even when we don't understand what happens to us."

Marisa's throat tightened. "That's hard for me to accept."

Elizabeth patted her hand. "I know. Hard for all of us, but it is best to accept that our loving Father knows more than we do."

"After my mother left the church..." She hesitated, not sure of the right way to say what she wanted. "Would you have been able to stay close to her, if you hadn't moved away?"

"You are thinking of the bann," Elizabeth said. "But even those who are banned can still stay close with family, if both sides want it. They must simply obey the rules."

She was tempted to ask about William's attitude, but that would probably not encourage any confidences. "So you didn't stay in touch with her?" They wouldn't have had any long telephone conversations, she supposed.

Elizabeth looked surprised. "We wrote, of course."

Of course. What was she thinking— people used to actually write letters to each other, instead of texting or emailing.

"She told you how she was getting along, then."

"Ja, for sure. She was so happy when you were born." Elizabeth smiled, clearly remembering that time. "We hired a driver to take us to see you. Mary Ann was not quite two, and she thought you were a baby doll."

Marisa exchanged smiles with Mary Ann. So there was already a bond between them. If things had been different, they might have grown up as friends.

Or wouldn't Barbara have wanted to keep up that relationship? Maybe she'd have found it a painful reminder of what she'd given up.

"Was she happy?" The question burst

out before she could censor it. "Did she regret the choice she'd made?"

Elizabeth didn't respond. Then she rose, and Marisa feared she'd offended her. But she held out her hand.

"Komm. I want to show you something."

Together they went into the next room—what must be the living room of the house. Several bookshelves, a couple of comfortable chairs and three rocking chairs, one of which had a basket of sewing beside it. One entire end of the room was taken up by a large quilt frame, with a quilt spread over its surface.

"Mamm is having a quilting this week," Mary Ann said. "We will all help to finish the quilt."

Marisa realized she was looking at the top of the quilt, beneath which were the layers of filling and the backing. It was like a sandwich of fabric, not yet joined together. That was what would happen at the quilting Mary Ann had mentioned.... Women would sit all around the quilt, stitching the layers together.

"The design is beautiful." She touched the quilt top lightly. Rows of patches of different colors seemed to ripple across the surface in shades that ran from dark to medium to light and back to the dark again in gentle gradations. She didn't know a great deal about quilting, but she knew enough to recognize the artistry shown in the quilt. It evoked an almost visceral response, as if it touched the emotions in a way she couldn't explain.

"Sunshine and Shadows," Elizabeth said. "That is the pattern, a very old one. I like the old ones best. They make me remember the generations of women who have made the same quilts."

Marisa nodded, her throat tight at the thought.

"It is called Sunshine and Shadows because it is meant to look like the pattern of sunshine and shadows moving across the land," she said. "That is also the pattern of our lives, ain't so? We have the gut things and the sad, one after another, but all part of who we are." She put her arm around Marisa's waist, drawing her close. "That was your mamm's life, too. Happy and sad things, all making up her pattern. Barbara understood that, I think. Do you?"

She had to clear her throat before she could speak. "I'm beginning to."

"Gut." Elizabeth gave her a gentle squeeze and then let her go.

She hadn't, perhaps, learned anything new, but Marisa was still oddly comforted. "When you read her letters, did anything change in the time leading up to her disappearance? Did she seem depressed or worried about anything?"

Elizabeth studied her face. Finally she gave a short nod. "I did not know whether I would show you this or not, but now I think that I must." She crossed the room to a carved wooden chest that stood against the wall, lifted the lid and returned a moment later with an envelope in her hand. "This is the last letter I received from Barbara. It came the week before..." She let that trail off and held the envelope out. "You should have this. You can decide if it means anything."

Marisa's fingers trembled as she slid the letter from the envelope. The folds were much creased, as if it had been read over and over. Very short, it didn't take up even a page, written in a round, school-girl hand. She touched the writing, realizing she'd never seen anything her mother had written.

*My dear cousin,* she read. *I don't know what to do. I wish that you were here, so that we could sit at the kitchen table together, drinking coffee and talking the way we used to. Maybe then I'd know. You'll say I should talk to Russ, but I can't. I'm afraid to talk to anyone about it. They—*

She must have stopped there, crossing out the pronoun and beginning again. *I know that if you were here you would help me. Perhaps William will, if he is able to forgive. Pray that I will do the right thing. Your loving cousin, Barbara.*

Marisa wiped away a tear before it could fall on the paper. Her mother's words, written so many years ago, still seemed to carry the weight of her worry. Not just worry. Fear.

"Did you answer her?"

"Ja, I wrote to say that I would get a driver to bring me on Saturday. I went, but when I got there, your mother was gone, and no one could tell me what had happened."

She looked from the letter to Elizabeth's face. "Did you show this to my father?"

"No. Maybe I should have, but she says she couldn't talk to him about it, so I thought I shouldn't. If I was wrong..."

"It probably wouldn't have made any difference." She slipped the letter back into the envelope. "May I take this?"

"Ja." Her cousin looked troubled. "Show it to anyone you want if you think it will help."

"Thank you." Impulsively she put her arms around Elizabeth, hugging her. "Thank you."

Elizabeth squeezed her, and her cheek was wet when she pressed it against Marisa's. "Denke. I am glad you have come back at last."

The back door banged, loud in the quiet.

"Ach, those kinder," Mary Ann muttered, leading the way back to the kitchen.

But it wasn't the children who'd come in. It was a man.

Marisa hesitated, not sure that was the right word. He had a man's height and breadth, but no beard, and his round face was unlined, as smooth and innocent as a child's. He stopped at the sight of her, clearly disconcerted at a stranger in the house.

Mary Ann smiled at him. "Ephraim, have you komm for something to drink for the men?"

He nodded, still looking at Marisa. It was the wide, unabashed stare of a young child, and she realized that he really was like a child. She'd heard that genetic illnesses and retardation affected the Amish in larger numbers than the general population, due to their small pool of ancestors.

Mary Ann began filling an insulated jug with lemonade. Elizabeth touched Ephraim's arm, urging him a step or two closer to Marisa. "Komm, here is someone you must meet. Marisa, this is my youngest brother, Ephraim. Ephraim, this is Cousin Barbara's daughter, Marisa. You remember Barbara, don't you?"

His eyes widened even more, if that was possible. His mouth opened in a chasm of what might have been horror. He uttered a harsh, guttural cry, tears spurting from his eyes.

Before anyone could move, he turned

and blundered out of the room, knocking over a chair in his blind rush.

Link ran his hand along the banister he'd been sanding. Smooth as silk. Once he'd finished, he'd put on a coat of stain and then varnish.

Painting would have been faster, but somehow that would have felt wrong. The craftsmen who had built this place, probably a hundred and fifty years ago, had taken pride in their work. He could surely spare the time to do the same.

Being back at work on the house, satisfying as it was, didn't entirely ease the tension that was riding him. He hadn't told Marisa his feelings about Tom Sylvester's mention of Uncle Allen's visitors. He'd let her believe that the only thing they'd come away with was the lead to the one man left who'd been working on the house that afternoon.

His feelings about Tom's reaction weren't facts, he told himself. Unfortunately, his conscience wasn't buying that excuse. He hadn't said anything to Marisa about it because it pointed right back at Allen again.

He stopped, hand on the railing, listening to the silence in the old house. If these walls could talk—what a cliché that was. But in this situation it was only too true. Something had happened here that day twenty-some years ago. Something that might answer the question of Barbara Angelo's disappearance. And they might never know what that something was.

*Certainly not if you keep withholding things.* The voice of his conscience spoke tartly, sounding rather like his mother.

Before he could pursue that, he heard something else—a real sound this time, not one in his head. A vehicle pulling into the driveway.

He walked back the center hallway and reached the family room door just as his brother approached the porch.

Trey raised a hand in greeting. "Hey. Glad you're here. Back at work again?"

"Trying."

Trey let the screen door bang behind him. "I thought maybe you'd be out following clues again today."

"Don't remind me. Marisa and I are supposed to catch up with Brad Metzger at the inn tomorrow. Seems like he's the only one left to see."

Trey nodded, opening the refrigerator door and helping himself to a can of soda. "Mom told me about your talk with Sylvester. At least it wasn't a total dead end."

"No." He hesitated. Easy enough to let it go at that, but he was beginning to think he had to talk to someone about his suspicions. And Trey was safe. Trey's interests and his were identical in this case.

He blew out an exasperated breath. "There is something more. I didn't mention it to Mom. Or to Marisa."

"Marisa was there, wasn't she?"

"Yeah. But she hasn't known Tom for the better part of a lifetime, like I have." He paused, marshaling his thoughts. "He was grousing about Allen...about his being too particular, complaining about the noise and the dirt, all that kind of thing. And he mentioned that sometime that week, Allen had been worse than usual, making them clean everything up before they left because he was expecting guests."

Trey's eyebrows lifted. "Allen? Guests?"

"That was my reaction, too. Funny thing was that Tom seemed to back away from that topic in a hurry. And when I asked him if he knew who any of Allen's guests were, he got defensive. Claimed he had no idea."

"You thought he was lying." Trey frowned.

"I thought something didn't ring true. But what would be the big secret about somebody coming here? Allan never entertained, as far as I know, unless it was somebody who had an old book he wanted. But Tom mentioned a meeting." Now that he'd put it into words, he could hear how feeble it sounded. "It's nothing, I guess. Tom probably just wanted us to go away so he could put his steaks on the grill."

Trey's frown deepened. "Maybe. But maybe not." He reached into his jacket pocket and pulled something out. That old journal of Uncle Allen's. "Mom found something in here that bothered her."

He took the journal from his brother's hand. "What? This wasn't from the time Barbara disappeared, was it?"

"A year or so later," Trey said. He nodded toward the book. "Check what he says on the first page that's marked."

The journal, he now saw, was decorated with some of the pink sticky notes Mom put as reminders on anything and everything. He flipped it open to the first one.

"Left-hand page," Trey said.

"September 1," he read aloud. "Didn't sleep again last night. I should have known better. I never should have gotten involved with them."

He looked up, his gaze questioning. "Them?"

Trey shrugged. "I don't know who. He doesn't name names, but there's a lot more in that vein—complaints about sleepless nights and bad dreams, vague references to people who caused trouble for him."

"Sounds like the old boy was getting paranoid." He'd rather think that than assume this had anything to do with Barbara's disappearance.

"Not so old then. He was a year younger than Dad." Trey rubbed the back of his neck. "I'd like to believe it's nothing, but I can't dismiss it, especially—well, go to the last reference Mom has marked."

Link flipped through the diary reluctantly. He didn't want this—didn't want any part of it. Closing around him, keeping him here. Maybe he was the one who was paranoid. He found the page. The writing straggled, the words uneven.

"I hate the very thought of that cursed bird. It's led to nothing but grief." The line trailed off, as if the pen had gone slack in Allen's hand.

Link slapped the book closed. "That makes no sense at all."

"Unfortunately, it does." Trey stopped, shook his head. "You never heard the full story of what happened back in June, when the Esch boy was accused of murder. Mom didn't want us telling you anything upsetting."

That nettled him. "Like I'm such a fragile plant. I know Bobby Stephens turned out to be a nutcase and almost incinerated you in the process of confessing to killing Dad. What could be worse that than?"

"Not worse, necessarily." Trey grinned.

"All right, so Mom was being overprotective. She kept saying you didn't need all the details to give you nightmares."

"I had plenty of my own nightmares," he said shortly. "Give. What details? And what does that have to do with Barbara Angelo's disappearance?"

Trey's face tightened. "There was a lot of ugliness surrounding the Esch kid's arrest. Jessica came here to defend him, hired by Mom. She started getting threats, marked with a black bird. A raven, to be exact."

"Sounds like something out of a comic book." But something stirred in the recesses of his mind, like a monster slowly surfacing and then sinking back into the mud.

"That's what we thought. But in the process of trying to figure out if it meant anything, Leo Frost finally traced the symbol to a secret society that flourished around here back in the 1700s."

Leo Frost, the attorney who'd taken Trey's finacée into his practice was also an old family friend.

He raised a skeptical eyebrow. "Get serious."

"I know. It sounds screwy. But Bobby..." Trey stopped, his face twisting as if he tried to hold back pain.

The sight jolted Link. Trey was the big brother, the strong one, the responsible one. He never showed weakness.

"Bobby was raving there at the end. He kept talking about how he shouldn't have used the sign to try and scare Jessica. That *they* wouldn't like it."

"*They* again."

"Right. Bobby apparently believed that the secret society existed, ready to punish him for screwing up."

Link's mind reeled. "You can't seriously expect me to accept that there's some secret society running rampant in bucolic Lancaster County, can you? What do they do—skulk around at night in white robes?"

"Nothing so crude. And no, I don't believe it, not really. But Bobby did. And now that." He gestured to the book in Link's hands. "I can't ignore the possibility."

Link felt like his head was about to explode. "Why haven't I heard about this? Did it become public knowledge?"

"The symbol was briefly in the news, but Bobby's efforts to kill me kind of eclipsed that. The rest of the story was bizarre enough without dragging in a secret society."

"I still don't believe it, but... Well, what do you propose to do?"

"See if there are any more diaries, for one thing. That's why I came over. And then...maybe we ought to sit down and talk this over. All of us."

"Including Marisa?"

"She's involved, isn't she?"

His gut tightened at the thought of bringing Marisa in on something so potentially damaging to his family. But did he have the right to keep her out?

He took a breath, trying to ease the tension. "Let's check for any more diaries first. And see what we come up with when we talk to Metzger. Then... Well, maybe you're right. But let's make sure we have all the ammo we can find first."

It had begun to rain shortly after Marisa left Cousin Elizabeth's farm—a steady, relentless downpour that turned the fallen leaves to a spongy mass on the ground. The gray atmosphere unfortunately matched her mood. She had a quick supper at the local cafe and headed back to her room.

She was alone in the bed-and-breakfast again. Two retired couples had come in for a couple of days, but left this morning. She must be getting used to it. The silence no longer felt vaguely threatening, and she didn't even bother looking out the window at the willow tree.

Once again she checked her cell phone for messages. One from her agent, saying she had an expression of interest in the Amish illustrations; nothing from her father. She flipped quickly to check emails. Nothing from him there, either, though she hadn't really expected that.

She put the cell phone on the bedside table and looked longingly at the bed. At the moment, her body felt as if she'd been flattened by a steamroller, but her mind jumped restlessly from one subject to another. She'd never sleep, and it would be useless to try.

Piling pillows against the headboard for comfort, Marisa pulled out her sketch pad. That would settle her mind.

She lingered at the drawing of her mother, walking away toward a misty wood. Marisa touched the figure lightly with her finger. Odd, now that she thought of it, that her imagination had pictured her mother in Amish dress even before she'd seen that Amish kapp in the suitcase.

Frowning, she tried to trace the image back to its origins. Useless. It had always been there, it seemed, in her dreams if not in her waking thoughts. Mammi, walking away.

Sometimes the dreams turned to nightmares. She'd see her small self running after the vanishing figure, crying out. But her mother never turned, never acknowledged the cries, and the child was left, a crumpled figure beside the road, sobbing.

What was she doing, letting herself think of that? Now her throat was tight with unshed tears, and her mind still would not settle.

Well, what did she expect? The talk with Cousin Elizabeth would have been enough to disturb her balance, even without the letter she'd produced.

Marisa had slipped it into the pocket inside the back cover of the sketch pad, and she felt with her fingers to be sure it was still there. *Don't get it out,* her sensible side insisted. *If you start puzzling over that, you'll never sleep.*

Unfortunately, she didn't need to look at it. She'd long since memorized the contents. She pulled her robe more tightly around her despite the room's warmth. Maybe the cold was in her soul.

What had her mother been afraid of that she couldn't talk to her husband about? And more to the point, what was Marisa going to do with the letter?

It was evidence. She ought to hand it over to the police or the DA. But as soon as they saw that reference to not confiding in Dad, they'd assume that he was the one Barbara feared.

She pressed her palms against her eyes, as if she could blot out the image of that page, but it was useless. She'd have to decide.

If her father was here, it would be simple. She'd show him—they'd puzzle it out together, wouldn't they? But he'd never talked about her mother in the past. What made her so sure he would now?

He'd have to, that was all. *Where are you, Dad? Why don't you call?*

She glanced down at the sketch pad, and the pencil dropped from suddenly nerveless fingers. Without thinking, she'd drawn a scene from a nightmare— Elizabeth's brother's face, distorted by the cry that came from his mouth when he heard who she was.

Elizabeth had tried to explain it away, saying that Ephraim sometimes reacted badly to strangers. But Marisa had seen how shaken Elizabeth had been. And there was no doubt in Marisa's mind that Ephraim's reaction had been because of who she was and not the fact of finding a stranger in his sister's kitchen.

Why? Tension prickled through her like an electric shock, making her legs twitch. Why? Did Ephraim know something? And if he did, was there any chance of finding out what it was?

Mary Ann had led Ephraim away, talking to him as soothingly as if he were one of her young children, and Elizabeth talked about him. Ephraim was capable of working under supervision, she'd said. He led a useful life as a valued member of the family—maybe more so than if he'd been in the outside world.

What could he know? He'd have been a boy when Barbara vanished—maybe in his teens at the most, but with the understanding of a six-year-old. Could he have seen something, heard something?

Marisa tossed the sketchbook aside and swung her legs off the bed. This was futile. She was exhausted, and her mind was running in circles. She had to shut down the speculation and get some sleep. Things would look clearer in the morning.

Rhoda always left milk in the fridge downstairs. She would get a glass of milk, drink it and go to bed, and all the while she would keep her mind focused on something other than the problems ahead of her.

She shoved her feet into slippers and went quickly out into the hall, where a low light burned all night long. It was sufficient to guide her to the top of the stairs. Downstairs, the desk lamp was also left on. She could see it as she descended, casting a small circle of yellow on the guestbook, leaving the rest of the hallway in shadow.

She reached the bottom, fingers touching the newel post, and started toward the desk. A step before she reached it, the lamp went out.

She froze, hands outstretched as if she balanced on a tightrope, and beat back an instant of panic. Stupid. It had burned out, that was all. She just had to feel her way along the desk, cross the few feet between it and the wall and find the switch that controlled the overhead lights.

Or she could forget the milk and go back up to her room. No one would know that she'd acted like a child afraid of the dark.

She'd know. She reached out, touched the edge of the desk and began to work her way along it.

She was fine, her sensible side insisted. Fine. Her fingers fumbled at the end of the desk. Funny that her eyes hadn't grown more accustomed to the dark. But it was cloudy out, so that the darkness that pressed against the window was only slightly less dense than that inside.

She reached out in the direction of the wall, took a breath and launched herself toward it, stepping cautiously, her feet making no sound in her soft slippers. For a disoriented second she thought she'd turned herself around completely. Then her groping fingers touched the wall.

The cool, flat surface reassured her. Now to find the switch—but unfortunately she didn't remember its exact placement. She moved her hand in a small arc. No switch. She tried again, widening the arc. Still no switch, and a tiny frisson of fear brushed her neck.

Stupid, she thought again, pushing it away, and in that instant her fingers found the switch—the old-fashioned kind with two buttons. She fumbled with it, pushed the button.

Nothing. No answering, reassuring glow of light from overhead. The whole house must be without power.

Just as if someone had turned it off at the main switch.

# CHAPTER THIRTEEN

Paralyzed, Marisa stood with her finger pressed against the button. She wasn't breathing, she realized, and took a slow, careful breath.

She couldn't let her imagination run away with her. Maybe the rain had knocked out the power. For all she knew, the whole town could be out. Rhoda wouldn't even notice, because they didn't use electricity in their wing. And she couldn't imagine trying to grope her way through the dark rooms to the door that led to their section of the house.

She could use her cell phone for a

light, but it was upstairs, on the table beside her bed.

No doubt there were candles some-place, probably in the kitchen, but she could spend the rest of the night feeling around without finding them. The only thing to do was to go back upstairs, get her cell phone and use its light to guide her to the Miller family's door.

Her fingers didn't want to let go of the security of the wall. She had to make a conscious effort to pull her hand back, to turn, to grope her way toward the desk.

There. Her fingers connected with a surface. But surely that was too high to be the desk. If she'd gotten herself turned around—

Again that irrational flicker of panic, and again she fought it. The room was the same in the dark as in the light. That was what her grandmother used to say when small Marisa had wanted a night-light. But in the end, Gran had always left a light on.

Marisa brought a mental image of the area into focus. The wide center hall, with the desk close to the wall that separated it from the kitchen. There was a desk, a chair. To one side a bookcase held books and brochures about Lancaster County and the Amish. On the far wall, a tall stand supported a Boston fern.

She slid her hand along the surface. No plant met her questing fingers. Instead they closed on a stack of brochures, the glossy paper smooth against her fingers.

All right, she knew where she was. The desk should be a quarter turn to the left. All she had to do was feel her way around it and she'd be at the stairs. No problem. She could do that.

She shifted her weight forward, preparing to take a step. A floorboard creaked—but not from her. Farther away, maybe in the kitchen. A chair clattered, a low voice muttered what might have been a curse.

She didn't dare breathe. She knew exactly what had happened. The chair at the end of the long table was in a direct line with the basement door. Someone had come stealthily up the stairs, presumably after cutting the power at the circuit box. Not someone who knew the house well. If it was Eli, he'd have known about the chair. And he'd have come with a flashlight as he had that first night.

Now that there really was something to fear, Marisa found herself unaccountably calm. She weighed her options. If the man stayed in the kitchen, she might be able to make it to the front door without being heard.

But why would he? If he'd gone to the trouble of shutting off the power, he wanted something. It was hardly likely there was anything valuable in the kitchen.

She found it hard to believe in a sneak thief, anyway. Someone had searched her belongings once before. Now he was back.

A pulse jumped in her throat. Not just to search. He had to believe he wouldn't find her room empty—not with her car parked outside.

Now the fear came in a cold, implacable tide. She fought it, but it was like swimming against a rip current. That had happened to her once, on holiday at the Eastern Shore. If not for an observant lifeguard, she'd have been pulled under.

She'd survived that. She'd cope with this. *Think, Marisa.*

The phone was on the desk. She could picture it, an old-fashioned black desk phone. Even if she could reach it without being heard, he'd certainly hear the sound when she picked up the receiver. She'd never manage to dial 911 before he was on her. The same thing was true if she screamed for the Miller's. And if he had a flashlight—

Of course he did. He'd have used it to find the circuit box. Probably he wasn't using it now because a moving light could draw attention if anyone happened to glance at the house. But if he knew she was there—

Her heart stopped at the thought of being pinned, helpless, in a beam of light.

Not helpless. She rejected the word. She'd fight back if she had to. But first, try to reach one of the doors. Get outside, away from the house, and start screaming.

If she knew where he was... She stiffened into immobility, not twitching a muscle, not breathing, and listened. She forced her mind to filter out the usual sounds of the old house—a branch of the forsythia bush moving against the window, the tick of the clock on the living-room mantel, loud in the silence. Anything else?

A faint creak, then another. He was moving—not toward her, but toward the stairs. If she'd gone that way, she'd have stumbled right into him.

Wait until he went upstairs and then try to make it to the front door? But what if he didn't do as she expected? Worse, what if he switched on a flashlight to make his way up the stairs? She could still be in his field of vision.

Her fingers closed on the corner of the desk. All right. She knew where she was. She'd edge away, toward the front door, ready to run for it—

Her fingers brushed a stack of papers on the corner of the desk, sending them fluttering to the floor with a soft ripple of sound. She sensed, rather than heard, the body coming toward her, seemed to glimpse a darker solid black against black, and a hand grabbed her sleeve.

She jerked back, but he had her, his hand hard on her arm, a swish of air as he raised something in his other hand. He was going to hit her; if he connected… She jerked to the side as the blow fell. It brushed her head and hit her shoulder, sending pain radiating down her arm—something hard and cylindrical, like a flashlight. The next blow would strike her head, and she couldn't lift her arm to fight back. He pressed closer, sensing his advantage.

*Please, please, I don't want to die here.*

Through the haze of pain and panic came the memory of the self-defense class she'd taken last winter, how the blow she'd almost inadvertently landed had stunned even the well-padded instructor. Drawing back her leg, she thrust with her knee as hard as she could.

He cried out, his grip slackening as he stumbled back. She ran to where the door had to be, felt it, found the dead bolt, twisted it and ran screaming out of the house.

Marisa huddled on the straight wooden

chair in Adam Byler's office, trying to gain control of the shudders that still shook her body. Reaction, she thought dully. That's all it was.

Someone had brought her a blanket—someone else had thrust a mug of hot coffee in her hands. She'd almost said that she never had caffeine at night because it kept her awake and then thought how silly that was. At the moment, she didn't see how she'd ever sleep, knowing the nightmares that would pounce on her.

"Now, Ms. Angelo," Adam began again, bending closer to her and looking faintly harassed. No wonder. Each time he started to take her over what happened, someone else came in, interrupting him. "Why did you go downstairs if you thought someone was in the house?"

"I didn't." She cut off the words, determined not to let her voice shake. "I thought everything was locked, and I—"

"But it was," Rhoda, white with shock, protested. "I know it. I went back to our house at around eight o'clock, and every door was locked then, I'm certain-sure."

"Yes, we do know that," Byler said. "The intruder forced the lock on the back door."

"Ja." Eli nodded, somber. "I saw. Who would do such a thing here in Springville?"

The chief didn't bother saying the obvious: that bad things happened everywhere. But this hadn't just been a random break-in. She studied Byler's strong-featured face. He didn't give much away. Did he really believe this was a matter of a sneak thief lashing out in a panic?

A shudder went through her, and she lifted the mug to her lips, taking a sip of the unpalatable brew. It was hot, that was all you could say in its favor.

"You went downstairs." Byler doggedly tried to get back on track.

"I felt restless." She thought of the letter, and her mind jerked away. She wasn't ready to show that to him, not yet. "I was going down to the kitchen to get a glass of milk. When I—"

The door burst open. Link surged through, looking so thunderous that she nearly quailed. Ignoring everyone else, he came straight to her, bending over her.

That wasn't anger in his face. It was fear. He was afraid for her.

"Are you all right?" The urgency in his voice had her wanting to comfort him.

"I'm fine. I—"

He put his hands on her shoulders. She winced, pain cutting her words off with a gasp.

"You're hurt." He peeled the blanket back with urgent fingers, his mouth tightening at the sight of her shoulder, which had begun to turn purple. He swung on Adam Byler.

"Why is she here? Why haven't you taken her to the hospital? She's not fit to be sitting here answering questions. You should—"

Adam held up his hand, stopping Link in mid-spate. "Ms. Angelo refused to go to the hospital, but I've already called Cliff Henderson. He's on his way now."

Link nodded, looking reluctant to give up his anger. "Don't you at least have sense enough to put an ice pack on this?"

Byler seemed to bite back a retort.

He opened the door. The patrolman was standing so close he nearly fell into the room. "Larson, get an ice pack and bring it here."

"Ice pack?" He looked blank.

"Fill a plastic bag with ice, fasten it, wrap a towel around it. You think you can manage that?"

"Yessir." The hapless patrolman gulped and lumbered away.

"Kid couldn't—" Byler cut off whatever he was about to say. Either he didn't think he should criticize the kid in front of civilians, or the language he'd been about to use wasn't exactly polite. He turned back to Marisa.

"I'd just gotten downstairs when the light on the desk went out." She said the words quickly, before anyone else could interrupt. "I thought it had burned out, so I felt my way over to the wall switch. That's when I realized the power was off." She took a breath, willing her voice not to quiver. "Then I heard someone in the kitchen."

Link moved closer to her, putting a hand on her uninjured shoulder.

Byler nodded. "It appears he broke in

the back door, went to the cellar and cut off the power, then came back upstairs."

"Why?" Link demanded. "If he was set on ripping off the place, he must have thought it was empty. Why bother with the power?"

Byler shrugged. "There's no accounting for what a kid hopped up on pills might do."

Convenient, but not true in this case. "He can't have thought the house empty," Marisa said. "My car was outside, and the light in my bedroom was on."

"Ja, that's true," Rhoda said. "I saw it myself when I was going up to bed."

Byler pivoted toward her. "Did you hear anyone? See anyone near the house?"

"Nothing. I'd have roused Eli if I had," she said. "I noticed nothing until I heard the door slam and Marisa screaming."

"I'm afraid I woke the neighborhood." Somehow that seemed to require an apology.

"Best thing you could have done," Byler said. "It scared him away—looks like he ran out the back, leaving the door open. Probably cut through the woods."

"You have someone looking for tracks?" Link said sharply. "He could have had a car parked somewhere."

"I'll be on it at first light." The chief's face tightened, as if he didn't care to be told his job.

"You should—"

She put her hand over Link's, and he subsided. She understood the helpless feeling, but getting the chief's back up wouldn't help matters.

The door opened yet again, this time to admit the patrolman carrying a dripping ice pack, followed by an older man carrying the traditional black bag. He took the ice pack, holding it gingerly away from his clothes.

"That'll do," he said, dismissing the cop with a nod. "Now, if…ah, thank you, Rhoda." This last in response to Rhoda's action as she took the dripping ice pack and dealt with it efficiently.

"What do we have here?" Obviously he knew who his patient was, because he came straight toward her, tipping her head back gently to look at her eyes.

"Marisa, this is Dr. Henderson," Link said, moving back a reluctant step.

"Retired doctor," he corrected, smiling. "But the good people of Springville keep calling me out. How is your vision? Seeing double, any blurriness?"

"Nothing like that. The blow brushed the side of my head and landed on my shoulder."

She sat still as gentle fingers explored her scalp and moved to her shoulder. He seemed to know what he was doing, and he was the very image of the country doctor, with his slightly baggy suit, thick white hair and keen eyes. In his seventies, at a guess, and he radiated an air of calm she found soothing.

"How did you get hurt?" Byler nodded to her shoulder.

"He grabbed me." She tried to say the words without reliving those moments, but it was impossible. For an instant she was back in the dark, fighting for her life. "He had something—a flashlight, maybe. I felt him swing it and jerked out of the way, but it hit my shoulder."

"Certainly a flashlight," the doctor said, pulling her robe away from her shoulder. "The marks of the cylinder are clear." He probed delicately, moving her hand and arm.

"Is that when he ran?" Byler persisted.

She shook her head and then wished she hadn't. "I felt the movement of his arm. He was swinging again. I...I kneed him as hard as I could, and he stumbled back."

There was a faint gasp from Rhoda, and the doctor chuckled. "Good for you, my dear." He held out his hand for the ice pack. "Let's keep this on for a while." He bent closer, effectively closing her off from the rest of the room. "Do you want to go to the hospital?" He asked softly. "You don't need to, but I can get you in. Maybe a quiet night would be a good idea."

Quiet. She knew what he was saying. He'd clap her in a hospital room where she wouldn't be bothered by anyone, including the police chief with his questions.

It was tempting. Very. But that would only be a postponement. She had to face what was happening.

"Thanks, but I'll be fine."

"Are you sure?" He looked concerned. "Where are you going to stay tonight?"

"We can sleep in the guesthouse," Rhoda offered. "That way Marisa won't be alone. You would not be afraid if we were there, ain't so?"

Wouldn't she? She wasn't so sure of that.

"Marisa will come home with us, of course." The patrolman must have left the office door open, because Geneva marched in, with Trey in her wake. Trey looked at Link and shook his head, spreading his hands wide, probably to indicate that he hadn't been able to keep his mother from coming.

"That's nice of you, Geneva, but—"

"No buts." Geneva brushed Link and the doctor out of her way, settling the ice pack into a more comfortable position. "We have a room ready for you, and I won't take no for an answer." Geneva put a surprisingly strong arm around her and helped her to her feet. "Right now you need a warm bath and a little mothering."

"I'm not finished questioning—" Byler began.

"That's enough for tonight." Geneva addressed him as if he were a rambunctious ten-year-old. "Tomorrow, right, Dr. Henderson?"

The two exchanged glances, and the doctor smiled, nodding. "That's my prescription, too. I'll give you something for the pain."

Link moved to Marisa's other side, putting his arm around her waist. "Let's get you out of here."

"One more thing," Byler said, clearly not ready to give up. "If this wasn't a random break-in, Ms. Angelo, what could the intruder have been after?"

She hesitated, her mother's letter clear in her mind. But no one could have known about that, could they? And she wasn't ready to tell him and start yet another round of questions.

"I have no idea," she said.

Whether or not Byler bought it, she had no idea. But she made the mistake of looking at Link.

He watched her, eyes narrowed. He knew she was leaving something out. And she suspected he wouldn't be content until he knew what.

. . .

Link worked his hands on the steering wheel as he drove toward Mom's house. Marisa hadn't spoken at all since they'd left the bed-and-breakfast after picking up some of her things.

Rhoda had packed for her—enough, apparently, for the night and the next day. But Marisa had gathered up her art supplies herself, working awkwardly with one hand. His effort to help her had been abruptly rejected.

Now—well, now he wasn't sure where they stood. But he had to break through her reserve. She was hiding something, and he had to know what.

He glanced at her. Against the dark outside, she was a pale profile, as still as a marble statue, her face set in lines of strain.

As if she felt his gaze on her, she stirred, the image breaking and reforming. "I hope I didn't insult Rhoda by leaving. I just couldn't face staying there tonight." Her smile flickered, painfully artificial. "I guess that makes me a wimp."

"Anybody would feel that way," he said. "Anybody. I'm sure Rhoda understands." He wanted to comfort her, but at the same time he wanted to press her. What was she hiding?

He shrugged, not liking the feeling that he knew her too well. Too well for such a short time, certainly. A short, intense time, in which their emotions had been scraped raw.

She moved slightly, touching her shoulder gingerly.

"Is the pain any better?" Doc Henderson had insisted she take one of the pain pills before she left the station. She'd clearly not wanted to take it, but in the end she had.

"A little better," she said, looking away from him and staring out the window at the dark.

This was getting him nowhere. He'd have to be more direct. "I take it you don't believe the comfortable explanation that this was a random break-in."

"Do you?" At least she was looking at him again.

"After everything that's happened? Not likely."

"No." She was silent for a moment. "I

don't think your police-chief friend is taking it seriously."

That startled him. "Adam? I wouldn't say that. Adam doesn't give much away, but he's a bulldog. He won't quit until he finds the answer."

"He doesn't seem to have been doing much about those shots that were fired at us in the woods."

"He investigated." Clearly Adam hadn't seen fit to confide in Marisa about it. "He found the place the shots were fired from, but that was it. No indication of who it was or why they were there." He paused, remembering what else Adam had said. "The fact that the place was so clean was suspicious in itself. A guy out target-shooting, even someone hunting illegally, wouldn't be so careful to pick up spent shells."

She stared at him for a long moment. "So he thinks it was deliberate."

"He didn't commit himself, not to me. But trust me, he's not blowing us off."

"I'm glad to hear that. But..." She let that trail off.

"But things are still happening. And we still don't know why." His hands knotted on the steering wheel. "I guess you don't want to talk about what happened tonight, but was there anything at all familiar about the man?"

"It was pitch-black. I couldn't see a thing."

"You could hear. Feel. Smell."

She shot him a lot of dislike. "I was fighting for my life at the time."

"Very effectively, too," he said.

Her smile flickered, and the tension ebbed.

"Thanks to that self-defense class. It's surprising how much it took to get to the point where I could actually think about hurting someone. But when he grabbed me, I—" She stopped, turning to look at him. "He was wearing gloves. I felt them when he touched me."

"Good. Anything else?"

She shook her head.

That didn't get them anywhere, and he didn't like the implication. The intruder had taken the precaution of shutting off the electricity. He'd worn gloves. If she hadn't been able to fight him off—Why had he really come?

He turned into the lane that led to the

house. Almost out of time. Once Marisa was inside, she'd be enveloped by Mom in full mothering mode. If he was going to ask, it had to be now.

He came to a stop in front of the house and turned to her. "Marisa, what was he after?"

"How would I know?" But she refused to look at him.

"I don't believe that. You know something...something you're not telling."

Her head went up and she glared at him. "And if I do? What about you? What about the things you're hiding from me? Do you think I don't know?" She thrust the door open and climbed out of the car.

# CHAPTER FOURTEEN

That went well. Link delayed getting out of the car and taking out Marisa's bag. He'd give her time to go inside and be swept up by Mom.

Sure enough, when he reached the front door, Mom already had one arm around Marisa. She snatched Marisa's small bag with the other hand, giving him a look that said she wasn't happy with him, and marched Marisa up the stairs.

Well, fine. He wasn't happy with himself, either. He was frustrated and annoyed, and his temper wasn't improved by seeing Trey giving every sign of wanting to talk.

"What?" he said, letting his irritation show.

"You want to tell me what's going on between the two of you?" Trey asked.

Link stalked past him into the kitchen. His brother followed him, obviously determined to get an answer.

"What makes you think something's wrong?" He opened the refrigerator door, stared at its contents and pulled out a bottle of milk.

Trey took a couple of glasses from the cabinet and set them on the table. "When Marisa walks in looking like a thunderstorm ready to break, followed by you ready to bite someone's head off, I'm actually smart enough to add two and two and get four."

Link poured milk into the glasses. Trey was safe enough—he never gave up a secret or let anyone down.

"When Adam asked Marisa what the intruder could have been after, she said she didn't know. That wasn't true. She knows, or at least suspects something."

Trey leaned against the quartz-topped counter, considering that. "You're sure?"

"I'm sure. Besides, she basically admitted she was hiding something when I pushed her on it. She accused me of doing the same."

"Hence the fireworks," Trey said. "Well, she's right about that, isn't she?"

Link drained his glass. Milk was supposed to be calming, wasn't it? "If she is...well, you know why. I'm not eager to focus attention on Uncle Allen."

"Morgans stick together, I get that. But maybe it's time to put that aside."

Link could only stare at him. "You say that? You're always the one to talk about the importance of family. Don't you remember all the lectures you gave me about not embarrassing the Morgan name?"

Trey grinned. "So I was a prig when I was a teenager. You don't need to remind me."

Disarmed, Link returned the grin. "Glad you realize that. Seriously, you think we should let everything come out? You, the responsible one?"

"Seems to me you've taken on plenty

of responsibility when it comes to Marisa's situation," Trey said, his tone mild.

"Not me." He snapped the words back instinctively. "That's not who I am."

The recoil went deep, maybe into his soul. Maybe kids were born knowing their place in the family. Trey was the oldest—the reliable, responsible one. Link was the daredevil, the rebel. Not good material for taking care of other people. Libby was the peacemaker, but with a strong strain of tomboy in her.

"Deny it all you want." Trey set his glass on the counter with a small clink. "I saw your face when Adam called to tell you Marisa was in trouble. You care about her."

He fought down the urge to throw something. "Even if I do, nothing's going to come of it."

"Why not?" Trey seemed determined to force him into confronting things that were better left alone.

"Think about it." He all but snarled the words. "Maybe our uncle killed her mother, in which case she's never going to want to see us again. Or her father killed her mother, and I'm instrumental in bringing that out. Same result."

"Could be," Trey admitted. "Or maybe there's some solution we haven't even considered yet."

"Maybe, but I doubt it. The obvious answer is usually the right one. And even if you're right...well, settling down isn't in my plans."

Trey was silent for a moment, frowning at nothing in particular. Then he rinsed their glasses, setting them in the sink. He turned back to Link.

"Whatever the truth is, I think we're past the point of hiding things. I say we all sit down together tomorrow and hash it over. Maybe if we're honest with Marisa, she'll return the favor."

"Or maybe not."

Trey shrugged. "Whatever. That's still the best chance we have at getting to the truth."

He'd argue, but unfortunately Trey was right.

"All right," he said. "Tomorrow." He moved toward the door. He'd go to bed, but he doubted he'd go to sleep very readily.

Trey followed him. At the doorway, he put his hand briefly on Link's shoulder. "Good. You'll see. There's no use in running away from things." He went on toward the stairs.

Link stared after him, knowing Trey was talking about more than just the current situation.

But Trey was wrong. Sometimes running away was the only answer, wasn't it?

Marisa was surprised to discover she'd actually slept through the night. That innocent-looking little white pill Dr. Henderson had pressed on her must have been more potent than she'd thought. She hadn't even dreamed.

She sat on the edge of the bed for a moment, assessing the damage. Not too bad—a tender spot on the side of her head, a few minor bruises where the man had grabbed her, and the huge purple one on her shoulder. She flexed her hand, tried to move her left arm, and decided she wouldn't be doing much of that for a few days. At least it was her left hand, not her right.

Grasping the graceful headboard of

the sleigh bed, she got slowly to her feet. The room was charming—a bow-front antique chest of drawers, a curved daybed, the sleigh bed covered with a quilt whose delicate colors seemed a bit feminine. Maybe this had been Link's sister's room.

She made her way toward the bathroom, becoming steadier as she walked. A hot shower helped. When she got out, she suspected she felt as good as she was likely to.

It proved impossible to get her hair up into a ponytail, so she had to leave it loose, curling as it dried. Dressing proved to be another issue. Fortunately she had thought to bring a shirt rather than a pullover.

She was still considering how to get her arm into the sleeve when someone knocked on the door. She clutched the shirt to her. "Who is it?"

"Jessica. I came to see if you need any help getting dressed."

"Thanks, I— Well, yes, I guess I do."

Jessica's smiling face appeared around the edge of the door, and she slipped into the room. "I thought you might. Let me give you a hand with that." She eased the shirt into place over Marisa's left arm and then buttoned it. "There. Anything else?"

"I think that's it." She hesitated, a question on her lips. "I didn't realize... Do you live here?"

"I have an apartment in town, but Trey called and said I should come over this morning." She paused, eyeing Marisa, and absently brushed a strand of sleek hair behind her ear. "They're planning a council of war this morning. I thought you should be prepared."

"Council...?" She was lost.

"I know." Jessica's voice warmed with sympathy. "The Morgan family can be a bit overwhelming when they decide to help you. That was my reaction when I met them. But honestly, Marisa, you can trust them. Us." Jessica squeezed her hand. "We all want to help."

The lump in her throat surprised her. Fortunately Jessica didn't seem to expect a response. She just led the way out into the hall and down the staircase.

Everyone was gathered in the dining room, including a white-haired man with

keen blue eyes whom Jessica intro-
duced as her law partner, Leo Frost.

"Mr. Frost." She nodded, hoping her
head wouldn't detach.

He inspected Marisa with a quick glance
and took her right hand in both of his.

"It's a pleasure to meet you at last,
Marisa. I'm sorry you've been having
such a difficult time of it since you arrived. Don't let that turn you against us,
will you?"

His tone was so warm that it was impossible not to believe he meant it, and
she murmured some probably incoherent response.

Really, she had to get control of herself. She was far too susceptible to kindness lately, and she ought to be wary.
That council of war Jessica had mentioned loomed in her mind. What, exactly, did they want from her?

Link replaced Leo, taking her hand
and submitting her to an inspection of
his own. "So, how do you feel this morning? Should you be up?"

Last night's antagonism had vanished,
and she could only be thankful.

"A little sore, but otherwise I'm fine."

He led her to a seat at the long dining-room table just as Geneva and her helper emerged from the kitchen, carrying platters of pancakes, bacon and scrambled eggs. The table already held two different types of breakfast cake as well as a clear glass bowl filled with fresh fruit. Geneva must believe they'd brainstorm better on stomachs filled to bursting.

As the food platters began circling the table, something else became clear. Geneva had obviously ordained that the situation not be discussed while they were eating, and she had a quick, reproving glance for any comment that veered in that direction.

Once the meal was finished and the dishes cleared, Geneva nodded to Trey, as if giving him permission. This was it, then.

Marisa's stomach protested her breakfast. She glanced quickly at Link, who sat on her right. He stared straight ahead, his profile forbidding. His lean, brown hand curled into a fist on the tabletop, the muscles on his forearm standing out.

Trey cleared his throat. Jessica, saying something to Leo Frost, faltered and fell silent.

"We've decided it was time for all of us to talk about this situation."

"Past time, given what happened to Marisa last night," Geneva put in.

Trey glanced at her, and she gave a rueful smile and shook her head. "I know, we decided you should take the lead. But when I think about what might have happened..."

"Thanks to Marisa's ability to defend herself, it didn't."

"It could have." Link's voice was harsh, his words clipped.

Before the brothers could begin an argument, Leo intervened. "Given the fact that we seem to be up against someone quite ruthless, I consider the relatively minor nature of Marisa's injuries nothing short of providential." He glanced at Marisa. "I don't mean to minimize your pain, my dear. But—"

"I know," she said quickly. "That blow was aimed at my head." She looked around the table, trying to assess their expressions. "Let me understand this.

You agree that this wasn't just a panicked burglar?"

"Yes." Trey seemed to answer for all of them. "And I could tell by Adam's expression that he didn't buy that comfortable theory either, whatever he said. Maybe he should be here."

"You're jumping the gun," Link said. "It's possible that Marisa's not ready to trust any of us."

She turned to face him, trying to ignore the pain in her shoulder when she turned her head. "I still don't know what you hope to accomplish. Trust you with what?"

Link met her gaze, and in that moment the battle was between the two of them. "Trust us with whatever you're holding back." Something that might have been concession appeared in his face. "And we tell you everything we know. Maybe, together, we can make sense of all this. If you're willing."

They were silent, all of them. Even Geneva, who looked as if she fought to keep from speaking.

*You can trust them,* Jessica had said. Heaven knew, she had to trust someone.

"All right," she said, and it seemed to her that the very room let out a sigh of relief.

"Good." Trey glanced around the table as if assembling a board meeting. "Well, we all know why we're here, then. Suppose I begin by recapping for Marisa what happened back in June."

Link stirred. "We can't be sure that's connected."

"No," Trey conceded. "But if there's a possibility, we need to put our cards on the table."

They'd be honest with her, in other words. And they trusted she'd be honest with them.

"Jessica came here in June to defend a young Amish neighbor of ours on a murder charge," Trey said. "As soon as it became evident that she was going to fight the case, she was subjected to harassment, vandalism and a series of threats."

Jessica looked as cool and collected as Marisa had always seen her, but she nodded slightly in agreement.

"The notes were marked with a peculiar design—something that looked like a hex sign of a bird. Leo was able to trace the history for us. It was the symbol of a secret society that vanished years ago."

Leo looked as if he'd like to contribute something at that point, but Trey swept on without giving him a chance.

"We eventually found the guilty person." Something that might have been grief darkened his eyes for a moment. "Someone I'd known and trusted most of my life. He'd killed our father, and he'd have killed me if Jessica and Leo hadn't interfered."

Jessica reached out to take his hand.

"In those last moments—well, I thought he was raving. He talked as if the Brotherhood was real and would punish him for involving it in his crimes." He caught Marisa's look and gave a wry grin. "Crazy, right? We thought he was off his rocker."

"Until we found something in Uncle Allen's journal." Link held out his hand to his brother, and Trey passed over the book she'd found in the library days ago. "You can see for yourself."

He opened the book to the first of

several sticky notes. Pink sticky notes, she saw. Undoubtedly Geneva's.

She bent over the page, reading the entry, frowning at the words Allen had written in the years after her mother's disappearance. Disjointed words, it seemed, talking about "them" and how they'd brought him trouble. How he couldn't sleep at night. A chill went through her. Because he was guilty? Was that what kept Allen awake nights? When he saw that she'd finished with each page, Link turned to the next one, holding the page flat. Most ramblings, none of it making a lot of sense, but all of it giving the impression of a man consumed with regret over something he'd been involved in.

When she'd read the final, sad entry, Marisa sat for a moment, staring at the faded writing. Nothing concrete, nothing to say outright that he'd had a hand in her mother's disappearance or knew who did.

And yet there had been something raw and distressing about the passages. It had clearly meant something to Allen Morgan.

She looked up then, glancing from one face to another. "Were there any more of these?" She held up the book.

"We searched every shelf," Trey said. "Maybe he stopped writing."

"Or maybe somebody got rid of them and just missed that one," Link added.

She considered that, still finding all this hard to believe. "What do you think it means? And how could it possibly connect with my mother's disappearance?"

"It might. Suppose for a moment that Allen and some others had decided to revive the Brotherhood," Trey said.

"Why?" Geneva sounded genuinely distressed. "Why would he want to do such a thing?"

"Mom, you know he wasn't just interested in the history of the area. He was fanatic about it. This Brotherhood idea was just the sort of crackpot scheme that would appeal to him."

"Goodness knows I didn't think very highly of Allen," Geneva said. "But there's no proof. And what would he want from something like that, anyway?"

"Power," Leo said. "That's what every secret organization is about, in essence.

It makes the insiders feel as if they have power over others. I'm sorry, Geneva, but you know as well as anyone how jealous Allen was of his older brother. He could never reconcile himself to coming second to Blake."

Geneva's brow wrinkled, her eyes filling with distress. "Blake wanted him to be a part of things. He did."

"I know." Leo patted her hand, his voice as tender as if they were the only two in the room. "There was just something twisted in Allen that wouldn't let him accept that. And I'm afraid Allen was involved in something."

Trey's eyes narrowed. "Why? What do you know, Leo?"

Leo folded his hands precisely in front of him. "It was years ago...thirty, probably. I didn't even remember it until this came up." He nodded toward the journal. "Allen stopped me after a historical society meeting one evening. Talked on and on about some research he'd been doing."

He gave an apologetic glance at Geneva. "You know how he could be when he got on one of his hobbyhorses. I'm afraid I was only half listening. In any event, he said he had a small group of like-minded individuals who were meeting together. He invited me to join them." He shrugged. "As I say, I wasn't really paying much attention, and frankly, I didn't have time for any more meetings. I begged off, and he never mentioned it again."

There was silence while they absorbed that. Marisa could only wonder that they were taking this so seriously. It all seemed so vague and faraway.

But then, so had her mother's disappearance.

"So there's a little confirmation that a group existed," Trey said.

"It fits with what Tom Sylvester said about a meeting at Allen's house that week," Link said.

Marisa had to readjust her thoughts from the distant past to their conversation with the construction boss. "I'd nearly forgotten that. You think it means something?"

"I think Tom wished he hadn't said it," Link said. "He backed away in a hurry when I asked who was there."

"I wish you'd listened a little closer, Leo." Trey swung toward the older man. "You didn't have any idea who those like-minded others were?"

"None." Leo spread his hands, empty. "It doesn't prove a thing, of course. But I can imagine a scenario where some people might be anxious that news of their activities not become public."

"You're not suggesting that they were doing anything illegal, are you?" Marisa could only think that sounded a little far-fetched for a group of history enthusiasts.

But Leo seemed to be taking it seriously. "The original purpose of the Brotherhood was to advance its members by any means possible, up to and including twisting the law to their advantage. I honestly don't know what they might have been thinking of, but it opens up some possibilities. They apparently met at Allen's house. Marisa's mother was the housekeeper there. Her suitcase was found there. Does that add up to something, or not?"

She found his words oddly compelling. Leo's calm, judicial persona seemed to add weight to the supposition. And did it fit with her mother's letter?

"Marisa?" Link's fingers brushed her hand. "What is it?"

Tell them, or not? But she already knew the answer to that.

"My mother's cousin, Elizabeth Yoder, gave me a letter she received from my mother shortly before she disappeared. A short note, saying she was afraid of something. She said she couldn't talk to my father. She said she knew Elizabeth would help if she were there. That she might have to turn to William and hope he would help her. That was all. But Elizabeth came to Springville a few days later to find that Barbara had disappeared."

"Did you tell Adam about this?" Link's hand tightened on hers.

"No." She didn't want to look at him.

"Why not? Don't you think that's important?" Frustration edged his voice.

She took a breath, trying to calm herself. "That comment about not being able to tell her husband. I thought the police would interpret that to mean she was afraid of him."

Their gazes met, crossing like swords. "It might mean that."

"And it might mean that she saw or heard something at your uncle's house that made her a threat to someone."

"To my uncle, you mean."

Leo cleared his throat. Marisa jerked her gaze away from Link's, to find that the others were watching them with varying degrees of surprise. She felt the heat flood her cheeks and wanted nothing more than to shove back her chair and walk out.

"There's no point in arguing among ourselves about what this might mean," Leo said. "I can certainly understand Marisa's concern for her father. But that just makes it more important that we reach the truth."

"And keep Marisa safe while we do it," Geneva added. She rose, coming around the table to Marisa and putting her arm around her gently, wary of her sore shoulder. "Don't you worry. We're going to deal with this, I promise. Together."

# *CHAPTER FIFTEEN*

Link glanced at Marisa's face as he drove down Maple Street. He hadn't told her where he was taking her...only that he wanted to show her something.

She hadn't protested. He had the sense that she'd had no emotional reserves left after that discussion this morning.

Now she moved, a bit restlessly. "Are you sure I'll be back in time to change before I go out with your mother?"

"Plenty of time." He still wasn't sure he liked the idea his mother had come up with. She had a dinner meeting of the Spring Township Historical Association at the inn tonight, and she'd decided Marisa should attend with her.

On the surface it was a logical idea. Any friends Uncle Allen possessed would probably be there. Marisa would be able to meet them, and Geneva would encourage them to talk.

He didn't know if he was more concerned about his mother's efforts to play detective or about Marisa. She'd already had a difficult twenty-four hours, and thanks to him, she was about to experience something that had to be emotional for her.

But it was too late to change his mind. He pulled to a stop in front of the house in which Marisa had lived as a child.

Marisa's gaze sharpened. She gripped the door handle.

He waited for an explosion, but it didn't come.

"Why did you bring me here?"

He made an effort to match her detached tone. "I thought it might help you remember when you were a child."

She stared down at her hands. "I'm not sure I want to remember."

"Is that why you haven't made an effort to see it?"

"I suppose so." She drew in an audible breath. "Well, now I've seen it."

"Not yet." He suspected she wasn't going to like this. "The house is unoccupied right now, up for sale. I got the lock-box code from the real-estate agent. We can go inside."

He could feel her resistance. He leaned toward her, feeling the by-now familiar surge of longing. It wasn't getting weaker. It was getting stronger. "I don't want you to be hurt." His voice showed too much emotion, but he couldn't help that. "I just want this to be over."

She closed her eyes for an instant. When she opened them, they were filled with tears, and his heart nearly broke. A faint smile trembled on her lips. "Guess I'm being a coward."

He couldn't stop himself. He had to touch her cheek. Her skin was warm and soft under his fingers. "You couldn't be a coward if you tried." His voice had grown husky.

For a long moment her gaze met his.

Then, suddenly, she nodded. "Let's go have a look."

Getting out, coming around the car, gave him a chance to regain his balance. He hoped.

He opened the gate in what had once been a white picket fence and frowned at its shriek. "Fred Whitney owns the house now, along with a few other rental properties. He's notorious for patching things together with binder twine and duct tape, then wonders why he can't get good renters."

Marisa glanced around the overgrown yard. "My mother had flower beds all along the fence. She'd be out there for hours, tending the plants." A spasm of what might have been pain crossed her face. "She let me help her. She showed me the differences between the different flowers, talking about them as if they were people."

Doubt was a lead weight in his stomach, but he tried to respond in kind. "You've seen my mother's gardens. She was the same. Once I pulled out a whole row of sweet peas, thinking they were weeds. She just laughed and helped me plant a new row."

She managed a more genuine smile at that. "She reminds me of my mother. Maybe that's why I can't ever say no to her."

"She has that effect on a lot of people." They moved toward the porch that ran the width of the frame house, and he took her arm as they went up the porch steps, avoiding a hole.

"The house was white when we lived here. With black shutters. There was a swing on the porch."

"It would have been a nice place to sit in the evening."

"It was." She looked at him as if he'd been sarcastic, and he realized his distaste had shown.

"I was reacting to how it looks now. Fred gives decent landlords a bad name. You'd never see the day when any of the Morgan rental properties would be in this condition."

"I didn't realize you had rental places." She stood back, giving him room to get at the lock box.

"Too many, Trey sometimes says. Our

grandfather and our great-grandfather, too, always believed money was safer invested in property. Now Trey's got the management of all of them, along with the other companies we own." He punched in the simple code—1, 2, 3. Took out the key.

He opened the door, but she stood for a moment, studying his face. "You don't handle any of that?"

"No." He wanted to leave it at that, but that would make it sound as if Trey had pushed him out. "It never seemed like my thing, so I left it to Trey. He's just like Dad, taking over naturally."

The front door opened directly into what was probably the living room. Marisa paused, putting up her good hand to touch her hair, smoothing it absently back over her shoulder.

His fingers tingled, as if he were doing it, feeling the soft curls running through his hands like water. *Back off,* he ordered his rebellious imagination. But he couldn't seem to lose the vivid sense of touching her.

"This was the living room." Luckily Marisa had no idea what he was thinking. "There was a braided rug on the floor, and I'd pretend the bands of the braid were roads for my dolls."

She sounded lost in the past, and the qualm of doubt seized him again. Was he doing the right thing, pushing her to relive the past? This little adventure had been Adam's idea, and at the moment he'd like to give Adam a solid punch on the jaw. If he tried, he'd probably end up flat on his back, but it might be worth it.

*Get her into the house,* Adam had said. *She'd go if you took her. She must remember something from that time, and there's no way of knowing what might help.*

Marisa moved, walking through the dusty, empty dining room. If she found it distressing, she didn't say so, just kept walking. She stopped when she reached the kitchen.

"This is the stove we had." She gestured toward the chipped surface of the gas range. "Mammi didn't like cooking on electric."

His heart did a stutter step at the sound of her voice. She'd slipped back into the time in her memory, probably quoting something she'd heard her mother say.

"It figures that Fred wouldn't have replaced it in over twenty years."

The urge to hit something grew. All very well for Adam to talk about helping Marisa remember. Adam wasn't the one taking the risk of hurting her.

She seemed stuck to the spot on the worn, old linoleum, and he touched her arm lightly. "Let's take a look upstairs."

She nodded, but as they started up the flight of stairs, he could feel her stress increasing.

"Is this the way you remember it?" Maybe if they talked it would dispel the tension.

She shook her head, pausing in the doorway of the first room. "This was Mammi's..." She stopped, seemed to realize what she'd said, and started again. "This was my parents' room. There was a quilt she'd made on the bed." She closed her eyes for a moment, as if visualizing it. "Lancaster Rose, she called it."

He nodded. "My mother has one in that pattern that an Amish friend made."

Tears filled her eyes again. She turned

quickly, nearly running into him as she hurried down the hall to the next room. He followed, heart thumping, trying to think of a suitable punishment for Adam.

"This was her sewing room." Marisa's voice was strained. "She had an old-fashioned treadle machine, and she made all my clothes." She closed her eyes for a moment. "Elizabeth and Mary Ann were talking about a quilting frolic. All the women of the family were coming to finish the quilt. My mother must have done that. Sometimes, when she was sewing, she'd look so sad. Maybe she was thinking about everything she gave up."

He touched her arm tentatively, not sure what to say or do. She was remembering, but she was hurting, too. "I'm sorry. I shouldn't have brought you here."

She shook her head, seeming to blink back the tears. "I'd rather remember, even if it hurts."

Down the hall to the last room, but when she reached the doorway, her energy seemed to leave her. He waited, letting her linger in the doorway, sensing that the heart of her emotion was here.

"My room," she said finally. "My father painted it yellow, because that was my favorite color." She crossed the floor, moving as if she walked through water. "My bed was here, by the window. If I couldn't go to sleep, I'd push the shade to the side and look out."

"I remember doing that. Kneeling on my bed and looking out at the stars." He came up behind her, needing to be close, not sure what he could do or say that would help.

Her fingers pressed on the window sill, and she gasped—a strangled breath that scared him.

"What is it? Are you all right?" He put his arm around her waist, needing to touch her.

Marisa put her palm to her cheek, cradling it as if to comfort herself. "I remember. I remember looking out one night. Mammi was there, under the oak tree." She pressed her finger against the pane, pointing. "She was with a man."

His mind spun. A man. A romantic triangle? Was Barbara's disappearance going to turn out to be that most mundane of matters?

"What man?" He forced the question out.

"I don't...I didn't recognize him. But he was Amish." A shiver went through her, and he drew her closer. "If I shut my eyes, I can see them. My mother and an Amish man, out there under the tree. They were arguing."

Her voice quivered, and he thought she was on the verge of tears. He took her hand, hoping just a human touch would be comforting.

"How do you know they were arguing?" He asked the question softly, afraid to push her.

She blinked, seeming to come back from a distance. "Body language, I suppose. Even a child can understand that." She rubbed her forehead. "That must be why it scared me so, seeing a man in Amish clothing in the yard at the Miller place. I connected it with that memory."

She swung toward him suddenly, and they were only inches apart. "Link, I just realized—it can't have been that long before she disappeared. I remember the doll I was holding, telling her everything would be all right. It was a cloth doll my mother had made for my birthday when I turned five that August."

Maybe this hadn't been such a bad idea after all. They were getting someplace, and it led away from his uncle.

And then her eyes filled with tears, and a shudder went through her.

"Marisa, I'm sorry..."

She shook her head, wiping the tears away with her fingers. "It's not that. I just...I remember hearing them quarrel. My mother and father, at night, when I was supposed to be asleep. I put my head under the pillow, but it was no use. I could still hear them."

"I'm sorry," he said again, longing to comfort her, feeling his own heart being wrenched open by her pain.

He pulled her against him. She didn't draw back, just settled her face against his shoulder with a sob. She'd accept comfort from anyone right now. He stroked her hair gently. This wasn't about love. It was about being there when she needed him.

"It'll be all right," he murmured, knowing he couldn't guarantee that. "It will."

They stood together for another moment. Then she drew back, fighting for composure. "I need..." Her lips trembled, and she pressed them together. "I need to leave."

She bolted from the room. He followed close behind her, ready to grab her if her headlong rush brought her to disaster.

Marisa hurried down the stairs, through the living room. She'd almost reached the door when she stopped. Stared at it.

"That day." Her voice was so choked that she sounded like a child trying not to cry. "I ran in from the school bus. I had a star on my paper. I wanted to show Mammi. But she wasn't here. She'd never not been here before."

He couldn't stand it. He reached for her and pulled her back into his arms, cradling her against him.

She sobbed, the tears spilling over, and buried her face in his shoulder again, holding on tight.

He held her close, murmuring softly, comforting her with words that probably didn't even make sense.

Who was he kidding? It was far too

late to worry about the risk of falling in love with her. He'd already fallen, so deep and hard he couldn't begin to think what he'd do about it.

Marisa entered the Springville Inn in Geneva's wake that evening, trying to concentrate on what was to come. There was no sense in reliving that visit to the house on Maple Street, at least not now. She'd probably be thinking about it, about Link, most of the night as it was.

The glass-paned door led into a wide, high-ceilinged center hallway. This must be the oldest part of the handsome Federal-style building.... The wings on either side looked newer, but blended with the brick core. To Marisa's right, an archway led into the inn's restaurant. To the left, an open area was furnished with groupings of love seats and chairs to encourage conversation.

And conversation there was. The historical group wasn't all that large—perhaps twenty to thirty people here altogether, but they made up in volume what they lacked in numbers.

"I don't know what those boys of mine

were thinking." Geneva paused, putting her hand on Marisa's arm. "If I came parading in here with the two of them when they've never shown the slightest interest in the historical association in the past, that would certainly rouse suspicion. But it's perfectly natural for me to bring you as my guest."

"I'm sure you're right." But Marisa did have a bit of sympathy for Trey and Link. They so obviously wanted to protect their mother, whether she wanted that protection or not.

"People will mingle with drinks and appetizers for about an hour before dinner," Geneva said. "That's the perfect opportunity to introduce you to anyone who might have been in Allen's confidence."

"Don't forget about Brad Metzger. I hope he'll be here tonight." The inn's assistant manager had been somewhat elusive when Link tried to pin him down for a talk.

"We'll find him. He usually makes an appearance at these events. If not, I'll make sure Owen Barclay rounds him up for us. Owen is the manager here, and he's very supportive of the association."

"Would he have known Allen?"

Geneva looked startled. "I suppose he would." She gave a slight shake to her head. "It's just hard to believe that any of these people might have guilty knowledge."

Surveying the well-dressed, obviously well-heeled group, many of them in the category euphemistically called seniors, Marisa had her own doubts. Still, a person might have helpful knowledge without having been involved.

"I hope Metzger will be open with us. Maybe it would be better to leave him to Link."

"Nonsense." Geneva squeezed her arm. "You have every reason for asking questions about that day. And with me there, he'll have to answer."

What might have sounded arrogant coming from anyone else was just the simple truth from Geneva. She was so used to her position in this community that she took it for granted. Metzger wouldn't refuse to cooperate if she was present.

"Geneva, how good to see you." The man who approached, both hands out to clasp Geneva's, was probably in his late forties, well-groomed and well dressed in a gray pinstripe suit that matched the artistic graying at his temples. He had the jovial, welcoming expression of the born extrovert.

"Goodness, Owen, you make it sound as if I haven't been around for years. You know I never miss a meeting." She evaded the embrace he obviously intended with what seemed the ease of long practice. "I'd like to introduce my guest. Marisa, this is Owen Barclay, manager of the Springville Inn."

"Ms. Angelo, isn't it?" He clasped the hand Marisa offered in both of his. "I've heard about your visit. One of the perils of small-town life, I'm afraid. Everyone knows your business."

She smiled, extricating her hand from his overlong grip. "Sometimes I think everyone knows more than I do."

"Marisa would really appreciate talking to anyone who remembers her mother." Geneva seized the opportunity. "I'm sure you do, Owen."

"I?" Barclay took a half step back. "Why would you think I'd know her?"

Was that alarm in his eyes? Marisa couldn't be sure.

"She was my brother-in-law's housekeeper for a time. You must have seen her when you went to meetings at Allen's place." Geneva threw herself into investigating with a little too much gusto.

"Meetings?" The dark eyes were veiled now, giving nothing away. "I'm not sure I ever attended any meetings there. Historical-association events, would they have been?"

"Perhaps." Geneva gave him what she probably hoped was an enigmatic smile.

"I can't say I remember—ah, I see those appetizer trays need refilling. Let me get the girls working on them." He faded toward the back precincts of the inn.

Geneva stared after him. "You know, I think I actually unnerved him. I wouldn't have believed it of Owen. He's always seemed so careful of his reputation."

Marisa squeezed her arm. "We shouldn't discuss him here. Someone might be listening."

"Nonsense," Geneva said briskly, not

bothering to lower her voice at all. "They're all too entranced with the sound of their own voices."

Geneva might prove to be a dangerous ally if she kept on this way. Fortunately, Leo Frost approached, and the twinkle in his eyes told Marisa he'd overheard.

"I'll have you know I prefer the sound of your voice to my own," he said, taking Geneva's arm. "Ladies, you look as if you need drinks and hors d'oeuvres."

"An iced tea for me." Geneva allowed herself to be led toward the table set up with beverages and appetizers. "I must say, Leo, that Owen Barclay—"

"Who else should I meet?" Marisa said, trying to head off anything too indiscreet.

"There are several old-timers in the association who knew Allen." Leo caught on quickly. Apparently he was used to dealing with Geneva. "I'll see who I can round up." He slipped into the crowd.

Marisa picked up a glass of iced tea from the table. "Let's save any discussion until afterward, all right? That way we won't have to—" She stopped, her stomach lurching. "Isn't that the district attorney?"

"Preston Connelly?" Geneva peered around. The DA stood in front of the brick fireplace, one elbow on the mantel, gesturing as he talked to a circle of people. "Probably. He used to be more active in the association. Now he generally just shows up when he's running for reelection."

"I hope that's not what you say about me." The woman who spoke was probably about Geneva's age, but where Geneva was all quicksilver and charm, this woman looked solid and sensible... like someone's grandmother, who would be more comfortable in the kitchen baking cookies. "Geneva, I see you're as indiscreet as ever. At least you had sense enough not to wear blue jeans to this event."

"Give me credit for some manners, Judith." Geneva waved a hand toward Marisa. "I'd like to introduce Marisa Angelo. Marisa, this is Judge Judith Waller. For all I know, she may be up for reelection."

The woman extended a strong, square

hand. "I'm not, as it happens. It's a pleasure to meet you, Marisa. I've heard
about you." She must have detected
something in Marisa's expression, because she gave a rueful smile. "Sorry.
That's a terrible thing to say to someone
on first meeting, but news does get
around."

"So I've heard." She was still getting
used to the idea that this maternal-look-
ing woman was a judge.

"I hoped Geneva would bring you tonight. I remember your mother." She
eyed Marisa. "You don't favor her a great
deal."

"I guess not. How did you know my
mother?" This was the first non-Amish
person, other than the Morgans, who'd
admitted knowing Barbara, and she
couldn't imagine how their paths would
have crossed.

"I met her when I went to some meeting or other at Allen Morgan's place.
She made the best apple walnut cake
I'd ever had, and I asked her for the recipe. I still make it, especially this time of
year when local apples are in."

As far as she could remember, she'd

never met a judge before, but she'd certainly never expect to be discussing recipes with one. "I'd love to have that recipe, if it wouldn't be too much trouble."

"Not at all." She waved her drink, which sloshed just short of spilling. "You're staying at Geneva's, aren't you? I'll email it to her."

"Good," Geneva said briskly. "About those meetings at Allen's place—what did you say those were?"

"I didn't." Judge Waller smiled. "But as I recall, we were discussing plans for an historic display at the library for Founders' Day. Allen wasn't much use on the practical matters, of course, but he did have a solid grasp of the early history of the township, to say nothing of a better library than the historical association."

"He never could resist an old book," Geneva said. "Acted as if they were his children."

Judge Waller nodded. "Speaking of which, I understand Lincoln is clearing the house. You will ask him to donate those reference books to the association, won't you?"

She was looking right at Marisa, as if assuming that she had anything to say about it.

"I...I think he's mentioned something like that. Geneva would really be the one to talk to him."

"He'll consider doing that," Geneva said. "After we've gone through all of them, of course. He's brought the most interesting ones to the house...Allen's old diaries and that sort of thing." Her voice seemed to ring above the surrounding hum of talk.

Marisa promptly choked on her iced tea. Maybe just as well, since that created a diversion. Geneva really was a loose cannon, announcing something like that here, of all places. She knew perfectly well there was only one journal.

Marisa realized Leo was the person patting her back and attempted a recovery. "I'm fine. Just went down the wrong way."

"Would you like a glass of water? Geneva, why don't you see if you can catch a waitress and get a glass of water for Marisa?" Leo's effort to distract Geneva was a little blatant, but it seemed to work. Geneva scurried off toward the kitchen.

"Trying to keep her discreet, Leo?" Judge Waller chuckled. "Good luck with that. Anyway, everyone in the township knows that Barbara Angelo's suitcase was found in the wall of Allen Morgan's house, and half the small boys are hoping to find a body. Naturally you're interested in anyone who might have been there around that time."

Here was plain speaking with a vengeance. Before Marisa could word a response, Leo intervened. "It's a good thing we don't elect judges based on tact, Judith."

She shrugged. "I call 'em like I see 'em. Always have. Still, Marisa, I forgot about Barbara being your mother. I apologize."

"That's all right." But if the woman valued plain speaking, she shouldn't object to a straightforward question. "Do you have any ideas about what happened?"

Ms. Waller smiled, displaying a strong set of teeth. "Since the matter could conceivably come before me officially, I'd better have no ideas at all. But I do have a word of advice." She included Leo in her glance. "Don't play detective. If there is a case, let the police and the district attorney's office handle it. Adam Byler is quite competent, and while Preston Connelly is a bit too political for my taste, he does know his job." She paused, her glance again going from Leo to Marisa. "Poking into it yourselves... Well, that might prove to be dangerous."

Seizing a drink, she forged a path into the crowd, which parted in front of her as she went.

Marisa turned to Leo. "Was that conversation as odd as I thought it was?"

"Rather strange." He was frowning. "But at the moment, I'm wondering where Geneva has gotten to. Do you see her?"

Marisa scanned the room, nerves jangling. Geneva...what on earth was she up to now? Link had been right to be concerned about how this would go. "There she is, over by the hotel desk." Her relief faded when she realized what Geneva was doing. She was deep in conversation with a man whose suit lapel bore a Springville Inn identification pin. There was no doubt in Marisa's mind that it was Brad Metzger.

Leo spotted her as well and gave an exasperated snort. "That woman will be the death of me. We'd better get over there."

When they reached Geneva, she had the grace to look slightly embarrassed.

"Here she is now. Marisa, this is Bradley Metzger. He's the young man Tom Sylvester was telling you about, and he'll be happy to talk with you."

How much had Geneva revealed in her artless chatter already? "That's good of you, Mr. Metzger."

"Brad, please. As I told Mrs. Morgan, I'm glad to help in any way I can." He gave a practiced smile that didn't quite reach his eyes. Slight and blond, he had a boyish look that belied his age, which must be over forty. He certainly didn't fit her image of a construction worker.

"Thank you. I understand you worked on the project at Allen Morgan's house that September my mother disappeared."

He nodded. "That's right. I was just out of high school, actually, and construction was a stopgap job until I found something more suited to my talents."

"I see." Obviously he considered working at the inn better than working with his hands. "According to Mr. Sylvester, on the day that my mother vanished, he was called away. He left you and another man to continue work on the drywall." Maybe it wasn't tactful to bring up that Sylvester had expected them to finish it.

"That's right. Len Barnhart and I. The two of us stayed until quitting time."

"Was my mother there the whole time?"

He glanced down, lashes hiding his eyes. "I'm not sure. We were working in the addition, you see, and she was someplace in the house. I remember she was in the kitchen for a while, because she brought us a pitcher of lemonade."

"And did you finish the drywall?" Leo put the question.

"Not all of it. That was too big a job for two men." This last was added quickly, as if someone had questioned it.

"Was my mother still there when you left?" She held her breath. This might

be as close as she'd come to recon-
structing that last afternoon.

He frowned, seeming to concentrate.
"Well, I'm not positive, you understand.
I know she was there when we were
having lunch, because that's when she
brought the lemonade. And she must
have been there a bit later, because she
had a visitor."

"A visitor?" Her heart jolted.

He nodded. "I happened to be taking
a smoke break, standing at the window.
Somebody was outside, talking to her
through the kitchen door."

"Did you see who it was?" Urgency
must have shown in her voice.

"He was turned away from me, so I
didn't get a really good look. About all I
can say is that it was a man. Oh, and he
was Amish."

Amish. Her breath caught. Barbara
had told her cousin she was in trouble.
She'd brought a suitcase with her to
work that day. And an Amish man had
come to see her that afternoon. Ezra
Weis? Her cousin William? Or someone
else Marisa didn't know about?

# CHAPTER SIXTEEN

Link paced across the living room and back again, glancing out the front windows as he passed, watching for headlights announcing that Mom and Marisa were back. Stupid, to be so stressed about their being out at night. This was Springville, not New York City.

Given the things that had been happening, he didn't actually find that very comforting. Bad things could hit innocent people anywhere, anytime. Nobody knew that better than he did.

His thoughts slid backward in time... back to Afghanistan. When they'd started rebuilding the school, they'd been told that four young girls had been killed in the original attack.

His heart twisted. Innocents, living in a dangerous place. At least he and his men had been professionals, out to do a difficult job.

The nightmares hadn't come in over a week, maybe because he'd been so preoccupied with the present danger. Was that the cure for post-traumatic stress— to get involved in something equally dangerous? He'd hate to think so.

*Please...* But he found he didn't know where that instinctive prayer was going. *Please let me forget?* That was the coward's way out. *Please protect Mom and Marisa?* That he could say with a whole heart.

He made another circuit of the living room, earning a glare from Trey, who was trying, or pretending, to read the newspaper.

"Mom won't thank you for wearing a hole in that rug." Trey tossed the paper aside. "What are you so jittery about? Nothing can happen to them at the historic-association dinner except that they might get bored into a coma."

"I'd have said nothing could happen to Marisa at the Miller's guest house. And it's a dark ride back from town. I should have taken them and picked them up."

"You offered, remember? And Mom said that when she got old enough to require a chauffeur, she'd hire her own."

"Right." The memory of his mother's expression provided a moment of humor, but it was short-lived. "You know Mom. Do you actually imagine she's being discreet? We have to face the possibility that someone at that meeting tonight could have been involved in Barbara Angelo's disappearance."

Could have been the person who attacked Marisa. His hands clenched. He'd been a fool to put his arms around her this afternoon. A fool to let himself think he loved her.

At least he hadn't said those words to her. It was bad enough saying them to himself.

"You can relax," Trey said. "I see the reflection of the lights."

Link spun, staring out the window.

Sure enough, the car was coming down the driveway. He suppressed the urge to go out and meet them. He'd been giving himself away far too much where his feelings for Marisa were concerned.

He heard the slam of the car doors, followed by their footsteps crossing the porch.

"We're home." Mom sounded exuberant. "I knew you boys would be waiting up for us."

"It's only nine-thirty, Mom." Trey gave her a quick hug.

"Really? I'd have said that speech lasted for at least three hours."

"It wasn't that bad." Marisa followed them into the living room. "I found it rather interesting."

"That's because you haven't heard Gerald Price's lecture on the Underground Railroad several hundred times," Mom said. "You'd think he'd want to freshen up his research, at least."

"Enough with the speech critique. How did you make out?" He looked questioningly at Marisa. She looked tired. "You're hurting, aren't you?"

"I'll take something. I'll be fine." She

sat down in the corner of the sofa with a barely suppressed sigh. "As for the more crucial aspect of the evening... well, it was interesting, wasn't it?" She glanced at his mother.

"It certainly was." Mom perched on the arm of the sofa, looking like a hummingbird pausing in flight. "Everyone we talked to acted suspiciously. I wouldn't be surprised to learn they were all in on Allen's little group."

"I'm sure that's an exaggeration, and you can't go around saying things like that," Trey said. "I don't want to have Jessica defending you on a libel suit."

Mom waved that away. "Owen Barclay certainly found an excuse to dash away when I asked him about meetings at Allen's house. Why would he do that if he didn't know anything?"

"Probably because he thought you'd turned dotty," Trey said. "You mean you came right out and asked him?"

"She did." A ghost of a smile flickered across Marisa's face. "And you should have heard her with the judge."

"Judith Waller? Is she still active in the association?" He remembered Judge

Waller from his misspent youth, when the thought of appearing before her and trying to explain himself had discouraged some of his crazier ideas.

"Somewhat." Mom's forehead wrinkled. "You know, that was odd. She jumped right into talking about Marisa's mother before I'd had a chance to bring it up."

"I'm sure it's just because she knew who I was." Marisa rubbed her shoulder absently.

"You ought to go to bed," he said roughly.

"I'm fine." She smiled at him, and behind the smile he read the memory of those moments when he'd held her and comforted her as she wept.

"No, but Judith did mention attending a meeting at Allen's house, saying that was where she'd met Barbara. She claimed it was a historical-association committee," she added darkly.

"Could have been," Trey said. "You're always going to committee meetings. Why shouldn't she?"

"Well, I think—"

It was a sign of how wiped out she

was that Marisa actually interrupted his mother. "Brad's revelation was more important, it seems to me." The fine lines around her eyes deepened, and he knew it wasn't anything good. "He remembered that day. He claimed that sometime in the afternoon, he saw my mother talking with an Amish man outside the kitchen door."

"I see." He kept his voice noncommittal with an effort and sat down next to her on the sofa. "Did he recognize the man?"

"No. Apparently he didn't get a look at his face. But if she took her suitcase with her that day..." Her voice died out, as if she didn't want to think about what that meant.

A love triangle? But that wasn't the only possibility. "We know she was frightened about something," he said. "And we know she was considering asking William Zook for help. It's possible he came to talk to her there."

"That's true." The look she gave him contained gratitude, probably because he hadn't jumped to the obvious conclusion.

"Or it might have been Ezra Weis," Trey said. "We know he was hanging around the Miller place at night. He could be afraid of what Marisa might find out about him."

Marisa's hand clenched...the only sign that prospect upset her. "It's possible. But since she told Elizabeth she was thinking of contacting William, that seems more likely."

"Either way, I'm thinking it's something Adam should be told," Trey said. "He can question people more effectively than we can."

Link moved his hand on the sofa, so that it brushed Marisa's, feeling the tension radiating from her. "Trey may be right. You said William wouldn't talk to you, but I don't think he'll refuse to talk to Adam."

He sensed her resistance. Finally she nodded.

"All right. Tomorrow. I'm too tired to think right now."

"Sure thing," Trey said. "Before you go up to bed, there's something I've been meaning to show the two of you. When we were talking about the raven symbol, I forgot I still had this. It's the pendant Bobby Stephens had, the one he apparently thought was his connection to the Brotherhood."

He held out something that dangled from his hand. Link reached for it, feeling an odd revulsion as it touched his hand. He stared at the stylized symbol, memory stirring.

"With this new information, maybe we don't have to worry about—"

"Where did you get this?" Link rasped the words, hardly able to form them.

"I told you. Bobby had it. What's wrong? You look like you've seen a ghost."

"Not a ghost." He had better control of himself now, but dread was pooling in the pit of his stomach. "But I've seen this before, or one just like it."

"What? Where?" Trey sounded rattled, and Trey didn't rattle easily.

Link sucked in a breath. "You remember the day I climbed down into the quarry? The day you had to pull me out?"

Trey nodded. Link could feel Marisa's gaze on him, but he didn't want to look at her, afraid she might guess at his half-formed fear.

"I made it as far as the mouth of the cave before I realized I couldn't get any farther. Libby kept yelling at me to come back, but I was delaying, not wanting to give up. I started looking around for something to prove I'd been there. That's when I spotted it. A tile, just like this one, half buried in the mud on the path outside the cave."

"What? Are you sure?" Trey grabbed the tile, staring at it as if it had answers. "What happened to it?"

"I stuck it in my pocket. Then I realized I couldn't get back up, and Libby started getting upset. I think it kicked around in my dresser for a while, but I don't remember." He met his brother's gaze. "More important, what was it doing there?"

Trey didn't speak for a moment, but Link could tell that his brother's thoughts were running along the same train his were. If this crazy story of the Brotherhood was connected to Barbara's disappearance—face it, to her death—then...

"How could anyone get a body down

there?" Trey's voice was as harsh as his had been.

Marisa gasped, her hand going up to cover her lips.

"I'm sorry," Trey said instantly. "I didn't mean—"

"Yes. You did." Her voice was steadier than he'd have imagined it could be. "You think my mother died that day. You're probably right. I don't see any other explanation."

His mother moved closer to Marisa, putting her arm around her gently. "If that's what you think, well, it would have been possible. There used to be an easy path down into the quarry. After it was closed by a rock slide, we put up the barricades."

"When, Mom?" Trey's tone was urgent. "When did that rockslide happen?"

He saw the startled realization in his mother's face.

"Why…I don't know, not exactly. But your father discovered it while he was taking a walk, and he came back and told me. I remember…" She got up suddenly and hurried out of the room.

"Where is she going?"

He patted Marisa's hand. "To look for Dad's property notebook from that month. He was meticulous about things like that. He'd have jotted the information down when he discovered it."

His mother was back in moments, holding the familiar brown leather notebook. She flipped through pages and then stopped, her face tightening.

"Here it is. 'Rocks have blocked the quarry path. No point in trying to clear it. Put up a temporary barricade, but I'll get someone to fix a more permanent one.'" She looked up. "It's dated September 30 of that year."

"So someone could have..." Trey began, stopping when Link shook his head.

He cleared his throat. "We'll have to check it out. Maybe it's best to see for ourselves before we get a full-scale police operation going."

Link nodded. His fingers wrapped around Marisa's, holding on tight. "We'll have a look first thing in the morning."

Marisa walked beside Jessica through the orchard the next morning. Ahead of them, Trey and Link wore hiking boots and carried ropes looped over their shoulders.

She glanced at Jessica's somber expression. "Is this dangerous?" She kept her voice low, not wanting Link to hear.

"Not really, as long as they're careful." Geneva, close behind them, answered. "I still wish they'd let me bring the dog. He may be old, but he'd sound the alert if there are any snakes around."

There was something else to worry about. "Maybe we should have called Adam and let him handle this."

"If we had, the news would have been all over the township in about a minute." Jessica's forehead wrinkled, and Marisa realized that she was worried, too. "Trey didn't want a stampede of people in here until we know for sure if…"

She let that trail off, but Marisa knew what she'd intended to say.

"If my mother's body is there. That's what we're all thinking, isn't it?"

Jessica shook her head. "The rational part of me says we're building a lot on something that might be pure coincidence."

"But it all fits," Geneva said. "Allen's

comments in his journal, his obvious fear and anguish over something, the tile Link found, the date of the rock slide."

"Not really evidence." Jessica's lawyer's outlook was evident. "But, yes, we have to look into it."

They fell silent. Marisa suspected that each of the other women was preoccupied with her own worries over where this was taking them, as she was. If they found nothing, that would simply be another dead end in a series of dead ends.

And if they did find what they all so obviously feared, she'd be plunged into grief and confronted with ever more serious problems. *Where are you, Dad? Oh, Lord, I'm so worried about him. Please...*

But did she really want to pray that she'd hear from him? She didn't have much confidence in her ability to keep that from the police, and what would happen then?

The woods closed around them, and they were forced into single file. The trees were alive with birdsong and movement, seeming to clash with the fear that hung over her. From what she remembered of that earlier trip into the woods, it wasn't far to the quarry path. Her chest tightened, as if her heart were being compressed. They'd know. Before long, they would know.

Link's tension was evident in every move he made. He gestured toward the fallen log where she'd been sketching the day the shots were fired. Showing Trey the spot, she supposed. She expected to feel that fear again, but her apprehension was completely absorbed by what they'd find at the end of this trek.

"I've never seen the quarry," Jessica said. "Trey said he'd bring me up here sometime this fall, but I didn't expect it to be under these circumstances." She touched Marisa's hand lightly. "I'm sorry. I can imagine what you must be feeling."

"For the most part, I just want to know. No matter how bad it is, knowing is better than wondering."

"I've often thought that about those poor people whose teenage children run away," Geneva said. "You read about it, and I can't imagine how that must be, always wondering, never knowing."

"If we do find something..." She let

that trail off, her throat closing on the word. "I don't know what will happen then."

"We'll have to call the police," Jessica said. "And I can just imagine what Adam will have to say about our interference. They'll launch a full-scale investigation, probably bringing in a forensics team from the state police, since Spring Township doesn't have those facilities. They'll rope off the area, but it will be a magnet for the curious, I'm afraid."

The men turned onto the quarry path and stopped, waiting for them. When Marisa reached him, Link gave her a tight smile that was probably meant to be reassuring.

"It's another thirty yards or so to the quarry. Don't go near the edge until we've checked it out. It may have crumbled since the last time anyone was up here." He gave his mother a stern look, probably thinking her the most likely person to dart ahead.

"We'll behave," Geneva said. "Let's get this over with."

Her sentiments exactly. As they started down the path, she managed to grab

Link's hand. "Are you sure you should be doing this?"

"I'm fine." His fingers tightened on hers and then released. "Better us than a stranger." He moved on in Trey's wake.

Was it? From her perspective, yes, but Jessica had probably understated the police reaction should they actually find what they feared.

They emerged into what at first seemed a clearing in the woods. Then her eyes adjusted to what she was seeing.

The quarry had probably been a harsh scar on the landscape at one time, but now the trees and scrub growth crowded in on it, softening its edges. It was an irregular oblong, probably less than a hundred yards wide at the widest point. The trees on the opposite side wore their autumn colors.

"They quarried here in my husband's grandfather's day," Geneva said. "It's been closed a long time."

Trey, holding onto a tree, leaned forward. "A little water at the bottom, but that's all. It's not too steep down to the cave, but the path is almost entirely gone. We'll need the ropes."

*Be safe,* she found herself saying silently over and over as the two men rigged up the ropes around a sturdy tree and put on safety helmets. *Please, be safe.*

Geneva's hand closed over hers. "I know," she said softly. "But Trey won't let him take any risks."

She nodded. Was she that obvious? It seemed so.

There couldn't be a relationship, she reminded herself, watching as Link prepared to go over the edge. Too many things stood between them. But he had held her when she wept for her lost childhood, and she had known then that she cared, maybe too much. It wouldn't be easy to say goodbye.

Trey raised a reassuring hand and then followed Link over the edge. Marisa heard a sharp intake of breath from Jessica, but then Jessica smiled and shook her head.

"I'm being foolish. It's just a simple rock scramble, and they have the ropes on if they should miss a step. There's nothing to worry about."

They'd both keep telling themselves

that, but Marisa didn't know how much good it was doing. A sharp breeze tugged at her windbreaker, and she zipped it up. She'd been warm walking up here, but now she felt the autumn chill in the air.

Geneva moved cautiously to one side of the spot where they'd gone over. "I think we can see from here, unless you'd rather not watch."

Better to know, she repeated, and edged into position next to Geneva. She was right: the two men were visible from here. She fixed her gaze on the top of Link's helmet, as if she could reach out across the space between them and keep him safe.

"The top part is the worst," Geneva said. "The path is completely gone. Once they get down another twenty feet or so, it should be easier going."

Now that it had been pointed out, Marisa could pick out the spot where the path had led downward. The top part was a steep drop, but they were nearly past that already. What had that been like for a child when Link had tried to climb down? She couldn't imagine. Geneva must have been terrified when she'd found out. But apparently the path had been there then.

Marisa followed the remnants of the path with her gaze. There was the cave they'd spoken of...a dark shadow surrounded by rocks. They'd made a guess that if someone were trying to hide a body, that would be the easiest place. But not the only place. A shudder went through her. There must be a couple of acres of tumbled rocks and brambles. How could they possibly search every bit of it? A body could lie there for a long time without being found.

Her hand was pressing into the tree trunk so hard that the bark was scoring her hand. She rubbed her palm, not daring to take her gaze off Link.

He was ahead of Trey. He reached the cave mouth and stopped, waiting for his brother. They seemed to confer for a moment. Then they turned on flashlights, bent over and disappeared into the cave.

Disappeared. Her mouth was dry. Vanished like Mammi.

She shook her head, not letting the

thought take root. That was stupid. Link was safe. She knew that. He was fine.

"Why is it taking so long?" She didn't realize she'd spoken aloud until she'd heard the words. "I thought Trey said the cave was quite small."

"It narrows down back quite a ways," Geneva said. "Unless it's changed since the last time I was in there...but of course that was over thirty years ago. It may have changed in that time. The rocks may have shifted."

Could they shift while the men were inside? That was yet another possibility to fear. The safety helmets were probably meant to protect them from that.

She clasped her hands together. Surely they were taking too long. Did that mean they'd found something? Or that they'd found nothing and were carefully searching for any sign?

*Please, please...*

The quarry was still, as if even the birds had stopped singing to wait in silence with them. The breeze rustled faintly in the trees. An orange leaf fluttered down, brushing her face before it drifted over the edge of the quarry and disappeared.

Something stirred in the blackness of the cave mouth. Shadows broke and re-formed, and Trey and Link came stumbling out into the sunlight again.

Link looked up, as if he searched for her. When she saw his face, she didn't have to ask. She knew. He would only look that way if they'd found her mother's body.

# CHAPTER SEVENTEEN

Trey was pulling out his cell phone almost before the men reached the top of the quarry. His conversation with the police was just background noise to Marisa, with all her attention focused on Link.

He stood for a moment, leaning against a tree as if for support. Then he came toward her, his face drawn.

"I'm sorry," he said simply.

She nodded, pressing her lips together, wanting to be sure her voice was under control before she spoke.

"Could you tell if...if it was my mother?"

Pain tightened his face. "There was

no way to be sure. I guess the forensics people will have to tell us. But..."

"But who else could it be?" She felt oddly detached, as if she floated above, looking down on the woman who was coming to terms with the fact that her mother had been murdered.

"I'm sorry," he said again. He reached out to her. Maybe he intended to hold her again, as he had the previous day.

But Geneva hurried over to her just then, putting her arms around Marisa. "I'm so sorry, my dear. I know you half expected it, but even so, it's a shock. We should get you back to the house."

"Adam said everyone should stay right here," Trey said. His face was nearly as ashen as Link's. "He's furious, of course. It probably wouldn't be a good idea to disobey him at this point."

"Well, I don't think we have to stay glued to this spot," Geneva said tartly. "At least let's get away from the edge."

They settled on a fallen tree trunk, worn almost smooth by the weather. "Are you all right, my dear?" Geneva sat next to her.

"I think so." She watched Link, who'd

propped himself against a tree again as he talked to his brother. "I hope Link didn't hurt himself. He's moving stiffly."

"I noticed," Geneva said softly. "But he won't thank either of us for mentioning it. I imagine Adam will get here quickly, and we can get back to the house."

That proved to be overly optimistic. They heard the police siren in a few minutes, but nothing seemed to move fast after that. She sat in a haze of misery, trying not to think as Adam, his temper seemingly under tight control, went over and over the situation.

After he'd had everything they could tell him, a lengthy discussion ensued over how to get men and equipment to the scene.

"Your best bet might be to bring what you need on ATV's or at least four-wheel-drive vehicles," Trey said. "You used to be able to drive right down the railroad bed, but it's grown over a lot since then. You can pick it up down at Mausteller's Corner."

"Near your uncle's place," Adam said.

"That's right." Trey's voice was even, but his fists were clenched.

Near Allen Morgan's place. Well, that wasn't so surprising, was it? That house was the last place her mother had been seen that day.

She tried to close her mind, not letting herself visualize what might have happened. But it was useless. The images crept into her mind anyway.

Link stretched, hand on his back, and grimaced. Her heart contracted. He'd hurt himself climbing down there. They should have realized he wasn't up to that yet.

Adam turned to him. "Link, how about taking the others back to the house? You can call Leo Frost, if you want, but don't talk to anyone else. Trey will stay here in case we need any directions for the state-police boys."

So Adam had noticed that grimace of pain. He was being tactful about it.

Link gave a quick nod and came toward them. In moments they were walking back the way they'd come.

The trip down went faster than the walk up had. Even so, Link was dragging by the time they reached the house. He slumped into a chair in the kitchen as soon as they walked in the door.

Geneva and Jessica exchanged glances. "I'll go and call Leo," Jessica said. "Come along and talk to him, Geneva. Maybe you can keep him from overreacting. He's not going to be happy about this exploit. I can just hear him. 'And you, an officer of the court.'"

Geneva nodded. "I'll tell him I dragged you along, protesting the whole way." They headed toward the living room, apparently having decided that she was the one to deal with Link.

She wasn't. He didn't look up when she sat down next to him.

"You're hurting. Can I get you something?"

He did look at her then, and the torment in his eyes cut her to the heart. "Nothing that will help."

Her heart twisted at the words. "Pain medication, or—"

"No." He snapped off the word. "I'm all right. You're the one who must be hurting. I hoped we wouldn't find anything."

She took a breath, trying to steady herself. "I've been given comforting lies for the past twenty-three years, and it hasn't helped. Please, just tell me what it was like."

He looked down at his hands, clasped on the table. He didn't speak. She put her hand over his, feeling his tension.

"Please," she whispered.

He moved then, wrapping her hand in his, giving her a bit of his strength and warmth. "The cave is smaller than I remembered." His lips twitched without humor. "Or maybe I'm bigger. We had to crawl back into it." His grip tightened painfully. "She...the body was clear at the back."

She forced herself to think of it rationally. "After all this time, there wouldn't be much."

"No." He sounded relieved that she understood that. "Just...bones. We didn't touch anything. The forensics investigators are going to have a fit as it is."

"You didn't see anything that would tell if it was my mother?" Her voice quavered on the words despite her best efforts.

Link shook his head. "Nothing. Just... whoever it was, they didn't die naturally.

Even without touching it, we could see that there had been a blow to the head."

She took a shaky breath, and it caught on a sob.

"Marisa..."

She shook her head. "I'm glad you told me. Honestly."

He nodded, but still he gripped her hand so fiercely that she felt the bones might crack.

"Is there something more?"

"No."

She put her free hand on his shoulder, and he winced away from her touch. "Link, you are hurt. You should see a doctor."

"Leave it alone." He let go of her suddenly, and her hand was numb. He shoved his chair back, lurching to his feet. "This isn't anything a doctor can help."

She rose, facing him, her mind stumbling through possibilities. "Something is obviously wrong. If you—"

She stopped, realizing what it was, what it had to be, and berated herself for a fool not to have seen it.

Say something, or let it rest? Instinct

told her to get it out in the open. She reached a tentative hand out to him.

"It reminded you. The cave, the body... It was like being trapped in the wreckage again, knowing your friends—"

"Don't." He knocked her hand away with a sudden, violent movement. "Don't, Marisa. I don't want your help. I don't want anyone's help."

He turned, nearly stumbled and righted himself. He walked away. He didn't look back.

She pressed her palm against her chest. Could you actually feel your heart breaking? It seemed so.

She cared so much. Too much. Maybe even loved him. But he was using his grief and guilt as a shield to keep everyone out, and if there was a way past that, she didn't think she'd be the one to find it.

The study door had been closed for nearly an hour, blocking Link out of Adam's questioning of Marisa. What could they find to ask her? She didn't know anything about how that body came to be in the cave.

He crossed the living room to the archway and glared at the closed door. Closing him out, just as he'd closed Marisa out earlier.

What else could he have done? Crawling into that cave, feeling the weight of rock and earth pressing down on him from above—it had brought back all those feelings, amplifying them until it had been all he could do not to panic.

And convincing him that backing away from her was his only choice, for both their sakes.

He yanked his thoughts from that to focus on the closed door. This was outrageous. The only comfort was that Jessica was in there, as well. When the DA arrived, she had quickly announced that she represented Marisa as well as the family, ensuring that she be present for any questioning.

Putting a hand on the archway eased the pain in his ribs, but not the pain in his heart. Everything would come out now. He couldn't protect any of the people he loved from whatever ugliness was headed their way.

The door opened. Marisa emerged,

looking spent. She started toward the living room but checked when she saw him.

He suppressed the words of concern that sprang to his lips. Far better that he not express the caring he felt.

"You were in there a long time. What on earth did they suspect you'd know about this?"

She shook her head, giving a small sigh. "You'd think there wouldn't be anything left to ask me, but they seemed to find things."

"You look as if you'd better sit down." He gestured toward the sofa.

She hesitated, as if she'd make some excuse to escape, but then crossed the room and sat down. "Same questions about my father. About anyone else who might have been around my mother at the time she...disappeared. 'I can't remember' isn't the answer they want to hear."

"They can't be sure that...well, that the remains are those of your mother." He took a chair at a safe distance from her.

"Apparently the tests will be rushed

through, so they'll know quite soon. The initial exam confirmed what you thought—a blow to the head, severe enough to kill." Tears filled her eyes, and she dashed them away impatiently. "I'm convinced, and I think Adam is as well, that it's my mother. This isn't going to go away soon, is it?"

"I guess not, unless they discover some physical evidence that points to the killer."

"He's gotten away with it all these years. He must have felt safe, until I came back."

"Your father—"

"My father had nothing to do with it." Her temper flared in an instant. "How can you even think that, with all that's happened here when he's been miles away?"

"That's not what I was going to say." He kept his voice even, although he wasn't as convinced of her father's innocence as she was. "Much as I hate the idea of publicity, this story is strange enough to be picked up by the national news, I'd think. So hopefully your dad will see that."

The anger drained from her face. "Yes...yes. I think you're right. I hope so."

"I know you're worried about him." They were talking like two polite strangers. He hated that, but it was better that way.

The study door opened again, releasing Adam and his cohorts into the hallway. Jessica followed, ushering them toward the door like a hostess whose guests have stayed too long.

"My clients will be available whenever you want to see them. As long as either Leo Frost or I am present, of course."

The DA gave her a frowning look, seemed about to speak, but then turned and went out. Adam, face somber, followed, trailed by a patrolman.

Jessica waited until the door had shut behind them before she joined them in the living room.

"I'm glad they're gone." Marisa clasped her hands in her lap. "I was beginning to think they'd never leave."

"They'll be back." Jessica shrugged. "They're just doing their jobs. Obviously Adam is embarrassed that his predecessor didn't take the situation seriously enough. And Connelly senses a big case to get him in the public eye."

"You're looking at it more rationally than I am," he said. "We're lucky to have you in the family."

"I'm the lucky one." Jessica's face softened, as it always did when she thought of his brother.

The doorbell rang, and Jessica's expression changed to one of annoyance. "If that's a reporter already, I'd better handle it." She went quickly out of the room, and he heard her heels click on the hall floor.

"She's amazing," Marisa said softly. "I don't know how I'd have held it together in there without her."

"If Connelly tries to bully you—" He didn't get that finished, because Jessica came to the archway.

"Marisa, there's someone to see you." A figure loomed behind her.

Marisa shot from the sofa, raced across the room and threw herself at the man whose arms spread to receive her. It looked as if Russ Angelo had turned up at last.

A few minutes later, Angelo was

seated on the sofa, one arm around his daughter. Link looked him over, trying to decide what he thought of the man. Angelo was stocky, heavily muscled, like a lot of men who spend their lives working outdoors. His dark hair was still thick and crisp, his eyes keen when he glanced at Link as if he knew that Link was assessing him.

Angelo ran a hand over the stubble on his deeply tanned face. "Sorry about how I look. When I finally got your messages, I figured I'd better just come. I was having trouble with the RV, so I borrowed a car from a friend and drove straight through."

"You should have called." Marisa's tone was gently scolding, but she smiled each time she looked at her father.

"You know how I feel about cell phones." He shrugged. "Figured the best thing I could do was get here. I stopped at the Miller place, but they said you were staying here for a couple of days. They also told me..." He came to a halt.

"We found a body this morning." Link got it out fast, before Marisa could break it more gently. He wanted to see how the man would react to a blunt statement.

He didn't get much. The man's face tightened as he took it in, but he had the kind of stolid face that didn't give much away.

"They can't be sure of the identity," Marisa added. "But under the circumstances—"

"About that." Angelo leaned forward, planting his hands on his knees. "Just what has been going on around here? I understand why you came to begin with, but it sounds as if things have gotten pretty darn complicated."

"That's putting it mildly." Jessica said. "I'm sure Marisa would like to fill you in, but I'd suggest we get to the police station before they find out you're here. It'll look better that way."

"We?" Angelo raised his eyebrows at her.

"It's up to you, of course. But I'm an attorney, so I can sit in with you and be sure you're treated fairly until you hire someone of your own."

That rattled Angelo; Link could see that in his eyes.

"They must be mighty eager to talk to me, it seems. Why—? Well, I guess that's obvious, isn't it? If my wife has been murdered, I'm the most likely suspect."

Marisa made a small sound of distress, and he patted her hand.

"No point in getting upset, honey. I didn't do it, and they'd have a hard time proving I did. But Ms. Langdon is right. If they've been looking for me, it's better if I go in on my own." He glanced at Jessica. "I'll take you up on that offer, thanks. Don't want to go putting my foot in my mouth the first time I talk to the cops."

"I'll go, too." Marisa stood. "Just let me get my things together, and we'll go back to the Plain and Fancy after you've talked to them. You look as if you could use some sleep."

She headed for the stairs. Link followed her, putting his hand over hers to stop her as she started up.

"Get a room for your father, but there's no reason for you to leave here. I'm sure Mom wants you to stay."

She drew her hand free slowly, maybe reluctantly, but her face was determined. "I want to be with him. And I'll feel safe with him there." She hesitated for the space of a heartbeat. "Besides, it's better this way."

The silence stretched between them, filled with all the things left unsaid. He wanted to speak the words that crowded his lips...the words that would make her stay. But he couldn't.

"Adam Byler wasn't that hard on me, honey." Her father reached across the restaurant table to pat her hand. "I wouldn't go so far as to say he believed me, but he was polite."

"Wait until you encounter the district attorney," Marisa said, pushing the remnants of apple crumb pie around on her plate. "He's more of a pit bull."

"Preston Connelly? Yeah, Byler said he'd want to talk to me tomorrow. Seems like I remember him, vaguely, from when we lived here."

"What kind of things did Chief Byler ask you?" Her tale of everything that had happened had taken them most of the way through the meal. Now it was his turn.

"Oh, not much." His gaze slid away from hers.

"Stop trying to protect me." *It just makes things worse.* "I'm all grown up now, and I need to know—even more than the police do."

"I guess that's true." He frowned, stirring his coffee absently. "I have tried to protect you, but in the end, that didn't do any good, did it?"

"No." She wouldn't compromise on that. She'd done her own share of trying to protect him, hiding her need to know about her mother. "I'll be a lot better off with the truth."

"Truth's a slippery thing sometimes." He took a sip of the coffee, made a face and added more sugar. "Your mother and I fell crazy in love, but I guess neither of us really understood how hard it would be for her." He shook his head, sorrow tugging down the lines of his face. "Now I can see that she needed a lot more support from me, but I was young and stupid. What did I understand? I thought she'd be happy, just being married, having a baby..."

"Did she regret the choice she'd

made?" It was the question she'd asked everyone, and everyone seemed to have his or her own take on it. Maybe, as Dad said, the truth was slippery.

"She never regretted having you." His voice was sure. "Don't doubt that for an instant. But I guess she felt isolated, like she didn't belong anyplace."

"I remember hearing her say that once. It was...sad." She blinked back tears.

"I thought it reflected on me if she wasn't happy. So we'd end up quarreling." He looked up at her. "The cops are onto that."

"Not from me," she said.

"No, of course not." Surprise registered in his eyes. "You didn't know. Did you?"

The truth, she reminded herself. "I heard, sometimes. After I'd gone to bed. I didn't understand."

"Honey, I'm so sorry. We never dreamed you could hear."

He looked so upset that she had to comfort him. "Don't worry about it. That was a long time ago." A long time, but it still lived in her dreams.

Dad ran his hand through his hair in a

characteristic gesture. "I messed up. But I never harmed your mother. When we found she was gone..." His face twisted. "I thought she'd left. I really believed that, and all the time she was lying there, dead."

She could visualize it too clearly, and a shudder went through her.

"Marisa, I want you to go back to Baltimore." He focused that look on her—the one that said this was not up for argument. "It's not safe for you here, and there's no reason for you to stay."

The look was effective, but she wasn't a shy fifteen-year-old asking to go to a party.

"I'm staying, so don't bother. Do you really think I'd leave you at a time like this? Anyway, I doubt that the police would let me go, now that it's an official murder investigation."

He winced, but nodded. "I suppose you're right." He stretched, reaching for the check. "I need to take a walk and get some of the kinks out. Process all this, too. I'll see you back at the Miller place, okay?"

She nodded, realizing it was more the

mental than the physical strain he wanted to deal with. "Just tap on my door when you come in."

By the time she reached the car, her mind had started churning again. The police, the DA... Surely they would get to the bottom of things. Or would they just pounce on her father as the most likely suspect?

Their knowledge of the quarrels made matters worse. She slid into the driver's seat and pressed her palms to her temples. She didn't like being that five-year-old again, hiding under the covers or running into her parents' bedroom and seeing...

She stopped, looking with amazement at the image that had just popped from the recesses of her mind. It was as if she had opened a long-closed door, and this had fallen out, as fresh as if it happened yesterday.

Herself, running along the hallway with hair ties in her hand, ready to have Mammi fix her braids for school. Opening the door, seeing Mammi kneeling on the braided rug, putting something into a black hole in the floor.

She blinked, looking at the image with adult eyes. A loose floorboard. Her mother had picked it up and put something into the recess underneath.

She reached for her bag to pull out her cell phone. Stopped. Who could she call? Whatever her mother put under that board wouldn't still be there, but if it was, who could she trust to see it? What if it contained something that seemed to incriminate her father?

She wrapped her fingers around the steering wheel. If anything was there, she had to see it first. Why not? It was still light out, perfectly safe. And unless the real-estate agent had changed it, she knew the code for the lock box Link had used.

She shoved the key into the ignition. Five minutes at most. That was all it would take to get into the house, run upstairs and find out if what she imagined was real.

# CHAPTER EIGHTEEN

A few minutes later Marisa stood on the porch of the house that had once been home. She wiped her palms on her slacks. Ridiculous, to feel so guilty. It wasn't as if she were going to steal anything.

*Aren't you?* the voice of her conscience asked.

No, she was not. If whatever her mother had put under that floorboard was still there, then it rightfully belonged to her. Or maybe to Dad, but either way, she would reclaim it.

She raised her hand to the lock box, held her breath and punched in the numbers. It clicked and swung open, and she grabbed the key.

She shoved the key into the keyhole, her fingers fumbling in her haste, and took a quick look around. The overgrown hedges on either side of the house effectively hid her from view. Only someone passing directly in front could possibly see her.

The door creaked open in response to the key. She started inside, reaching up to close the lock box. If anyone did come by, the place should look as normal as possible. Heart thudding, she went in and shut the door behind her.

Quiet. Even the faint sounds from the street didn't penetrate here.

It should feel odd, even frightening, to be alone in the empty house, but it didn't. Dusty and ill-kept as it was, the house wasn't really silent. It echoed with the sounds of her childhood.

A small version of herself, counting the steps loudly as she went up and down. That must have nearly driven her parents crazy, but she'd been so proud when she could count them all. Mammi, singing softly in Pennsylvania Dutch in the kitchen, with the aroma of baking cookies drifting through the house. Daddy coming in the door from work, calling out, "I'm home. Where's my girl?"

The memories were comforting, even if that time had ended in pain and grief that she hadn't been old enough to understand.

But she'd better hurry. Already the shadows were deepening in the house as the light faded outside. All she had for illumination was the penlight on her key chain.

She went up the stairs quickly, intent on what had to be done, and went into what had been her parents' bedroom without hesitation.

In the room she stopped. The image was clear enough in her mind of what she'd seen that day, but the room looked so different without furniture.

The double bed would have been about there, she guessed, with an oval braided rug beside it. The rug had been flipped back a little, brushing against Mammi's knees as she knelt.

Marisa dropped to her knees on the dusty floor, studying the boards. Wide and uneven, they were marked with knotholes. They must have shrunk at one time, leaving cracks between some of them, filled now with dust and who knew what else.

Her hands moved over the boards, testing each one. Press, feel for movement. Pry at the cracks, breaking a fingernail. Nothing. They seemed as solid as if they hadn't come up since the day they were laid.

She sat back on her heels, frustrated. Maybe she was overestimating how much space the bed had taken up. She moved to her right, adding another layer of dust to her already filthy slacks, and began the whole process over again.

Press, pry, wiggle. Move on to the next, her heart sinking with every failure. Could her subconscious have made the whole thing up?

She pressed on the next board and felt it move under her hand. Her breath caught. This must be it. If only—

A sound broke the silence, freezing her in place, stomach clenching. That had sounded like a moan. She listened, ears straining for any sound.

Nothing. She was able to breathe again. Old houses made noises, that was all.

But her movements were more frantic as she worked at the board. This had to be it—she was sure. It moved, but didn't come up. Something to pry it with?

She scrabbled through her bag, coming up with a nail file. This should do it. She ran the point of the file all the way around the board, as if she were loosening a cake in a pan. Slid the wide end under the board, using it as a lever. With a reluctant creak, the board came up.

Her heart stopped. The crevice beneath it wasn't empty. Amazingly, against all odds, a metal box sat there, thickly coated with dirt.

She lifted it out and used up every tissue in her bag to get it clean enough to see what it was. Small, maybe ten inches square. The lid had been painted with a design, and there was enough of the paint left to identify a Pennsylvania Dutch hex sign—a stylized flower.

She should take it and run, but the feeling that drove her was stronger than mere curiosity. She had to know for sure that this was Mammi's.

The lid resisted her pressure, and she had to resort to the nail file again. The box popped open. Papers, yellowed and fragile, but intact. She pulled out the top one, unfolding it.

A brief note to her mother, agreeing to meet her—*At the crossroads. I will see you at four. Your cousin, William.*

Pain gripped her. Her mother had needed help. She hadn't turned to Daddy. She had turned to her cousin.

Her fingers tightened on the note, and she shoved it back in the box, closing the lid. She'd take the box back to the inn and go through the contents piece by piece. Then she'd decide what to do with them.

She stood, clutching the box, and turned toward the door. And the sound came again. A groan, louder this time, coming from downstairs.

She had to go downstairs. There was no other way out of the house. Regardless of what waited for her there, she had to go.

Moving cautiously, she edged along the hallway, hand on the wall, to the head of the stairs. There she stopped, listening.

Nothing.

Scarcely daring to breathe, she eased down a step, then another. One more and she should be able to see most of the hall. If someone was there, she'd see.

She stepped down, staying against the wall, praying the stair wouldn't creak. She could see the length of the hallway now, but the shadows were deeper than when she'd gone up the stairs. Someone could be in those shadows, waiting.

She felt in her pocket for her cell phone and pulled it out, tucking the box under her arm. Careful. If someone was there and she tried to call, he could be on her long before the police got here.

She slid down another step, then another. Nothing moved in the shadows. There was no sound but the beating of her own heart, loud in her ears.

A few more treads and she'd reached the bottom. Just as she stepped down she heard it again—a moan, coming from the kitchen. A gasp. A word that might have been a cry for help.

She clung to the newel post, torn by

indecision. A few steps would take her to the door. She'd be out, safe.

But she couldn't do it. If someone was hurt, she couldn't run in the opposite direction.

She moved quickly now, back the hallway, cell phone clutched in her hand, finger poised to hit 911. The kitchen door stood ajar. She put a hand on it, pushed it gently. Opposite her, the back door to the porch was open, letting in a chill breeze.

She saw nothing at first, and then she realized the dark shape on the floor wasn't a shadow. It was a person. A man, stretched out, hand reaching as if pleading for help.

She took a step closer and knew him. It was Ephraim, Elizabeth's youngest brother, who'd cried at the sight of her. He lay prone on the floor, blood seeping from the back of his head.

*Just like Mammi*, she thought. *Just like Mammi.*

Marisa felt as if she'd been in the hospital waiting room for hours, but when she glanced at her watch, she saw that it had been less than an hour. She was alone, except for the young patrolman Adam Byler had left with her. To guard her or to protect her? She had no idea.

She crossed the room to the window, rubbing her arms with her hands. It wasn't cold in here, but a chill had settled deep in her bones.

It had gotten dark outside while she'd been waiting, and a light rain was falling. The parking lot's surface glistened, and the streetlights had a hazy glow.

Poor Ephraim. Did he even know what had happened to him? Their brief interaction hadn't been enough to give her much understanding of him.

She'd ridden in the ambulance with him to the hospital, telling the paramedics she was his cousin. They'd looked at her a little oddly, but they hadn't argued.

If he'd awakened during the trip, someone should be with him. But he hadn't. The instant they arrived at the emergency-room door, he'd been whisked off. She'd been left to worry and pray.

The door began to move. Her breath caught. The doctor...but it wasn't. It was Adam. He glanced around the room.

"Your father's not here?" His voice was edged with suspicion.

"There's nothing he can do." That was true. But what also true was that she didn't know where he was. She'd called the B and B and gotten no answer.

Adam's expression said he knew what she wasn't saying. "Let's go over—"

The door opened, interrupting him. Her relief was muted by the fact that the person who entered was her cousin William, closely followed by Bishop Amos and Ezra Weis.

"Ephraim." William had a tight rein on his emotions, but she could sense his anguish. "How is he?"

"I don't know. The doctors are with him. They said I should wait here for word."

"What happened? What did he say? How did you find him?"

Bishop Amos put a hand on William's shoulder. "Let Marisa tell us what happened." Ezra stood silently behind him, his face bleak.

"I'd like to hear that, too," Adam said.

Ignoring him, she focused on Bishop Amos, since he was the only one looking at her without an accusation in his face.

She didn't want to tell them. She was afraid of what else the box might contain.

But when an innocent like Ephraim was attacked, the time for caution was gone.

"I remembered seeing my mother put something in a hiding place under the floorboard in her bedroom. It didn't seem likely that it was still there, but I couldn't ignore the possibility."

"How did you get in?" Adam asked. He probably suspected her of breaking a window.

"I noticed the lock-box code Link used the other day. It hadn't been changed." She took a breath. "If the box was there, it belonged to me."

"And was it?" Adam's tone was even now, giving away nothing of the suspicion he must feel.

"Yes." She pulled it from her bag, holding it carefully between her hands.

"But what about Ephraim?" William clearly couldn't be silent any longer. "Why was he there?"

"I don't know. Really. I heard a sound in the kitchen. I... It sounded like someone in trouble. I went and saw him." Her throat tightened as she relived that moment. "I called the paramedics."

"Did he say anything? Anything that would tell you what happened?" Adam pressed.

"He was unconscious. I rode with him to the hospital, but he didn't wake up." *But he will, won't he?*

"Why? Why was Ephraim there?" William took a step toward her.

"Didn't you send him?" She would not let William intimidate her.

"I send him? Why would I do that?"

She gestured with the box. "To get this. To keep me from reading the note to my mother from you."

She opened the box and took out the topmost paper. She didn't want to part with it, but she forced herself to hand it to Adam.

He read it, frowning, and held it up so that William could see it. "How about it, William? Did you write this?"

William's face worked. They all stared at him now, even his friend, Ezra. Expecting an answer. "Ja," he said finally. "I wrote it."

"I think you must explain," Bishop Amos said.

William nodded. "Ja. All right. I see I must tell it all. I heard from Barbara. She said she had to see me. That she was in trouble and I was the only one who could help."

Behind him the door opened. Link came in, and Adam held up a hand commanding him to silence. He looked faintly rebellious, but he obeyed.

"I went to that house, in the evening. She came out to the backyard to talk to me."

"It was you I saw then." Marisa knew it was true the instant she said the words. "You and Mammi were arguing."

"You saw?" He gave a short nod. "She said she had to get away. That I had to help her. But she wouldn't tell me what it was all about."

"What was she afraid of?" Adam's question was sharp.

"You think I didn't ask her? She wouldn't answer. Said it was dangerous. That I was safer if I didn't know anything. That she had to go away for the sake of her family."

Marisa's tension eased ever so slightly. If that was what Mammi had said, it sounded as if she was trying to protect them. But from what?

"You're sure that's what she said?" Adam probably didn't want to hear that. He was busy looking for evidence against her father.

"Ja." William shrugged. "So I said I would help." He nodded to the letter. "I said I'd pick her up, but..." He stopped, looking as if he struggled with himself.

"But what?"

"I was delayed. So I sent Ephraim to Allen Morgan's house to tell her I would be late, so she wouldn't be standing there at the crossroads."

She could feel Link's tension even through the distance that separated them.

"What happened?" He grated out the words.

William pressed his lips together, as if holding back something painful. "Ephraim came back when I was harnessing the horse. He was that ferhoodled we couldn't make out a thing he was saying. Just kept crying when we tried to get him to tell us."

Adam and Link exchanged looks, and she knew what they were thinking. Ephraim had seen what happened to her mother that day.

"I drove there, fast as I could." William shook his head. "The house was empty. I looked, I called for Barbara, but she was gone, and I didn't know what to do."

"Ephraim..." Her heart hurt for the little boy in a man's body. "He never spoke?"

William shook his head, the movement heavy. "When we tried, he'd get so upset he couldn't sleep for days. It was cruel, to treat him so."

"You should have gone to the police," Adam said. Probably he felt he must say that, but she could see the sympathy in his eyes.

"Ja, for sure. But then..." William shrugged. "It seemed best to let it be. I thought maybe Barbara had gotten an Englisch friend to take her to a bus station."

She wanted to blame him. Wanted to blame someone. But she understood. He'd been afraid for his younger brother and had assumed Barbara had gotten safely away.

"Why do you think Ephraim went to the old Angelo house today?" Link put the question, frowning as if he tried to piece things together.

"I don't know."

Ezra moved slightly. "If he wanted to see Marisa, that's where he'd go, because he knew that was where she lived then, ain't so?"

It made a certain amount of terrible sense to Marisa. "He was trying to warn me. That's it, isn't it?" Her voice broke. "The man...whoever it was, must have found him there."

"Or followed him there." Link seemed to be on the same wavelength. "He may have feared what might happen if you and Ephraim came together."

"That's speculation," Adam said. "When—"

The door opened. This time it was the doctor. His gaze searched the room until he found her face.

"How is he?" She held her breath, afraid of the answer.

"He's not out of danger yet. He has a severe concussion, and there may be some brain swelling." The doctor glanced at the three Amish men. "You're family, too?"

William nodded. "Will he get better?"

"We'll have to monitor him closely for the next twenty-four hours, but if nothing more serious develops, I think he'll recover."

"Can he talk?" Adam went straight to the point that mattered to him.

"He hasn't recovered consciousness, but he is muttering a little. You can't question him, if that's what you mean, but you can see him. And the family can sit with him."

Adam gave a terse nod. "Larson, come along. I want a guard on his door at all times." He went out, trailed by the patrolman. William and Bishop Amos followed.

Ezra made as if to go after them, but then he stopped. "There is something I must say to you." His voice rasped, as if the words hurt him. "You were right. I was in the Millers' yard those nights."

It took an effort to bring her thoughts back to the moment when she'd looked out the window and seen someone. Seen Ezra. Her instinct had been right.

"But why? What did you want?"

"Nothing. Nothing. I chust..." That trailed off. He seemed to struggle to start again. "I heard Barbara's daughter was there. I couldn't sleep. I wanted to see you, but it didn't seem right." He held up his hands, palms empty. "I cannot explain very well. But I never meant you any harm. You are Barbara's child."

He didn't wait for a response, just turned and went out the door.

Barbara's child, her mind repeated numbly. After all these years, he still grieved.

She blinked back tears, not sure she could take any more. "I'm going."

Link put his hand on her arm. "Wait a minute, Marisa. Please."

She fought against the warmth that went through her at his touch. There was no future in letting herself hope.

"I should go. Ephraim doesn't need me, now that William is here." She pulled her arm free.

"Tell me something first. What on earth possessed you to go there without telling anyone? Are you trying to put yourself in danger?"

Anger came to her rescue. "Who would you suggest I tell? You?"

He took a step back, emotions battling in his face. "What do you mean?"

"You've made it clear you don't want to take responsibility for anyone. Fine. I get that. You're not responsible for me. And if you want to become the same kind of unhappy loner your uncle was, I'm certainly not going to stop you."

She yanked the door open and rushed through it. But there was no need to hurry. He wasn't coming after her.

The tide of anger carried her along until she reached the ground floor of the hospital. She was following exit signs down an empty corridor when she realized the truth—she had left her car parked in front of the house in Springville.

She'd have to call for a taxi. She turned, ready to go back to the lobby. She certainly wouldn't ask Link for a ride, not after what she'd said.

What had possessed her? It might be true, but that didn't mean she should have said it.

Her footsteps echoed on the tile floor,

and she was so tired that the hallway seemed to stretch on indefinitely. She had to find Dad, tell him what had happened.

A sense of movement behind her...a vague shape glimpsed from the corner of her eye. And a blow sent her tumbling into blackness.

# CHAPTER NINETEEN

Adam tugged Link out of Ephraim's hospital room, where William and Bishop Amos sat on either side of the boy's bed while Ezra stood at the window.

Link glared at him. "Ephraim could say something that will solve this whole thing. Someone should be listening."

"Bishop Amos will tell us if that happens," Adam said. He frowned at the Larson kid, who looked like he was playing dress-up in his uniform. "No one goes in but family. Check with Bishop Amos. Right?"

The kid nodded. Gulped. "What about the doctors and nurses?"

Adam suppressed a sigh. "Yes, let them in. But make sure you check their ID badges."

"Yessir. You can count on me."

Adam didn't look as if he found that reassuring. He glanced at Link. "I've got to get back to the scene. Why don't you go home?"

"We've got to talk first."

The elevator doors opened, letting out a group of Amish who were probably looking for Ephraim. A nurse scurried after them, herding them into the waiting room.

"I don't have time—"

"Make time." Link all but snarled the words, impelled by a sense that time was just what they were running out of. "In here." He propelled Adam through the door to the chapel. Thankfully it was empty.

"Two minutes," Adam said. "I have to get back. There's got to be some evidence pointing to the identity of the third person who was in that house. Assuming there was anyone else there."

Link fought down an intense desire to grab him by the shirt. "If you think Marisa hit that boy, you're crazy."

Adam sighed. "Personally, I think that Marisa Angelo is exactly what she seems to be. But I have to do my job. And I'm not so sure about her father. We haven't located him yet this evening. He seems to drop out of sight just when he's wanted."

Link shook his head, hoping that would clear away the clouds. "I know you have to suspect the husband, but I think we're missing a piece."

"Missing?" Adam snorted. "If anything, we've got too many pieces—the husband, the Amish angle—either the boyfriend or the cousin, to say nothing of this whole business of the Brotherhood."

"That's just it. There are so many possibilities that we're forgetting how we came to find Barbara's body. The raven tile."

Adam frowned, but he gestured with one hand. "Go on. I'm listening."

Link tried to order his thoughts. "If I hadn't remembered finding that tile years ago near the cave, we'd never have gone looking there. That has to mean something."

Adam lifted an eyebrow. "You realize that train of thought leads back to your uncle."

He knew, only too well. "Nothing but the truth is going to do for us now. When you combine the tile I found near where the body was hidden with those cryptic mentions in Allen's journal, where does it lead?"

Adam's impassive expression sometimes fooled people into thinking he was dumb. He wasn't. A keen mind worked away at the problem.

"Okay. Just supposing. Suppose Allen was involved in a small group that was trying to resurrect the Brotherhood. A group of people who'd advance each other's interests in any way, including bending the law. If someone—Barbara, say—overheard or saw something, one of those people might think she had to be gotten out of the way."

Link nodded. "Here's what I'm thinking. This person attacked her at Allen's house while she was waiting for it to be time to meet William. Hid her suitcase in the wall, but he'd be smart enough to know he couldn't get away with putting the body there. And he thought of the quarry."

"Your uncle is the most likely person to fit that scenario," Adam said.

Link frowned, dissatisfied. "What could she know that would threaten him? He never worried about his reputation, as far as I know. He didn't have to worry about losing a job or a family if something adverse came to light."

"True. But other people in his little group might not have been in the same position," Adam said. "Someone could have had a lot to lose."

"If Ephraim saw the person who killed Barbara..." Link frowned. "The killer might not have been sure how much he'd seen. Or he might have felt safe, knowing Ephraim's condition, believing he'd forget all about it or didn't understand what he saw. But then Marisa came back, and her presence upset Ephraim—maybe made him remember."

Adam nodded slowly. "I like it. It uses more of the pieces than any other scenario. But we still need evidence, so I've got to get back to the house. You going home, or to see Marisa?"

Edginess had him almost twitching. "I don't think Marisa wants to see me right now."

"She's been through a rough experience. She cares about you. Who else would she want to see?"

Link shrugged him off. "Don't play Cupid, Adam. The role doesn't suit you."

Adam pulled the door open. "Deny it all you want. I know what I see." He went quickly down the hall, headed for the stairs.

Link followed more slowly, taking the elevator down. Adam meant well, but things between him and Marisa were more complicated than Adam would believe.

Even so, he wanted to see her. Reaching the ground floor, he headed for the parking lot. It was just that he was smart enough not to start anything between them.

*Smart enough?* a small voice inside inquired. *Or scared? Scared that if you get too close, you'll let her down?*

That didn't have any good answer.

He crossed the parking lot toward his car, zipping up his jacket against the light rain that was falling. Forget it for now. By this time, Marisa would be falling into bed back at the Miller place. Tomorrow...well, maybe tomorrow things would be clearer.

Just as he reached the car, the text signal sounded on his cell.

He jerked it from his pocket impatiently and realized it was from Marisa. No, not Marisa. Just her phone.

**If you want to see her alive again, come to the quarry. No police, or she dies.**

He stared at it, disbelieving, for a long moment. Then he flung himself into the car, mind churning with incoherent prayers, started the car and peeled out of the parking lot.

Adam would kill him for not calling, but he couldn't take the chance. Not with Marisa's life.

If this was a trick—he grabbed the cell phone from his pocket, steering with one hand on the rain-wet road. Punched in her number.

The phone rang. And rang. No answer.

No sooner had he clicked off than it rang. He snatched it up, heart pounding. "Marisa?"

"This is Russ Angelo. Where's Marisa? She hasn't come back to the B and B, and I can't get her on her phone. I got your number from your mother."

"I don't...know." *No police,* the text had said.

"What's wrong?" Russ's voice sharpened. "I can hear something's wrong. What is it? Has something happened to her?"

Link hesitated. But she was Russ's daughter. He had a right to know.

"I got a text from her phone. Someone has her. He told me to meet him at the quarry. No cops."

Russ absorbed the blow with a sharp intake of breath. "Where are you?"

"Just coming off the highway toward Springville. On my way to the quarry."

"It's a trap," Russ said flatly.

"Yeah. I'm still going."

"I'll meet you there."

Link could think of a whole host of reasons why that was a bad idea. "You won't know the way. I'm not waiting."

"I don't want you to wait. I know where it is. Just go."

"Right." Link clicked off, shoving the cell phone back in his pocket. What did he have in the car that could be used as a weapon, if it came to that? A tire iron. A flashlight. That was about it. All he could do was get there.

And pray he'd be in time.


Someone groaned pitifully. Marisa would help, but the pain in her head was so intense she couldn't move to go to them. Then she realized that she was the one who had groaned.

No wonder. Her head felt as if it would fall off. As if that would be a relief.

She had to open her eyes and make some sense of this. Was she in the hospital? Her eyelids were as heavy as her head, but finally she got them open. She couldn't see.

Panic ripped through her. Was she blind? She blinked, trying to focus. Or trapped in a place where the darkness was so intense that no light could penetrate?

She had to concentrate. To beat back the panic before it controlled her.

*Please. Please. Help me.*

She closed her eyes. Opened them again. Was it her imagination, or had the blackness thinned just a little? *Think, Marisa. Think.*

Air moved over her, stirring her hair. She was outside, then. The rain had stopped, but the ground beneath her was saturated. She shivered from the cold. She had to get up. No matter how her head hurt, she couldn't just lie here, a rock cutting into her cheek.

She tried to push herself up. Couldn't. Her hands were tied in front of her—her feet bound, too. Panic came again; the panic of being helpless, at the mercy of the person who'd brought her here.

*Help me.*

She listened, straining her ears. Wind rustling the leaves of a tree. The call of a night creature. Nothing that sounded man-made.

All right. She wasn't helpless. If she

could move, she might loosen the bonds on her feet. She could get out before he came back.

She swung her legs, trying to get enough leverage to get her knees under her. Move, move.

The ground disappeared from beneath her feet. For a terrifying moment she was falling...and then she got her feet back on solid ground. Panting, afraid to move, she dug her fingers into the dirt.

She knew where she was now. On the edge of the quarry where her mother had been buried. A sob choked her. She battled for control, trying to think. To remember.

The hospital. She'd been there with Ephraim...Ephraim, who'd been struck down in the kitchen of the old house. And then the man who attacked Ephraim had come after her. The empty corridor, the sense of someone behind her, a faint, oddly familiar presence. He'd struck her. Brought her here to the quarry. The person who killed her mother attacked Ephraim, attacked her. He was cleaning up loose ends. Who next? Link?

Her heart seemed to crack. That bitter accusation would be the last thing she said to him.

No. She wouldn't give up—lie here and wait to be killed.

Flexing her fingers, she pressed her hands against the ground. She edged her bound hands forward. *Slow, easy, don't tip toward the side.* An inch at a time, she moved her hands. Finally she was up on her elbows.

She could see now—stars, bright against a dark sky, a sliver of moon, the dark abyss that was the quarry. Close— even closer than she'd realized.

She had to get farther away before she could attempt to work her hands and feet free. Wriggling? Rolling? Either had a risk if she overbalanced, but she had to try.

Holding her breath, she listened. Was there a change in the night sounds? If so, she couldn't detect it.

She edged her feet and legs over, a precious couple of inches farther from the edge. Then the rest of her body, her shoulders and head.

Again. Wriggle, shift, gain ground.

Confidence rising, she pressed her feet against the ground. If she could roll...

The edge crumbled, falling away beneath her feet, too fast for thought. Clutch her fingers into the ground, grasping at roots, clinging tight, seeing the steep drop to the rocks below. *Please, please.*

A last rock fell, sounding a distant punctuation as it hit the quarry floor.

She pressed her face against her hands, scarcely daring to breathe. Terrifying to think of moving again, even more terrifying to lie here, helpless.

If she could find a sharp rock, maybe she could cut the bonds on her wrists. She explored them with her fingertips. Not rope. Strips of cloth. Why would...

And then she realized. He didn't want rope marks on her wrists when she was found. Her death was meant to look like an accident.

*No.* Desperate, she pressed her palms down. She'd have to risk rolling, praying—

Fierce light pierced the darkness, pinning her to the spot. Heart thudding against her ribs, she narrowed her eyes, trying vainly to see against it. He was here.

"I wouldn't struggle." The voice was a gruff male whisper. "You'll fall."

*Help me.* From somewhere deep inside, courage welled. "That's what you intend anyway, isn't it?"

"Smart girl. Too smart."

Not much, but things began to click together in her mind. Scent, sounds, a vague impression of size and shape.

"You may as well stop hiding behind the light. I know who you are."

Silence for an instant. Then the beam flickered upward in a quick flash, and she saw the face she knew she'd see. The district attorney, Preston Connelly.

# CHAPTER TWENTY

Right about now he could use those night-vision goggles he'd had in Afghanistan. Link paused, listening, when he reached the old railroad-bed trail, hearing nothing but the normal sounds of the woods at night. He set off at a trot down the trail. The tire iron he'd stuck in his belt thudded awkwardly against his leg, but it was the only weapon he had to protect Marisa.

Thinking of Marisa brought on a cold fear that clutched his heart and turned his bones to jelly. He focused instead on the man whose call had brought him here. Used the fury to propel himself forward.

*Please, God, Please, God...* The incoherent prayer sounded in time with the thudding of his feet. He didn't need to say the words—God surely knew his prayer, when Marisa filled his thoughts. If he didn't get there in time—

*No, don't think that. Think tactics.* He had one advantage here that he hadn't had in Afghanistan. This was his home turf. No matter how well the killer knew this territory, he knew it better. Most of his boyhood had been spent in these woods, and he knew every inch.

The log drag, for instance. It slanted up through the woods at an angle just where the path to the quarry broke off. He'd go that way, instead of the more obvious trail. It would bring him up to a slight rise over the spot where the old path down into the quarry had been.

That was where the killer would have Marisa. That was where he'd gone to dispose of Barbara's body in that cave. Where he'd dropped the telltale hex tile.

That had to be it. The person who'd texted him hadn't been Amish. He'd been someone involved in Allen's group—someone to whom Barbara had become a threat. That was the only thing that made sense.

The killer also had to still be living here, in the area and in a position to follow developments in the case. Now, obviously, he thought that Marisa and Link were getting too close to the truth.

When Link reached the trail that led to the quarry, he had to risk turning on his flashlight for a moment, shielding it with his hand. There was the log drag, a shallow depression in the earth where long-ago loggers had followed the natural curve of the ground to bring logs down from the mountain. Nearly buried in leaves, so no one who wasn't looking for it would spot it.

He started climbing, staying to the uphill side of the drag to avoid rustling the leaves. No point in advertising his presence. He had no illusions about the killer's intent. He and Marisa weren't supposed to survive the night.

Pain gripped his heart. He'd die without ever telling Marisa he loved her, and that suddenly seemed the worst thing that could happen. He had to find a way to save her.

It wasn't far to the top. He forced himself to stop, to steady his breathing and clear his head. Now he had to move cautiously. Even a snapped stick might reach the killer's ears. He crept toward the spot where he'd be able to see the quarry.

He heard them before he saw them. Marisa—that was Marisa's voice, and the relief that flooded him was so strong he knew he hadn't expected to find her alive. Another step, and he could see them. The man had a flashlight in one hand and a gun in the other, both trained on Marisa.

She was standing, hands tied in front of her, dirty and disheveled but otherwise apparently all right. So far.

And she was defiant.

"You can't hope to get away with this." Her voice sounded strong. "People will realize I'm missing. Link. My father. The police chief. They're probably looking for me already."

"Morgan doesn't need to look." The

voice was familiar, and it took Link a moment to absorb the truth. Preston Connelly.

In an insane way, it made sense. Connelly fit everything he had thought about the killer, and the district attorney was someone with a lot to lose. That made him doubly dangerous.

"What do you mean?" Now fear edged her words—fear for him.

"Your boyfriend is probably rushing up here right now to protect you. When he gets here, there'll be an accident. People won't be all that surprised, you know. Distraught over finding your mother's body, you came up here in the night, and Link followed you. Maybe you tried to kill yourself. Maybe it was an accident. Everyone knows Link hasn't been the same since he came back from the war. The ending is the same. You both fall to your deaths."

His heart stuttered, and he was far more frightened than he'd ever been in Afghanistan. This was Marisa.

He took a long, slow breath, focusing on the situation. He was maybe twenty feet above them. Even after he got to the bottom, he'd have to cover another eight or ten feet to Connelly in the open. The tire iron wasn't going to do him much good until he got a lot closer.

He started down toward them, treading as carefully as if he stalked a grouse. Slow, painfully slow, feeling with each foot before he dared put his weight on it.

"Hold your hands out," Connelly ordered. Holding the flashlight with his arm, he approached Marisa, yanking the bonds from her wrists. Before she could move, he swung at her with the gun—a backhanded blow that sent her staggering toward the edge of the quarry.

His heart stopped until he saw her catch herself, teetering for balance close to the edge.

"Stay put," Connelly ordered. "It doesn't matter to me if you go over before or after Morgan arrives."

He had to move faster. She was balanced on the edge. The rocks could crumble, she could lose her focus. He had to reach her—

A twig snapped, sounding like a gunshot in the night woods. Connelly was on it in an instant.

"I know you're there, Morgan." He might not know exactly where Link was, but he knew where Marisa was. He pointed the gun at her. "Come out now, or I'll have to use this on her."

No choices left. He felt for the tire iron, loosening it, holding it ready in his hand. Then he climbed down, making no effort to hide his progress. He'd have to hope he could find a chance to over-power Connelly, hope that Angelo would get there in time to help.

He emerged into the clearing at the top of the quarry, his eyes fixed on Marisa. He didn't know if she could see his face, but he tried to give her a reas-suring smile. "Are you okay?"

"Not bad," she said, clearly not dar-ing to move.

"Over there." Connelly gestured with the gun, motioning him toward Marisa.

He'd have to pass fairly close to Con-nelly to get to her, and obviously Con-nelly wanted them to go over the edge close together. That would be his best chance to jump the man.

"Isn't this an odd role for you, Con-nelly?" He moved slowly, deliberately.

"You're supposed to be upholding the law."

"Don't bother stalling." Connelly waggled the gun. "No one is coming to help you."

"You sure? Maybe I called Adam after I saw your note."

"You wouldn't be that stupid. And he has no idea I'm involved."

Link shrugged, flexing his grip on the tire iron he held behind him, praying Connelly couldn't see well enough in the dark to know he had something. "You sure? We figured it out. I don't suppose he'll be far behind."

"No one has suspected me in all these years. I don't think they'll start now. Marisa was the only wild card. I thought she might have seen me talking to her mother out in the yard the night before she died."

"I didn't." Marisa sounded surprised. "I only remember seeing her with Cousin William."

"What about the tile?" Link said, desperate to distract him. "You must have had a few bad moments when you heard

I found it. I'm guessing there's something about it that identifies you."

"Move." Connelly wasn't easily rattled. "I'm not going to stand here explaining myself to you."

Another step. Two. Soon he'd have to make a move, but Connelly watched him intently. He might not want them found with bullet holes, but he'd shoot if he had to.

"You killed my mother." The accusation ripped from Marisa's throat, and Connelly's gaze flickered for an instant.

All he'd get. Link launched himself toward the man, lifting the tire iron, but then they were grappling for the gun, no chance to swing it, no chance to do anything but fight for the gun, pray Marisa was all right—

The gun went off, and pain burned across his thigh. He staggered, Marisa cried out, he was losing his grip...and then a figure hurtled out of the woods, charging straight at them. Russ Angelo grabbed for the gun and sent it sailing in an arc across the clearing.

Connelly threw them off, diving after it, the pair of them launching themselves after him, and in an instant they were tussling on the ground. Not for the gun, thank God: that must have disappeared into the layer of leaves. They were getting him. He was no match for the two of them; they'd have him—

Connelly lurched away, losing his balance, stumbling toward Marisa. The ground began to crumble, Marisa screamed—

And then it was Connelly screaming, arms windmilling as he went over. The scream cut off.

Link dove for Marisa, catching her hand as the edge beneath her went completely, rattling away to the quarry floor. But he had her, holding her tight by one arm with her body swinging in space. He gripped with all his strength, grabbing for something, anything, to hold on to with his other hand.

"You can't...I'll drag you over." She gasped the words.

His hand caught a tree root, snagging it, and confidence poured into him. "I will never let you go." He held her until Angelo reached him. Together they pulled her up and into their arms.

. . .

They huddled around Geneva's kitchen table like a group of shipwreck survivors, Marisa thought. She wrapped her hands around the mug of tea in front of her, welcoming the warmth. She had had a hot shower and was now bundled into an aqua fleece robe that belonged to Geneva, but she still felt chilled to the bone.

She looked across the table. Dad had exchanged his muddy clothes for jeans and a sweatshirt that must have belonged to Link's father.

As for Link... She searched for signs of pain but found none. Adam had wanted him to go to the ER, but he'd insisted the bullet had just grazed his leg. He'd see his own doctor in the morning, if necessary.

Despite the wound, despite the exertion that must have exhausted him, Link looked better, in a way, than she'd ever seen him. Peace and confidence gentled his expression. He saw her watching him and smiled...a small, private smile just for her, and her heart turned over.

"I still don't understand what drove a man like Preston Connelly to do such a thing," Trey said. "Even if he was involved in Allen's little group, surely what they were doing wasn't illegal."

"It may well have been." Leo Frost's white hair was rumpled, and she suspected he'd been roused from bed by Geneva's call, but his eyes were alive with interest. "Twenty-three years ago, Connelly was a smart young attorney with his eye on advancement. If he was trading favors with anyone for a leg up the ladder, he might well have bent the law. And if that came out, he could kiss a political career goodbye."

"He said that he came and talked to my mother the previous night, but I didn't see him." It was a struggle to keep her voice steady, but she made it. "I suppose he tried to pressure her to keep silent. Maybe threatened her. That's why she packed that suitcase—she was leaving to protect us."

"Yes." Dad's voice roughened. "She was still Amish in the way she thought. She wouldn't have wanted to do anything that would draw attention to herself. It would never occur to her to go to the police. She'd just try to disappear back into Amish life." A world of sorrow and regret seemed to weigh on him.

"It wasn't your fault, Daddy," she said softly.

"The blame belongs on Connelly." Link patted his shoulder awkwardly. "Nobody else."

"Unless Uncle Allen knew about it and did nothing," Trey said. "Whether we'll ever know the truth of that..."

"You'd never have known it from Connelly, even if he hadn't died the way he planned for you." Leo's tone was precise. "He knew the system too well."

"I understand why he went after Marisa." Adam accepted the coffee mug Geneva handed to him. "He was afraid she might have seen him. But why was he so intent on eliminating Link?"

"I think I know." Geneva slipped her hand into the pocket of her fuzzy pink robe, her cheeks as pink as the material. "Today I went through the boxes of Link's old toys in the attic. I found this."

She dropped it on the table, and it lay there looking vaguely ominous. The tile, with its menacing hex sign.

"I had no idea what happened to it,"

Link said, making no effort to touch the thing.

"Look on the back," Geneva said.

Adam flipped it over. They could all read the initials incised on the back.

"PLC," Adam said. "Preston Lawrence Connelly. He'd have had trouble explaining that away."

"He must have been afraid you'd produce it," Marisa said, looking at Link, marveling at the fact that they were both still alive. "Or remember the initials."

"I'll take this," Adam said, lifting it. "It's evidence, even though Connelly has escaped a trial."

"Good by me. I'd be just as happy not to see it again." Link stood. "Now I think Marisa ought to get some sleep, if nobody minds."

Nobody did, it seemed. There was a general murmur of agreement.

"I've got to call your sister back. She's been calling every half hour, wanting to know what's happening and threatening to fly home." Geneva headed toward the kitchen phone. "Russ, if you don't mind waiting a moment, I'll get a bed ready for you for what's left of the night."

Marisa rose, discovering that her knees still had a distressing tendency to buckle, and took the hand Link held out. His fingers closed warmly over hers.

When they reached the stairs, he paused. "Maybe I should carry you up. You still look wobbly."

"Don't you dare. With that wound on your leg, we could both come tumbling down." The words were meant to be light, but they quivered when she thought how close they'd come to a much worse fall.

"It's okay." He closed the slight gap between them and stroked her hair with a gentle hand. "We're all safe now."

"Thanks to you." She looked up at him, finding that tears blurred the image of his face. "When I started to fall, I thought..."

"Don't," he whispered. "Don't relive it."

"I want to. I want to remember how you caught me. Held me. You said..." She let that trail away, not sure he'd want to be reminded of those words.

"I said I'd never let you go." His fingers caressed her cheek, and there was a steady glow in his eyes. "I meant it. I love you, Marisa. You were right about me. I was trying to keep from being responsible for anyone, ever again."

"You don't have to..."

He smiled and echoed her words. "I want to. When I knew he had you, I realized just how stupid I was. Nothing in this world could have kept me from getting to you. Not even myself."

A tear spilled over onto her cheek, and he wiped it away.

"Well?" he said. "I told you I love you. Are you just going to leave me hanging here?"

She shook her head. "I wouldn't do that to you." The tendency to tears vanished. Her mother was still gone, but she no longer had to wonder what had happened, and the hole in her heart was nearly healed. It just required one more step of faith on her part. "I love you, Link Morgan. And I will never let you go."

Apparently they were the right words, because the sun seemed to come up in his face. He bent to kiss her, and then they didn't need any words at all.

# *EPILOGUE*

Link stood against the back porch railing at the house that had once belonged to Allen Morgan, watching the crowd that milled around the yard for the auction. They'd lucked out with the weather—mid-November could be miserable, but it was a clear, chilly day, perfect for the stand some of Marisa's Amish cousins had set up to sell hot chocolate and funnel cakes to the auction-goers.

Trey came over and stood next to him, surveying the men who'd gathered around the contents of the barn. The harrows and plows might be a little rusted, but someone would find a use for them.

"Any regrets?" Trey said, lifting an eyebrow in his direction.

"About selling this place? None at all. I'm glad to be rid of it, and a new young family taking up residence will be just the thing to chase out all the unhappy memories."

He'd been fortunate to find a buyer quickly once the renovations were finished. He'd thought the publicity might scare people off, but just the opposite had been true. After the remnants of furnishings and equipment had been sold at auction today, there would be nothing to tie the Morgan family to this place.

"You may be right about that. Mom said it was a happy house once, before Allen moved in. It can be again."

His mother had been right about a lot of things. And Marisa had, as well. He had been on the road to turning out like Uncle Allen, letting his fears dictate his future and failing to understand how good his relationship with his brother could be.

"Too bad we'll never know the truth

about the extent of Allen's involvement," Trey said.

"Maybe that's just as well."

He'd been frustrated for Marisa's sake that she'd never know the details about how her mother died. But she knew the important thing, after all—that her mother had never wanted to leave her.

As for the rest, they could pretty well imagine how it must have happened. Connelly surprising her, probably when she was getting ready to meet her cousin. A quarrel, a blow, blood on the suitcase and an unconscious, maybe dying woman on his hands. Connelly had panicked, stuffed the suitcase behind the half-finished wall to hide it and then taken Barbara away.

He glanced toward the food stand, where Ephraim was unloading a wagon filled with bottles of apple cider. Once he'd recovered, Ephraim had finally told the secret he'd held for so long. He had come to the house to deliver William's message, and he'd seen Connelly. He'd consistently broken down at that point, but it seemed clear in context that he'd seen Connelly putting Barbara's body in the trunk of his car.

"Looks like Ephraim's doing all right." Trey was apparently following the direction of his thoughts. "I'm glad it didn't come to a trial. I'd have hated to see him put on the stand."

Link nodded. "Marisa has built a nice relationship with him. He's still pretty leery of me, but I'll keep trying."

"That's right. Got to stay on the good side of the in-laws," Trey said, grinning a little. "Here comes Marisa with some spiced cider for you, so I'll leave you two alone."

He strolled off, waving to Marisa as he went. She handed Link a steaming cup and looked after him. "Where's your brother off to?"

"He's being tactful. Leaving us alone."

She smiled, leaning against the porch next to him, her shoulder touching his arm. "That is tactful."

"Surprising for my family, I know. They so seldom leave anyone alone."

She leaned her head against his shoulder. "You shouldn't talk about your boss that way."

"Trey's not exactly my boss, as he's been reminding me ever since I took over the construction business. We're partners." He slid his arm around her. "Like you and me."

"Not quite, I hope."

"No, not quite." He glanced down at her left hand, never tiring of seeing his ring there. The pearl and diamond ring had belonged to his great-grandmother, and she insisted she loved that far more than anything new. "Sure I can't talk you into getting married any sooner than April?"

Her low laugh held a world of confidence in his love. "I think we can wait, for your mother's sake. She already has one wedding to deal with next month."

He'd never understand the fuss women made over weddings, but if it made Marisa and his mother happy, he was all for it. Besides, by then the house he was building for them would be finished, and they could move right in. It was on a great piece of land down the road from Marisa's cousin William and his family, with a small woodlot and a trout stream that Russ was already enjoying.

"I almost forgot." Marisa dug into her pocket and pulled out an envelope. "This came in the mail, and your mother thought you might want to see it right away."

He flipped it over, saw the address and the foreign stamps, and his heart seemed to stop. He felt again the scorching heat of an Afghanistan summer, squinted against the unforgiving sun.

He ripped it open and scanned the note that was enclosed, and then read it again to be sure he understood.

"Link?" Marisa put her hand on his. "Is something wrong?"

"No." He cleared his throat. "Actually, I guess it's something right. It's from the headmaster of that school. He thought I should know that the villagers found the courage to rebuild. He enclosed a picture." He showed it to her—a simple building, with a double row of smiling kids lined up in front. "He translates the sign for me. It says the school is dedicated to the brave friends who died trying to rebuild it."

The picture blurred before his eyes, and instead he saw the faces of those who died that day.

Marisa squeezed his hand, and he blinked, coming back to the here and now, to the woman he loved standing beside him and the new life they were about to begin.

"Something good came out of all the bad things that happened to both of us," she said softly. "I don't think we can balance one against the other."

"No. But we can let it remind us to live every day without regrets." He drew her a bit closer. "That's good enough for anyone."

\* \* \* \* \*